The Easter Egg Murder

by

Patricia Smith Wood

Aakenbaaken & Kent   New York

The Easter Egg Murder

Aakenbaaken & Kent   New York

akeditor@inbox.com

ISBN: 978-1-938436-10-9

Dedication

To my wonderful father, the late Thomas J. Smith, Deputy Assistant Director, FBI (Retired) who first told me the story about the unsolved murder of Cricket Coogler, and who encouraged me to write.

And to the late Tony Hillerman, author of the popular Lt. Joe Leaphorn and Sgt. Jim Chee mysteries set on the Navajo Reservation, for providing much needed information about the Coogler case, and for encouraging me to go forward with the fictional version.

Acknowledgements

The mental picture of the lonely writer slaving over a typewriter in a cold garret somewhere in Paris sounds romantic. But all the writers I know have a team of friends, family and other writers who encourage them and help with the journey of completing and publishing a book. I have a stable of wonderful people who were with me through that journey. This is where I get to tell you about them.

My talented and published critique group brought me into their midst at the most auspicious time of my life and offered me support and guidance. Many of them read the entire manuscript. Thank you to Margaret Tessler (who introduced me to the group), Mary Blanchard, Charlene Dietz, Edie Flaherty, Jeanne Knight, Betsy Lackman, Marcia Landau, Jan McConaghy, Joan Taitte, Mary Zerbe and the late, talented Ronda Sofia who unfortunately did not live long enough to see her work published. Thanks to two other wonderful writers who read parts of the story and offered suggestions: Joseph Badal and Earl Staggs.

Thanks to all the excellent instructors at the conferences I've attended over the years. The Hillerman Writers Conference allowed me to meet some wonderful authors who generously shared their knowledge and encouragement. Special thanks go to Sandi Ault, who taught classes of great value and mentored me more than I could have imagined.

Thanks to the other friends who agreed to read and critique the book in all its versions: Pat Priebe, Lois Twyeffort and Richard Turner. That's service above and beyond the call. Also a big thanks for Ann Paden who gave it her professional editorial critique and seal of approval.

Then there was my very special, hunky FBI agent, literary critic/advisor, who made sure I didn't endow the FBI with more juice than they have.

When I needed help with editing (more than once) my long-time friend, Joan Taitte, stepped up and did an amazing and thorough job. She's wonderful, even if she did want to do away with the cat.

And finally, I could never have finished this project without the love and support of my amazingly understanding and supportive husband Don and my equally precious daughter Paula. They both gave their best evaluations and encouragement and made sure I had the time and the kick in the pants when I needed it. Aren't families wonderful?

Prologue

Sunday, April 9, 1950

The high desert of New Mexico is a lonely place to die. Only coyotes, jackrabbits and prairie dogs would have heard the screams. Even the moon hid its face, leaving the distant stars the sole source of light.

The boys watched the early gray dawn melt away as the sky above the Manzano Mountains flushed pink with a new morning. A hawk circled high overhead, drifting lazily with the current. To the West, Los Huevos Peak reflected the sun's first rays, and to the South, the small town named for the peak was barely visible.

Charlie, Jake and Freddie loved the desert in the early morning. They loved catching lizards at the foot of Los Huevos Peak, especially when those creatures were still lethargic from the previous night's cold. But today was Easter and there was a price to pay—their parents had ordered them to return in time for Mass. Already they regretted making such a promise.

They left their bikes beside the narrow dirt road and walked toward the rock formation, Charlie in the lead.

Something strange caught his eye, and he stooped to pick up a red high-heeled shoe. He was about to toss it away when he noticed the bare foot protruding from behind the boulder.

He gazed at it, uncomprehending, and yelled to Jake and Freddie, "Hey you guys! Come over here and take a look at this!"

The other two boys ran to join Charlie but stopped short when they saw the foot. Freddie turned pale, his jaw dropped and he gulped air.

Jake stared, wide-eyed. "Is that a real foot?"

Charlie moved farther to the left so he could see behind the boulder. The red shoe slid from his hand and landed on the ground with a soft plop.

"Oh, Jeez," he moaned. "Oh, God!"

Jake joined Charlie and stood on tiptoes to see over his shoulder. He instantly regretted it. A woman in a red dress lay on her back, arms crossed over her chest. One leg stuck out straight from her body, the foot shoeless. The other leg was bent at the knee, its foot encased in the mate to the red shoe. Her clouded eyes stared blindly at the pink tinged sky. A crimson scarf encircled her neck, and her long, black hair, littered with leaves and debris, fanned out from her bloodless face in a tangled mass.

A gust of cold wind touched down and ruffled her hair, then moved on, stirring the sand and sending it skyward in a slender spiral.

Charlie shivered. Lizards would never entice him back to this place.

1

Sunday Morning, April 9, 2000

"Why didn't I just kill the jerk when I had the chance?" She muttered, mostly to herself.

The question had periodically occurred to Harrie McKinsey for the past thirteen years. It was a dumb question. She could never kill anyone, even her ex-husband, no matter how big an ass he was. But if anyone ever needed killing, it was Nick Constantine.

"Did you say something?" Ginger Vaughn looked over the top of her glasses.

"I said why would anyone murder someone and then drive all the way out to the desert to dump the body?" Harrie frowned. Why did reading about murder always bring Nick's image to mind?

Ginger shook her head and grinned. "Oh, I don't know. How about, the desert is deserted, and a body could lie out there for months before being discovered?"

"Okay, let me rephrase that. If the murderer took the trouble to take the body out there, why wouldn't he at least bury it? Why leave it there where those kids could find it?"

The two women had worked seven straight days on their latest editing project, and they were beyond tired. They had started the business six months earlier and were now getting some good clients. Their first big break came when Ginger's godfather, Senator Philip Lawrence hired them to help with his book about his senate career. Then, three weeks ago, he hired them to transcribe and edit his new manuscript about the real-life murder of a young woman half a century ago. This job presented numerous challenges. For one thing, they might need to do some of the research work for him, and they needed an assistant. So far, no candidate had survived the first interview.

Ginger looked on as her best friend struggled with the coffee maker. They had instantly bonded that first day in seventh grade in 1974. In school the boys used to call them Mutt and Jeff. The blue-eyed, raven-haired Ginger was a good four inches taller than Harrie, who was barely five feet, five inches. They made quite the picture. She joined Harrie at the sink.

"Sweetie, what's wrong? You've been agitated all morning. Something's bothering you."

Harrie took a deep breath and let it out slowly. She flashed Ginger a crooked grin, but her hazel eyes looked tired and puffy. "I had the dream again last night."

"The one about the body?"

"Yep, and it woke me up. I couldn't get back to sleep."

"Was there something different about it this time?"

Harrie shrugged. "I think so, but I can't remember what. My heart was pounding, and I had this awful sense of dread."

Ginger remained quiet as she finished filling the coffee pot. She turned back to Harrie, her jaw set in determination. "You're coming home with me. Steve is cooking on the grill, and you and I need a break."

"No way. I won't intrude on your family cookout. You've barely seen the boys all week, and Steve must be annoyed with us by now. All we've done is work, work, work."

Ginger raised an eyebrow. "You know better than to argue with me. Even when I'm home, my sons are way too busy with soccer, homework and girls to miss having Mom around. They are, after all, fourteen-years old. Besides, you need to think about something besides that crazy dream."

Harrie smiled at the picture of authority, the much taller Ginger with hands on hips and chin set in a "do-not-argue-with-me" look.

"Gee, how can I refuse an invitation like that?"

Ginger's face softened. "Well, obviously you can't. At precisely 1:30, we lock up and go spend the rest of the afternoon sitting on my patio, drinking wine and thinking only of wonderful food and friends."

Harrie looked out and saw dark clouds gathering over the Sandia Mountains, backdrop for the east side of Albuquerque and ever-changing canvas for its fickle spring weather. At the moment, they fit her turbulent state of mind. She forced her focus back to the manuscript.

"Not to change the subject, but do you remember hearing anything about this murder from Senator Lawrence when you were a kid?"

"Not really." Ginger smiled as she thought back. "He and Dad spent hours talking about all kinds of things, but I didn't pay much attention."

Harrie said, "I wonder why he's writing this particular book now. He's not even finished with the Senate book."

"I don't know. But he seems really fired up to get into this one."

"He wasn't even living here when it happened, was he?"

"I don't think so." Ginger's face lit up. "Why don't you ask him tomorrow afternoon? I'm going over to his house to take the pages we've finished, and it would be a good opportunity for you to see him again."

Harrie hesitated. "I don't know. To tell you the truth, he intimidates me."

Ginger's mouth dropped open. "You're kidding me! Why?"

"Remember what happened at your wedding? After Steve introduced me to Nick, the senator walked over, gave me a stern look and said I should be careful. I don't remember him saying a dozen words to me before that day. He obviously didn't approve of Nick."

Ginger said, "I never told you this, but I found out after you divorced Nick that Philip knew some damaging things about him. At that time he didn't indicate what, just that you should have been more cautious."

Harrie frowned. "Why didn't you say something before?"

"Because by the time he told me, Nick was gone. Things happened so fast with you two. You eloped and then five months later you're broken hearted, financially ruined, and left hung out to dry. When Philip found out you were divorced, he felt bad he didn't warn you more thoroughly."

Harrie shook her head. "I'm surprised he paid any attention. After all, he didn't know me that well."

"Philip told me Nick had some connection to illegal gambling. Steve and I talked it over and decided we didn't want to burden you with that information." She grinned at Harrie. "We kept a close eye on you."

Harrie smiled at the memory. "Yes you did. You and Steve also started trying to fix me up with someone before the dust of Nick's departure had settled."

"Good thing we did. Otherwise, you and Mark wouldn't have met."

Harrie's throat tightened, and she turned away.

Ginger groaned. "Oh Harrie, what a stupid thing for me to say."

Harrie swallowed hard and turned back to smile at her friend. "It's okay. It's been five years, after all."

Ginger rushed to hug her. "Hey, you take all the time you need. I only remember how happy you were. I try not to think about what happened."

"It's okay. I rarely fall apart anymore. Bu for the last couple of weeks it's been on my mind more than usual. Maybe it's working on this manuscript." Harrie's shoulders sagged. "I think about that poor girl and the way somebody left her out there. It's a miracle they discovered her before the scavengers did."

The distant rumble of thunder filled the awkward silence.

"Come on," Ginger said, "let's finish up these next few chapters before we leave for the day."

Harrie said, "Woman, you are a slave driver. Remind me to complain to my union rep."

A pleasant rhythm settled around them as they worked. When Ginger announced it was 1:30, it surprised Harrie that time had passed so quickly. With her concentration on work interrupted, her mind drifted back to the unsettling dream from the night before and the nagging question that accompanied that memory. How did last night's dream differ from the others? Why couldn't she remember? She kept seeing the body of a woman stretched out on the ground. But there was something else. What?

She sighed and went to gather up her belongings. In the restroom, she touched up her lipstick and smoothed her hair. She studied her face in the mirror. *You are a mess, woman.*

She returned to the conference room in time to see a brilliant flash of lightning followed by a loud crack of thunder. Harrie jerked reflexively. Now she remembered what was different about the damn dream. Another body lay beside the strange woman. With a sick feeling, she realized the second body in the dream was Senator Philip Lawrence.

2

"Uncle Daniel, you should see this."

Jonathan Templeton handed the old man a section of the *Albuquerque Morning Sun*.

Daniel Snow was ninety-two and it showed. His skin was almost translucent. His gnarled hands shook as he took the newspaper. He brought it close to his face and squinted at the caption. "Why should I look at the Arts Section?" He tossed the paper on his desk. "Give me the front page."

"I think you'll be more interested in this." Jonathan retrieved the paper and turned to the Book Section on the back page. "Let me read it to you."

"This better be good. I'm not in the mood for that artsy fartsy crap."

Jonathan smiled at his uncle's grumpiness and read aloud.

Former U.S. Senator Philip Lawrence, who recently signed a six-figure contract with Random House for the story of his 24-year-career in the United States Senate, announced he is also working on another book about the murder of Kathleen "Chipper" Finn, a cocktail waitress who died fifty years ago today. Her body was discovered on Easter Sunday morning, 1950, in the desert outside the gambling town of Los Huevos, thirty-five miles southwest of Albuquerque. The newspapers of the day quickly dubbed it 'The Easter Egg Murder.' They had a field day with the sloppy investigation by the local sheriff. It prompted a change of venue for the murder trial of Manny Salinas, a prominent figure in the boxing world at the time. He was acquitted, and no one else was ever charged with the crime.

Jonathan paused and looked at the old man. Daniel gestured impatiently at him to continue.

District Attorney Daniel Snow, who personally prosecuted the case, left the District Attorney's office in 1952 to run for Attorney General. Snow's campaign was successful due to his stance against open gambling in the state. He promised to close down illegal casinos in Los Huevos and to fight government corruption. He maintained the young woman's death was the result of the lawless activities in that small town. In 1957, he was appointed to fill the empty seat created by the death of U.S. Congressman Joseph D. Calloway. He held that seat until 1964 when he abruptly resigned and became a virtual recluse at the family estate.

When asked about his new book, Senator Lawrence, a longtime associate of Congressman Snow, would not comment on the possibility of new evidence in the case, nor would he speculate on who he thought was involved in the young woman's death.

A full minute passed before Daniel spoke. "Find out who he's working with on this. He must have someone editing the manuscript. And see if you can get his agent's name."

Jonathan took a deep breath. "Uncle Daniel, what about Eric?"

"Jonathan, do you trust me?"

"Of course, Sir."

"Then go along and do as I ask. Everything will be fine."

Jonathan nodded and left.

Daniel Snow looked down at the newspaper on his desk, not really seeing it. He tried not to think about his son, Eric, and the threat now rearing its ugly head again after all these years. Most of all, he tried not to think about a girl named Chipper.

3

Ginger looked at Harrie. "Are you okay? You look awful!"

"I just remembered something about my dream."

"Want to tell me about it?"

"Not yet. I need time to think some things through."

"Such as?"

Harrie looked down at her hands, framing her words with care. "I may need to tell Philip about my dream, and I'm not sure that's a good idea. You know how people sometimes get when I talk about the dreams."

"I guess it depends a lot on what has you stirred up. Why do you think it's necessary to tell Philip about your latest nightmare?"

"Because I think someone is sending me a message through this dream."

Ginger watched Harrie. "And why would you think that?"

Harrie brushed aside the question and asked one of her own. "Do you remember when Mark died?"

"Of course I do. Shortly before your third wedding anniversary."

Harrie nodded. "January 15, 1995."

She could still feel the chill from the cold, damp air. It had been snowing that evening and the quiet that comes with soft falling snow made the night seem so peaceful. That was shattered when two detectives rang her doorbell shortly before midnight. She knew instantly what it was.

Mark McKinsey was a detective with the Albuquerque Police Department for over a decade when Ginger and Steve introduced him to Harrie in 1991. He made it clear from the beginning he was interested, but her brief, disastrous marriage to Nick Constantine still haunted her.

Mark was a big, sturdy man with a dependable, safe feeling about him. Their dating slipped into a comfortable routine. They had dinner together on his nights off and quiet weekends visiting the cafes and shops of Old Town, especially Treasure House Books and Gifts with its trove of books and gifts devoted to things Southwestern.

During a romantic dinner On Valentine's Day, 1992, he asked her to marry him. After the meal, they ordered coffee, and Harrie chided him about his use of cream. She always took hers black.

The wedding was in May and she anticipated a quiet, uneventful life with this wonderful man who loved her without question.

Then three years later on that terrible night in January, Mark and his partner went to question a possible witness in a murder investigation. After they knocked on his door and announced they were police officers, he opened fire, mortally wounding Mark and severely wounding his partner. By the time Harrie got to the hospital, Mark was in a coma. He died minutes after she arrived. She hadn't been in an emergency room since that night and prayed it would stay that way.

Harrie forced her mind back to the present. "Do you remember how depressed I was?"

"I'll never forget. You were like a zombie."

"Did I ever tell you what happened that helped me start to heal?"

Ginger shook her head. "Not really. You said something about a dream, but you never explained. I always wondered, but I didn't want to ask."

"It was the first time I had one of my really vivid dreams, and I wasn't ready to share it with anybody. Remember when we were kids, I told you about my grandmother and how she used to visit people in her dreams?"

Ginger nodded. "I remember thinking you had the neatest grandmother in the whole world!"

"I always thought so." Harrie smiled as she pictured her grandmother. "Anyway, on Valentine's Day the year after Mark died, I felt depressed, as usual, and I went to bed early. That night, my grandmother came to me in my dream and said she had a surprise for me. She told me to go to my kitchen. When I did, Mark was sitting there at the kitchen table, sipping coffee, just like he always did. I was stunned, but happier than I had been in ages. I sat down opposite him, and he said, 'Why are you so sad?' I can still remember the feeling of pure joy at seeing him there, and I said, 'I'm not sad now that you're here with me'. He smiled at me and said, 'I've always been here with you. Just because you don't see me doesn't mean I'm not with you. I'll always be around when you need me, but you've got to get on with your life. There are so many wonderful things ahead for you.' He reached across the table and touched my hand, and I felt his warm skin against mine. The next morning, I woke up with the sun shining through the bedroom window. My hand was in the sunbeam, and I felt the same warmth as in the dream when Mark touched me. It was so real!"

Harrie looked off into space.

Ginger sat very still and waited for Harrie to go on.

"When I went to the kitchen, I was still thinking about the dream and how it comforted me. I poured myself a cup of black coffee, just like always. I sat down at the table, and my heart almost stopped beating." Harrie's eyes filled with tears.

Ginger whispered, "What happened?"

Harrie smiled and brushed away the tears. "I looked across the table, where Mark always sat, and there was his favorite coffee mug. In the bottom of the cup were the remains of cold, creamed coffee."

4

Monday Afternoon, April 10, 2000

"Names, please?"

"I'm Ginger Vaughan, and this is Harriet McKinsey. We're here to see Senator Philip Lawrence."

Harrie and Ginger had worked all morning on the revisions for the senator's manuscript. After a quick lunch, they drove to Canyon Estates. The security guard checked his clipboard, nodded, and reached for the button to open the huge iron gates.

"This place is like a fortress, but it's gorgeous," Harrie commented. The homes lining the main road displayed a profusion of colorful flowers, and the golf course looked almost too meticulous to actually play on.

The sun was out, and the clouds of yesterday were only a memory. Their cookout on Sunday had been wonderful. But today, Harrie was again apprehensive. Last night had brought a repeat of the same bad dream.

Harrie brought her attention back to the upcoming meeting with Senator Lawrence. "Does he know I'll be with you?"

"I called him just before we left the office." Ginger looked over at her. "Still worried about that dream?"

"Yes. I think the senator is in danger."

"Why?"

She hedged. "It's just a feeling."

After the dream about Mark four years ago, Harrie experienced other unusual ones. Sometimes she would dream about something and find out later it had actually happened. Other times she felt she was supposed to deliver a message to someone. She believed these messages and intuitions were from Mark. She didn't talk about it much. Most people seemed to discount dreams as nothing more than a person's imagination set free by the sleep state.

Harrie said, "I'm reluctant to mention anything to him without knowing what his reaction might be. He might think I'm a nut case."

Ginger laughed and patted Harrie's arm. "Let's just see how it goes. You'll know what to do."

An older woman with short-cropped gray hair answered the chime. Her face lit up when she saw Ginger. Ramona Sanchez had been the senator's housekeeper for many years. She ran the house with quiet efficiency and doted on her employer. He tended to be a loner and seldom left the comfort of his spacious home. Ramona shopped for groceries, prepared all his meals and kept the house in immaculate condition. She also fiercely guarded his privacy.

Ginger introduced her to Harrie and said, "Is he ready for us?"

"He's in the library. Go on in, and I'll bring some iced tea."

The senator's home was quiet and comfortable. Harrie believed houses had an energy all their own, related to the people who lived there and the events that transpired within their walls. At Ginger's soft knock on the library door, a deep, mellow voice responded, "Enter."

Walnut bookcases lined the room from the gleaming hardwood floors all the way to the ceiling. A library ladder with books stacked on the bottom step stood against one section of shelves. A black leather sofa and chair, positioned on an elaborate Persian rug, occupied the library at one end along with a sturdy conference table. A huge walnut desk dominated the other end, and Philip Lawrence sat behind it. He had white hair and fierce black eyebrows. A smile creased his craggy face when he looked at them.

"I am a lucky man. It's not every day two lovely ladies come calling on me." He chuckled. "In fact, it almost never happens."

He wasn't much taller than the five-foot-five Harrie, but his stocky build, barrel chest and muscular arms made him look younger than his seventy six years. He enveloped Ginger in a bear hug. "How's my girl, and how are Steve and those boys of yours?"

"We're all fine, Philip. And those 'boys of mine' are young men of fourteen now. They're so busy these days with school, soccer, girls and homework, we only see them at mealtimes!"

Philip chuckled, "Just you wait, my dear. It won't be long before even mealtime won't bring them home. Where does the time go?" He released Ginger and turned to Harrie.

"My goodness, Harrie, it's been a long time since I've seen you, hasn't it?"

"Yes, Senator, it has."

"I hope you'll relax enough to call me Philip before you leave today."

He guided them to the sofa and then seated himself in the matching chair. Ramona brought a tray with iced tea then closed the door as she left.

Philip looked at Harrie. "When Ginger called today, she said you might have questions for me?"

Now that she was here, she didn't know how to start. The senator was still as intimidating as she remembered him. She took a sip of tea before proceeding. "Well," she took a breath and plunged ahead, "I know you were a newspaper reporter for a time, but I gather you weren't in New Mexico when the crime happened. I'm curious. Why do you want to write about this old unsolved murder?"

When he didn't say anything for a moment, Harrie wondered if the question was too personal. He looked at her with those dark, penetrating eyes.

"For one thing, it was a turning point for politics in the state. It's entirely possible that without that unfortunate woman's murder, I would not have become a United States senator."

"Look," she said, "I feel a need to tell you something, but I'm afraid you'll think I'm a nutcase. You see, for a few years now, I get this sort of . . . well, I have these unusual experiences . . ."

"Harrie has weird, vivid dreams," Ginger said. Harrie felt her face flush, and she looked down at her shoes to avoid his gaze.

"Oh, really?" A smile played across his face.

Harrie lifted her chin and straightened her shoulders.

"Yes, really." She knew she sounded defensive and tried again. "Sometimes I get messages for people. Maybe it's a word of encouragement for someone going through a difficult time. It could be that a person lost something, and I know where to look. Then sometimes . . . well, sometimes I get warnings."

Philip studied her. "So are you saying you have a message for me?"

Harrie relaxed a little. "Yes sir, I think I do."

"Well, Lord knows I could use encouragement, or maybe I lost something. Tell me, my dear, which is it?"

She looked him in the eyes, searching for the right words. "I've had a recurring dream since we started work on this manuscript. I don't understand all of it, but I believe the dream I've had for the last two nights contains a message for you." She continued to look into his eyes, willing him to believe her. "You're in danger. Someone doesn't want this book published." She swallowed hard. "I believe someone wants you dead."

5

Philip looked at Harrie for a long time. The room was eerily quiet around them with only the grandfather clock's soft ticking measuring the passing seconds. The leather chair whooshed as he pushed himself up.

"Ladies, I'm about to trust you with something I've only shown two other people. I hope to assure you I'm quite prepared for any problems."

He went to one of the bookcases and withdrew a volume from the shelf. He reached in behind where the book had been. There was a soft click, and the section swung noiselessly out into the room. A door, which appeared to be made of steel, was behind the bookcase. Philip tapped numbers into a keypad next to the door, and the door opened.

He flipped a switch and light bathed a small room. The air smelled slightly stale and felt warmer than the senator's library. Philip touched another control beside the light switch, and cool, fresh air flowed from a vent near the floor. Sturdy metal shelves stood against the wall opposite the door. A desk, typewriter, chair and small dormitory refrigerator were arranged at the end of the room. There were no windows. The walls were covered with framed photographs, plaques and awards. Harrie noticed a complex control panel on the wall to the right of the door. Above it was a flat panel monitor suspended from the ceiling. Philip punched some buttons and the monitor blinked to life.

A picture of the library appeared on screen. After a few seconds, that image dissolved into one of the front entrance to the house. The screen changed again and showed Ginger's yellow VW parked in the circular driveway. Harrie watched in fascination as the picture changed to several more locations before it came back to a new image of the library. The camera zoomed in on the table where the iced tea pitcher and glasses sat. Harrie glanced at Philip and saw that he manipulated a small joystick to operate the hidden camera.

He chuckled. "I imagine this must look rather eccentric to you."

"Philip, what is this all about? Why did you build this room?"

"It's a safe room. In some circles they call it a panic room, although I don't really care for that name."

"But why? Why do you need a safe room?"

He smiled. "Maybe I anticipated Harrie's warning." Then his face became serious. "Over the years in public office you acquire enemies. Occasionally, someone decides to seek retribution for real or imagined grievances. I don't anticipate trouble, but I am prepared for it. I also have something else to show you."

He unlocked a side drawer in the desk and withdrew a fat, rubber-banded folder. "This contains all the newspaper clippings I saved about Chipper Finn's murder. I have copies in a safe deposit box at my bank. Having the original clippings here helps me connect to the past as I dictate the chapters of the book."

His face softened and took on a look of sadness. "There's something about yellowed newsprint saved long past its time that puts things in perspective. Some people toss away newspapers without a second thought, just as they sometimes toss away a life." He ran his fingers over the bulging folder, his thoughts apparently lost somewhere in the past it represented. With a sigh, he rejoined them in the present.

"When you leave today, I want you to take this folder back to your office. But first, I'll go over some of the articles with you. Let's go back to the library where we can be comfortable."

He handed the folder to Ginger, and they reentered the library.

Harrie looked around for the hidden camera. She tried to remember the exact angle she'd seen when it focused in on the iced tea tray. "I give up. Where is the camera hidden?"

Philip's eyes twinkled. "You never saw it, did you?" He pushed the library ladder along the railing and climbed to the top shelf where he pointed to one volume among a series of leather-bound books with ornate gold markings on their spines. "It's embedded right here within this curlicue. Very effective, don't you think?"

They went to the conference table and settled in.

"You should acquaint yourself with the news coverage surrounding Chipper Finn's murder. Feel free to keep these clippings for the next few days. First, though, I'd like to tell you the way I saw the story develop."

He leaned forward in the chair and paused as though collecting his thoughts. "Kathleen Finn, also known as 'Chipper,' was a young woman barely twenty years old. She was very beautiful, and she supposedly had numerous boyfriends. She worked in Los Huevos at a gambling joint in the spring of 1950."

Philip paused when Harrie and Ginger exchange looks. "Do you have a question?"

Harrie said, "I thought gambling was illegal in New Mexico until the compact with the various Indian tribes. So how could there have been a 'gambling joint' in Los Huevos in 1950?"

Philip smiled. "Gambling was officially illegal in New Mexico in 1950, but that didn't mean there wasn't any. On the contrary, we had quite a bit of illegal gambling here. Everybody wanted to make a buck, and gambling seduced people into thinking they had a chance at doing just that."

Ginger frowned. "Why didn't they just go to Las Vegas?"

"In those days, Las Vegas was just a small desert town. There wasn't much going for the town besides the gambling. And remember, air travel was a luxury in those days, and driving to Vegas in cars without air conditioning was uncomfortable to say the least. Even the Mafia hadn't fully appreciated its potential."

Ginger asked, "Was the Mafia involved in New Mexico?"

He nodded. "New Mexico was actually their first choice. It had more to offer than Nevada. It was remote, but had convenient railroad service. The weather was better, too. All they had to do was push through the legislation to make gambling legal. In the 40s, especially, the state was wide open with plenty of corrupt politicians eager to take money for their favors. Stories are told about Bugsy Siegel meeting with a group of these politicians in Santa Fe, and he almost made a deal. But something went wrong. In the end, Bugsy settled in Las Vegas, Nevada, and the rest is well-known history. The politicians who protected the gambling establishments in New Mexico hung on a long time. Los Huevos was the last place closed down in the reform."

"What caused the reform?" Harrie asked.

"Basically, it was Chipper Finn's murder. Because the Ventana County sheriff conducted such a sloppy investigation, the FBI became involved. The man arrested for the murder had his civil rights violated in a particularly painful way. Three law enforcement officials ended up in federal prison. A grand jury convened to take testimony about corruption, not only in Los Huevos, but in other parts of the state as well. The grand jury authorized raids on gambling establishments. One-armed bandits and other gaming devices were destroyed. Los Huevos was never the same."

Philip took a few clippings from the folder. "Go ahead and read through these."

Harrie noticed the headline of the first article – *Easter Egg Murder Shocks Small Town*. "Why do they call it the Easter Egg Murder?"

Philip chuckled, "Well, they discovered the body on Easter Sunday morning, and it was found at the base of the mountain called Los Huevos. You know," he said when she gave him a blank look, "the eggs?"

She grinned. "Of course. So much for my Spanish vocabulary."

She resumed her reading and saw what Philip meant about the slipshod investigation. The next clipping featured a grainy newspaper photograph. Harrie squinted at the shadowy image and realized she was looking at a photo, taken at the scene, showing the woman's body.

Her throat felt tight, and her mouth went dry. She thought she smelled the faint odor of cool sand and vegetation—like early morning in the desert. Fear flooded through her like summer rains rushing through the arroyos. She had seen that image before. Not in a yellowed old newspaper clipping, but in her full color dreams. It was the same body she saw in her nightmares laying next to Senator Lawrence. Her head spun and her vision blurred.

6

Harrie reclined on the sofa, her head low and her feet raised by pillows. Philip had insisted she rest after her brief faint. It had happened before.

After the blood flowed back to her head, she told him about the image's strange appearance in her dreams. She didn't mention seeing the Senator's body. Instead, she asked how he had become involved in the Easter egg murder.

Philip gazed at the ceiling. "For about eight months in 1945, I was stationed in Albuquerque training for a special mission that became unnecessary when the atomic bombs were detonated over Hiroshima and Nagasaki in August that year. The Japanese surrendered shortly thereafter, and I received early release from my enlistment. I was only twenty-one. I had left college to enlist, and it made sense to go back to school. I enrolled at Georgetown University and took night classes under the GI Bill. But I kept thinking about the New Mexico landscape. It was so different from New Hampshire where I grew up. There was a freedom in the open spaces and the clean dry air. I wanted an excuse to return. I even subscribed to the *Albuquerque Morning Sun*. I remember thinking it would be interesting to try my hand at being a reporter. Then one day I saw the story about Kathleen Finn's murder, and it captured my imagination."

Harrie was drawn into the Senator's story. She understood why he had been such an effective politician. His voice was deep and resonant, and he had the actor's ability to hold the attention of his audience.

"In 1950," he continued, "I had just completed a year of pre-law when an old army buddy looked me up. Eddie had stayed in Albuquerque after the war, working for the *Albuquerque Morning Sun*. He was getting married and taking on a new job, and he volunteered to put in a word for me if I wanted his old job at the paper. I decided I could complete my law studies at UNM. So I packed my bags for Albuquerque and landed the job."

Ginger asked, "Why did they assign you the Finn murder?"

"Chipper worked in Los Huevos, but she was an Albuquerque resident. The paper wanted background information and human-interest stories about her. I was assigned to see what I could come up with as filler pieces."

Philip stopped talking when the grandfather clock chimed three times.

"Oh no," said Ginger. "I was so engrossed, I lost track of time. Harrie and I have another appointment. Do you think we could talk again soon?"

Philip pulled himself up from the chair. "Of course. Take the material, look it over and call me when you're ready to talk again. I'm an old man who likes to have a captive audience for his ramblings."

"I enjoyed every minute," Harrie assured him and meant it.

Philip walked with them to the front door, but stopped Ginger as she started to open it. He reached into his pocket and pulled out the set of keys they had seen him use earlier. He removed two from the ring and reached for Ginger's hand. She watched as he pressed the two keys into her palm and carefully folded her fingers over them.

"They're duplicates. Put them someplace safe. If anything should ever happen to me, use the big one to get into the desk in my safe room and take custody of all my files. Would you do that for me?" His dark eyes watched her intently.

"Don't say things like that," Ginger protested.

"Please, Ginger, I need you to make this promise."

She sighed. "If that's what you want, I promise."

"Oh, I almost forgot." He took a slip of paper from his pocket and jotted down some numbers. He put the paper in Ginger's hand, along with the keys.

"That's the combination to get into the room. Keep it with you, okay?"

She looked into his eyes. "Okay, but you have to promise me to be careful, and not let anything happen to you."

He patted her on the shoulder and opened the door for them. "I promise I'll be extra careful." Then he looked at Harrie. "You two promise me something. Do not tell anyone, and I mean *anyone*, about these keys or the safe room. Will you do that?"

Both women murmured their agreement. Ginger hugged him one more time, and they left.

"He's really something." Harrie mused. "Why do you think he was so insistent you take those keys?"

"I don't know. Sometimes he can be very dramatic. Remind me to put them in the key cabinet in the vault when we get back." She abruptly changed the subject. "Hey, I want to talk about you. Are you really okay? You had me worried in there, Kiddo."

"I'm fine, I just got dizzy. When I saw the photograph, I remembered it from my dreams. I didn't realize exactly what I had seen until that moment.

The image of a woman, lying there on the desert floor in that strange pose startled me. It was such a shock to have it all come together like that."

Harrie hesitated, considering whether she should tell Ginger about the other body in her dream. She decided to wait. Maybe there was nothing to it. There was no sense getting her friend more alarmed. She looked over at Ginger and saw the doubt still there. "For goodness sake," she teased her, "will you stop worrying. I'm really not all that frail, you know."

Ginger gave her an appraising look. "Okay. But if you don't mind, I'm going to keep my eye on you until we're safely finished with this project. I'm feeling more than a little uneasy about all this. I think you've managed to spook me out, thank you very much."

They laughed and Harrie sensed the tension easing somewhat. They waved to the guard at the gate as they exited, and Harrie noticed he made another notation on his clipboard. Ginger chuckled. "I'll bet they have cameras posted all around here and know what every visitor does every minute they're here." While stopped at the traffic light at Academy, they discussed their next appointments where they hoped to hire their administrative assistant and all round "Girl Friday."

When the light changed and they turned west on Academy Boulevard, Harrie noticed a black SUV parked in the turnout just outside the gate. She laughed and shook her head. "Don't look now, but I think all this murder and mystery is getting to me."

Ginger didn't take her eyes off the road, "Now what? Did you see another body?"

"Hardly. But if I were an alarmist I might think that black SUV that was parked outside the gate is following us."

Ginger groaned. "Please do *not* add more intrigue to this situation. Philip's drama of the keys and safe room door code is enough for one day."

"Okay," Harrie said, "but don't blame me when it turns out I'm right."

"Trust me," Ginger said and looked over at her friend, "it's just another case of your vivid imagination at work. I swear, woman, you should put that mind of yours to good use and write a book of your own."

Harrie snorted. "Yeah, right! That'll be the day!"

7

Monday, April 10, 2000, Late Afternoon

Harrie and Ginger had planned for months before opening Southwest Editorial Services. Ginger had been a high school English teacher for years, teaching Creative Writing. Harrie had her bachelor's degree in English but had also taking courses to qualify as a paralegal. She'd worked at a law firm for more than ten years where she routinely prepared briefs and other legal documents for the attorneys. Now they had taken the plunge and established their own business.

At first, they worked from Ginger's house, taking over a spare bedroom. When this arrangement proved to be unworkable, a small inheritance from Harrie's grandmother and an equally small withdrawal from Ginger's savings account allowed them to lease a small space.

The fledgling company offered transcription, editing, and résumé preparation to writers, professors, and graduate students, mostly at the University of New Mexico. They both relished leaving their old jobs for something that would allow them more flexibility and a chance to run their own company.

When Philip Lawrence offered his goddaughter and her partner the job of transcribing and line editing his book about his career in the United States Senate, they found themselves with more work than they could comfortably handle. They hired a series of part-time typists. When the senator added the new book about the cold case murder of Kathleen Finn to their workload, they realized they had to get a full-time assistant. They hoped to find the ideal person during the afternoon's interviews.

After the next to last candidate departed, Harrie moaned, "If this is the best we can get, we might as well stop sleeping and do all the work ourselves."

They had interviewed three strange candidates. First came the gum-smacking high school senior with her exposed midriff revealing a pierced belly button. Next was the vampire-wanna-be, a black-draped young woman who announced she couldn't type. They didn't bother to ask whether it was because of her long dagger nails or lack of skill. But the topper was the woman who resembled a female prison guard straight out of the Third Reich. She reminded Harrie of the horrible Miss Trunchbull in the movie *Matilda*.

Ginger grinned at her friend. "Hang in there a little longer, Sweetie. The next one is the one. You'll see."

"And you know this how?" Harrie crossed her arms and raised her eyebrows.

"Because, she's the one I told you about who worked for the managing partner at Steve's law firm. I met her years ago, and really liked her. The partners depended on her completely."

They heard the front door open, and Ginger introduced Harrie to their final appointment of the day.

Caroline Johnson was an attractive woman who looked to be in her early fifties, tall and slender with a graceful elegance. She had short and smartly styled blonde hair. Skillfully applied makeup completed the business-professional appearance. She wore a dove-gray business suit and carried a slim briefcase from which she produced two papers.

"Hello Ms Vaughn. Nice to see you again. I brought you each a copy of my résumé."

Ginger said, "Please, call me Ginger. We're not that formal around here."

Caroline smiled and nodded. "Ginger it is, then."

They spent the next half hour discussing the job requirements and the salary. As Harrie listened to Caroline discuss her employment history, she couldn't believe their luck.

Harrie said, "Forgive me, Caroline, I can't help but wonder why you're willing to consider this position. From what I see on your résumé, this job seems far below your skill level."

A gentle smile played across Caroline's face. "I suppose it does look strange from your perspective. When the law firm hired me almost thirty years ago, I had just finished paralegal training. I considered myself lucky to have such an opportunity and wanted to learn all I could. I worked for the senior partner for more than twenty years. When my employer died a year and a half ago, I was devastated and took a month off to think about my future. I went back, but lasted only two months. It just wasn't the same anymore. I told the remaining partners I needed a change. I had invested my money well, and could afford to take a chance on doing something else."

"What did you do?" Harrie asked.

"Well, for as long as I can remember, I wanted to own a bookstore. I love books and being around them. So I opened a small bookstore in a strip mall on Louisiana, just north of Menaul. The timing was bad, though. Within six months of opening my store, that huge discount chain, Books, Bagels and Things, opened two blocks down the street in the mall."

"And you decided to throw in the towel?"

Caroline sighed. "I suppose that's what I did. I found a couple that wanted to open an arts and crafts store, and they were delighted to take over my remaining lease."

"It must have been very disappointing for you," Ginger said.

"It was, but I found the experience taught me something important about myself. My dream of owning a bookstore was more fantasy than reality. The books were great. Dealing with all the customers wasn't. So I decided I wanted something that could make use of my skills, doing work I enjoyed. I didn't want the stress or pressure I had at the law firm. And, as I said, I'm financially secure enough that the salary really isn't important. So to me, this seems perfect."

Ginger asked Caroline to step outside for a few moments so that she and Harrie could discuss their decision.

Caroline rose. "Certainly. Take all the time you need. I don't want you to feel rushed to make a decision."

After Carolyn was out of earshot, Harrie said to Ginger, "You do realize we're not executives, and this woman is an executive assistant?"

Ginger laughed. "You may not think of us as executives, but we own this enterprise. We run it, we direct it, and we need a keeper! Besides, she's content with the salary we're offering. What could be better?"

"True, but don't you think she's overqualified? Isn't it strange she's willing to take this job?"

Ginger nodded, "Okay, but I think she explained all that. If it's something less stressful she wants, I can see why she considers this the ideal spot. Do you have other reservations?"

"I guess not . . . not really. If you think she'll work out, I'm all for it. God knows, we'll never find anyone remotely as good as she is to take this gig."

"So it's agreed, we'll tell her she has the job if she wants it."

Ginger asked Caroline to rejoin them and said, "We'd like to offer you the job."

Caroline beamed at them. "I'd be delighted to accept."

Harrie said, "How soon could you start?"

"Well, this is Monday. How about I start first thing Wednesday morning?"

Harrie was surprised. "That's wonderful, but we need to get you a desk and supplies."

Caroline picked up her briefcase. "Don't worry about that. I'll do an inventory first thing Wednesday, and we can discuss what you have in mind for any equipment or furniture."

Ginger sighed. "Didn't I tell you, Harrie? This woman is a keeper. Okay, it's a deal."

They walked to the front door. Caroline paused and turned back to them. "I think you should know something. I drove by here earlier to make sure I knew where you were located so I wouldn't be late."

Ginger and Harrie listened politely, waiting to see where this was going.

"As I drove by, I noticed a black SUV parked across the street. It had tinted windows and seemed somehow out of place. Then, when I returned for our appointment, I saw it had moved into this parking lot. I could tell somebody was inside, and I had the strangest feeling they were just sitting there, watching."

Harrie felt the familiar coldness start up her neck.

"Just now, while I was waiting and you were deliberating, I looked outside, and the car is still there. I thought you should know."

8

Tuesday Morning, April 11, 2000

Harrie stood under a tree, or at least it seemed to be a tree. It was so dark, she couldn't tell. She didn't know why or how she got to this place. She smelled wet grass and damp earth. There was a noise, like an animal moving through the bushes. She strained her eyes to see. The dark clouds above parted, revealing a full moon. In its glow, she could just make out a shape that appeared to be a person. She sensed it was a man, and she held her breath as he approached her hiding place. He wore dark clothing with a hooded jacket that covered his head. Dark shadows hid his face.

She watched him move closer, and a cold, clammy sensation washed over her skin. She strained to hear, but there was no sound. She pressed against the tree, willing herself invisible, and watched, terrified. He stopped, listened, and slowly turned his head in her direction. The moonlight shone on him, and where there should have been a face, there was nothing but a featureless head. Harrie squeezed her eyes shut. A scream rose up in her throat, but nothing came out. She felt completely paralyzed. A loud, shrill buzzing broke through the silence.

Her eyes snapped opened, and the darkness disappeared. Harrie's oversized Siamese cat, Tuptim, lay sprawled across her chest, watching her intently. Her clock radio buzzed angrily. She dislodged the possessive cat, fumbled for the off button and moaned. The clock face showed six-thirty.

Sleep still clouded her brain. *Damn, what was that all about? Why do I keep having these creepy dreams?* She sat on the edge of the bed trying to shake off the dream. She looked down at Tuptim rubbing against her legs and purring lustily. "Tuptim, my little love, I don't have time to think about this today. I'll think about it tomorrow."

The fear in the dream faded somewhat in the shower, and she forced herself to concentrate on the warm water and fragrant bath gel. *Concentrate on the good*, she scolded herself. *Don't let the bad stuff into your head.*

She thought about Caroline Johnson. It was a stroke of luck she was available and wanted the job. But was it really luck or something else? Caroline was perfect for the job. *So why are all these questions running through my head? It's not as though Caroline is a stranger.* Steve and his friends from

Snow, Tessler, Knight & McConaghy knew her and recommended her. Harrie leaned into the shower and let the water cascade over her head.

Harrie's self-imposed deadline to finish reading all the newspaper clippings was in jeopardy. She found it difficult to concentrate. Her thoughts drifted to Senator Lawrence. What did he know about that long-ago murder that would make someone threaten him now? But had he really been threatened? She thought so. What else could her dream of him stretched out next to the dead girl mean?

Last night's dream was completely different. In this one, she was the one threatened. Was it because a car had been parked outside their office last night? What logical reason did anybody have to watch them? All these thoughts and questions swirled inside her head and it started to ache. Enough, she thought. This won't get the reading done.

As Harrie started a list of things she wanted to clarify about the news stories, Ginger came in and sat in the chair across from her.

"Do you think we should try to make an appointment with Philip for this afternoon or wait until tomorrow?"

Harrie considered the situation and her own current mental state as she looked at the pile of papers on her desk. "I don't know. There are several items I want to go over with him, but I first want to finish reading these articles he gave us. But if we wait until tomorrow, Caroline will be here, and we need to spend time with her."

Ginger shook her head. "I wouldn't worry about Caroline. I'm sure she can teach us a few things about running this place."

"I suppose you're right. How about this? Let's go over these folders until lunchtime. We could send out for sandwiches from the deli and eat in the conference room while we work. Maybe we could be finished with most of them by this afternoon in time to see him. Would that work?"

"Let me call him and see what his schedule is this afternoon. If he's agreeable, we can take back whatever we've finished and you can quiz him about your list." Ginger left to place the call.

Harrie started to put the finished folders in her briefcase, but it wasn't there. She tried to remember if she had brought it in from the car. *Okay, I'm officially losing it! I can't even remember what I did three hours ago!*

"Ginger," she called out as she grabbed her keys. "I'm going to see if my briefcase is in my car."

It was a bright, sunny, New Mexico day, and she wished she'd had the presence of mind to grab her sunglasses. She put her hand up to shield her eyes from the intense light and promptly dropped her keys. She was bending down when a deep voice said, "Do you need help, Miss?"

Harrie rose and swiveled toward the voice simultaneously. Her feet flew out from under her, and she landed unceremoniously in the grass. Before she could move, she felt strong arms pull her up and put her back on her feet.

Flustered and angry with herself, she now confronted a tall, dark-haired man watching her through sunglasses. A faint smile creased his ruggedly handsome face.

"Is it your habit to sneak up on people like that?" She sounded snippy and antagonistic even to herself. She felt unusually jumpy today.

"I'm sorry Miss. I didn't realize I would frighten you. I only meant to help." The smile was gone now, but he didn't look unfriendly. In fact, Harrie thought he looked concerned and downright gorgeous. A lock of his dark hair lay on his forehead in a way that reminded her of Christopher Reeve in *Superman*.

Then 'Sunglasses' spoke again. 'Are you hurt?' He bent to look in her eyes, his hands bracing her shoulders.

Oh, that voice! He even sounds like Superman!

"No, thank you. I'm fine." She attempted to regain her composure. "You were kind to help. I didn't know anyone was behind me, that's all." She tried to disengage herself from his steadying hands.

"Well, you do seem a mite jumpy, if you don't mind my saying so." The grin was back as he released her shoulders.

She looked down, avoiding his gaze. "I dropped my car keys. Thanks for your help, but I'm in a bit of a hurry, and I have to find those keys."

Sunglasses leaned over and picked up something "Are these the keys you're looking for?" That grin again. *Honestly, men can be so damned annoying.*

She drew herself up to her full five feet five inches, and reached for the keys. She realized her nose just about reached the top of his chest. She managed a tight smile. "Yes, thank you very much. These are, indeed, my keys." *Yes, indeed, being stilted and tight-assed should show you're in control!*

Sunglasses dipped his head in a small bow. Then he turned and walked across the parking lot. Harrie gazed after him until she realized she had not moved. She quickly turned away, flustered again.

She unlocked her car and found the briefcase on the front passenger seat where she had put it that morning. She grabbed it, and headed back inside. As she headed back inside, Sunglasses was nowhere in sight, but just turning out of the parking lot and heading south on Wyoming Boulevard was a black SUV with tinted windows.

9

Harrie and Ginger settled in the conference room with sandwiches and bottled water, each engrossed in her own pile of newspaper clippings. Harrie reread the article with the dead woman's photograph, but carefully avoided looking at the picture again. She read the account of the young boys' grisly discovery, and felt herself drawn back in time, experiencing what she imagined the public did in 1950 as they read these articles. *BODY DISCOVERED IN DESERT IDENTIFIED*, the headline proclaimed.

Information on the identity of the remains discovered in the desert near Los Huevos was released today by Ventana County Sheriff, Hugo 'Smiley' Hernandez. Kathleen Finn, age 20, a resident of Albuquerque, was discovered on Easter Sunday morning by three Los Huevos youngsters who were lizard hunting in the desert. Sheriff Hernandez released the victim's name after her mother, Mrs. Ovida Finn, was notified and made the identification at Green Haven Mortuary.

Details of the young woman's death are being withheld pending further investigation, but Sheriff Hernandez indicated he expects a quick resolution of the case. Mrs. Finn told sheriff's deputies that her daughter, known to her friends as Chipper, was working in Los Huevos to pay for her school tuition. 'She was a good girl, a loving daughter. Somebody evil did this to her, and God will punish them,' Mrs. Finn told a reporter as she left the mortuary. Besides her mother, Finn is survived by her brother, Bryan.

Harrie made a few notes and picked up the next article, *ARREST MADE IN FINN MURDER*.

Sheriff Hugo 'Smiley' Hernandez announced today that his deputies have arrested Manny Salinas, a well-known local prizefighter. Hernandez told reporters Salinas was involved with Miss Finn. They were seen together the night she was murdered, leaving a nightclub in the gambling district of Los Huevos. Sheriff

Hernandez stated he was 'confident that Salinas is the culprit. It was well known that Salinas was very jealous and possessive about Miss Finn. They recently broke up but he wouldn't leave her alone. So it's obvious that he decided if he couldn't have her, nobody would. It shouldn't take long to get him convicted and executed,' said the sheriff.

"Well, nothing like having the sheriff solve the case before it even goes to court," Harrie muttered.

Ginger looked up from her reading material. "What are you talking about?"

Harrie handed the article over for Ginger's inspection. "Old Sheriff 'Smiley' Hernandez laid it out for the press that Salinas is guilty and here's his motive and let's just hang him. He implied they didn't really need a trial. There's no way they would have found an unbiased jury with such prejudicial remarks to the newspapers."

Ginger said, "From what I've read in my stack, 'Smiley' Hernandez ended up on the losing end. It looks like Salinas was acquitted by his trial jury, and Sheriff Hernandez and some of his buddies went to jail."

Harrie nodded. "Those are the guys Philip was talking about yesterday."

"That's right. It says here, the sheriff, a deputy, and a state police captain decided to take a detour before delivering Salinas to the jail in Albuquerque. They stopped the car between Los Huevos and Albuquerque and took Manny off in the desert, not far from the place where Chipper Finn's body was found, but over the county line. They questioned him again, and it got rough. Manny was a fighter long enough to receive quite a few punches to the head, so he wasn't the sharpest knife in the drawer. He just kept insisting he was innocent. The more he denied, the more they pounded him. Finally, something else happened, which was apparently too graphic to be included in the newspaper article at the time. Anyway, somehow the FBI got involved in investigating the sheriff and the others, and they were convicted of violating Salinas's civil rights. They were all sent to federal prison."

"So they acquitted Manny Salinas."

"That's what it says here. Maybe the jury found out what the sheriff did . . . it doesn't explain."

Harrie pondered this. "Do they ever mention any other possible suspects? I didn't find anything in my stack indicating they even seriously looked at anyone else."

Ginger shrugged. "That I don't know. There seems to be a gap in the coverage. We'll have to ask Philip when we see him this afternoon." Ginger looked at Harrie quizzically. "Do you feel okay? You look tired and a little pale."

"I had another dream just before I woke up this morning, and it left a bad feeling."

Ginger studied Harrie's face. "Tell me about it."

She described the eerie setting and the faceless man. "That's about all there was to it. Nothing happened. It was just spooky. I'm nervous and irritable, and I'm having a hard time staying focused. " She rubbed her neck, willing herself to relax. Then she brightened. "Maybe some caffeine would help."

10

"Who was the man in your dream?" Ginger maneuvered through the traffic on Montgomery Boulevard.

"I have no idea. He was creepy, that's all I know. I'd rather focus on our meeting with Senator Lawrence."

Ginger nodded. "Okay. Then let's discuss the handsome stranger you met this morning."

"What's there to tell? Anyway, I never said anything about him being handsome. I really don't remember what he looked like. He was just a guy who scared me to death."

"Well, that might be easier to believe if I hadn't seen him myself. I also saw how flustered you were."

"You were watching me?"

"You mumbled something as you rushed outside. I got to the window just in time to see you drop your keys and focus your attention on finding them. Then I saw this good-looking guy walk up behind you, and you fell on your backside. Very unladylike. I started to rush out to help, but I saw he'd stepped in to haul your ass up off the pavement. So, I decided to let nature take its course." Ginger had a smug little smile as Harrie looked over at her.

"Exactly what were you expecting to happen after that?"

"Oh, I don't know, maybe that he would introduce himself and ask your name, and then he would offer to buy you a cup of coffee. Then you might feel comfortable enough to accept a real date with the guy, providing he was willing to hang around with absolutely no encouragement."

"You are positively determined to get me hooked up with someone, aren't you?"

Ginger feigned surprise. "Now why in the world would I do that? Why do you suppose I would want my best friend in the whole world to find a nice, respectable, loving male companion? Do you think I want you to be alone for the rest of your life?"

Harrie shook her head. "I'm just not ready. Maybe I'll never be ready. Anyway, what's the big hurry?"

"In case you've forgotten, we both turn thirty eight this summer."

Harrie grimaced. "Why do people say you 'turn'? It sounds like we become sour milk."

Ginger sighed. "You need to think about your biological clock. You've always said you wanted kids. If you wait much longer, that isn't going to happen."

Harrie felt her throat tighten, and she looked out the window. She took a long breath and let it out. "I can't worry about that right now. If it happens, it happens. If it doesn't ..." the unspoken words hung there.

Ginger looked at her friend. "Are you afraid to meet someone?"

Harrie started to make a flippant remark, but stopped before it reached her lips. "Yes, I guess I am," she admitted. "I haven't had such good luck with men. The marriage to Nick was a nightmare. Then Mark came along, and he was wonderful. I had just started to feel safe when they came to my door that night ..." She broke off and swallowed hard.

"Sweetie, I know you felt your life was over. For a long time, I thought you would never come out of it, but you did. It's been five years now. Every time I try to introduce you to someone, or when you meet someone on your own, you back away. You find something wrong with everyone before you even get to know them. Why can't you just try?"

Harrie didn't answer the question directly. "If something happened to Steve, would you try again?"

"You know Steve is my love and my life. He drives me crazy sometimes, and I'm sure he also has moments when he wonders why he wanted to marry me. But we have a wonderful life and two great kids. However, if something happened to him, I hope I'd have enough strength to go on and make a new life somewhere down the line. I know you have enough love in you to reserve a special place for Mark and still be able to love someone new. You told me yourself he sent you a message that you needed to move on. You said he would always watch over you. But he also said you had a life to live, and you'd better get on with it. Didn't you tell me that?"

Harrie looked at Ginger and grinned. "The light is green, you know. That woman behind us will start honking if you don't go now."

"Okay, okay. Lecture is over, but you get my drift, right?" She eased her foot onto the gas pedal.

"I do indeed. You want me to stop the pity party and get a spine, and" she held up her hand, "you want me to give the next poor sucker a break."

"Well, that's not the way I would have put it, but, yeah, that's pretty much it."

"Okay, if I promise to at least meet one of your bachelor buddies, will you give it a rest? Honestly, you're worse than my mother."

"Fine. Insult me all you want, but you know I'm right. And what do you mean 'one of my bachelor buddies'? Do you think I have them stashed in a closet somewhere?"

"I wouldn't doubt it. You always seem to have one who needs an escort for some party. I'm surprised you haven't tried to fix me up with Senator Lawrence!"

"Now there's an idea worth exploring," Ginger teased.

"Please tell me you aren't serious." Harrie looked alarmed.

"Oh, get over yourself. What would a famous, distinguished man like Philip Lawrence want with a skinny kid like you? Besides, he has his own tragic love story."

Harrie's eyes widened. "You never told me anything about a tragic love story. What happened?"

"Some other time. It'll take too long. One night soon, come over for dinner and I'll fill you in."

"This is a trick, right? You lure me to your house with the promise of good food and wine. Then, when I least expect it, you bring him out."

"Bring out who?"

"One of your closet bachelors, of course."

"No, I think I'll watch the parking lot in our complex. Eventually the tall, dark and handsome guy will show up again, and when he does, I'll be ready for him. I'll march out there, introduce myself, and tell him you are too shy to approach him yourself."

"Oh, my God, I'll bet you would. Well, you better pray he doesn't show up again, because he'll think you are a lunatic, and he'll have you arrested for stalking him. Then I'll have to call Steve to get you out of jail."

They were both laughing so hard they almost missed the turn into Canyon Estates. The mood in the car had definitely lightened. Harrie felt better than she had all day and was ready to get back to work. Maybe tonight she would sleep without the dreams.

11

Tarnished silver clouds hung over the Sandia Mountains as Harrie and Ginger drove through the gate of Canyon Estates. The smell of moisture hung heavy in the air.

Harrie craned her head to get a better look at the sky. "Do you think it's really going to rain this time?"

Ginger laughed. "Get serious. You know I haven't had my car washed yet. It can't possibly rain until I do that."

As they parked, a dust devil passed over the car like a ghostly apparition. Ramona answered the door and led them to the library.

Philip read and approved the edited pages of his book. Then he asked Harrie, "Did you read those articles?"

Harrie shifted in her chair. His directness and commanding presence were unsettling. "Most of them, but I sort of skimmed through the rest. There's one thing we wondered about. What did the sheriff and his buddies do to Manny Salinas? It didn't say specifically in the news articles."

Philip sighed. "What they did to poor old Manny was really horrible. They took him out in the desert, stripped his clothes and put a bicycle lock on his testicles. They thought that would force a confession out of him."

Harrie gasped. "That's awful! How did they get away with it?"

"They didn't. Manny told his mother what happened, and she went straight to the FBI. They discovered the corruption that had been going on here for years. As I told you, gambling was rampant during that time, and officials were bribed to look the other way. It went all the way to the state government in Santa Fe. It was said that some of our congressional delegation were also bought and paid for. There were people who thought one of those higher office holders might have been involved with Chipper Finn or at least had some knowledge or involvement with her death."

Harrie shook her head. "It's hard to believe things were that bad. If they started cleaning things up, why didn't they ever find her killer?"

"Is that your real question?" Philip Lawrence was certainly direct.

Harrie took a deep breath and plunged ahead. "Okay. Who do you think murdered Chipper Finn?"

Philip studied her face for a moment with those penetrating eyes. She could imagine him in a courtroom or on the floor of the senate, evaluating his opponent, looking for the weak points. She reminded herself she wasn't an opponent and had no reason to feel intimidated.

After what seemed like minutes, he spoke. "Well, that is the question, isn't it? I'm not prepared to answer just yet. Who do you think the culprit is?"

Harrie didn't know what to say. Why ask her? Why would he think she knew anything about it? Then she remembered telling him about her dream. She said, "I didn't know anything about this case before we started editing your book, so there's no way I would know."

Philip patted her hand in a soothing way. "Maybe there is. I sense you have an unusual gift. Call it intuition, psychic ability, whatever you want, but you do sometimes know things, don't you?"

Harrie didn't want the conversation to continue in this direction. She looked to Ginger for help, but Ginger just sat there.

"I had a strong sense that you were in danger. I saw the body in the dream – the one I then saw here in the clipping – and I knew something else bad was going to happen." She looked at him, her eyes pleading for understanding.

"What about the dream you had last night?" Ginger gave her a questioning look. "You said you saw a man. Maybe that's the person who's the threat."

"But he didn't have a face, and I'm not even sure it was a man. It was dark, and he, or whoever, was dressed in dark clothes and wearing a hooded jacket or sweater. Maybe that didn't have anything to do with this," Harrie finished lamely.

Philip watched her thoughtfully. "Then why do you think you dreamed something so frightening? Do you often have such nightmares?"

He sounded like a psychiatrist, and it was somewhat annoying.

"I doubt I have them any more often than anybody else. I've just had some since we started working on the book. Maybe I'm more open to suggestion than the average person." Harrie paused and tried to sound less defensive before she continued. "You have more answers to these questions than I do. You were there. You investigated. I don't know anybody connected with this case except you, and I don't know anybody like this spooky character from my dreams."

Ginger spoke again. "What about the guy outside the office last night?"

Philip finally shifted his attention from Harrie to Ginger. "What guy?"

Ginger explained about their interview with Caroline Johnson and the person in the black SUV outside their office. Philip's concern was apparent.

"Did anybody get a license number on this SUV?" he asked.

"No," Ginger said, sounding contrite.

"Did you happen to notice what kind of SUV it was?"

"You mean was it a Ford or a Chevrolet or something?"

Philip nodded. "Yes. It would help to know that."

Harrie shook her head, and looked at Ginger. Ginger shrugged her shoulders. "Who knows anymore? They all look alike to me."

Philip spoke carefully. "I want you to stay alert and pay attention to what's going on around you. If somebody really is watching you, we need to find out who and why."

"There's no reason for anybody to be watching us," Harrie said unconvincingly. "We don't know anything."

Ginger said, "What about Sunglasses?"

Philip looked confused. "Sunglasses?"

"That's what Harrie called the guy she encountered in the parking lot this morning. He may have driven a black SUV, too."

Harrie protested. "I did not have an encounter. He just helped me up after I slipped. I don't know what kind of car he was in. I don't even know if he had a car. Maybe he was walking or just got off the bus."

Philip shook his head. "Ladies, we have to talk about this. Let's sit over here, and you can explain just what you mean about him helping you up off the ground." He looked at Ginger. "And I need to know why you think he was driving a black SUV."

Philip settled himself in the leather chair. Ginger related what she had seen through the office window that morning. Philip asked Harrie questions to get her part of the story.

"So you don't think you've seen this man before?"

Harrie shook her head. Philip looked at Ginger, and she thought it over before she spoke.

"You know, I didn't recognize him exactly, but he does look sort of familiar."

Harrie almost choked on her coffee. "You never said anything about that. How would you know him?"

"I don't know, but there was something about him. It'll come to me. Give me a chance to sleep on it. I didn't think it was important at the time."

"Tell me about this woman you interviewed," said Philip.

"Caroline Johnson, and we did more than interview her. We hired her. She's our new office manager. She'll be fabulous." She explained that Caroline had worked at Snow, Tessler, Knight, and McConaghy and was the managing partner's assistant.

Philip frowned. "She was Jacob Snow's assistant?"

"Yes. Is there some significance to that?"

"Perhaps. Did I tell you there were two brothers and a brother-in-law in the practice? Jacob Snow was the youngest and became the managing partner in 1952. Then there was Peter Templeton who married Rachel Snow, the middle sibling. Rachel was close to Daniel's age. They were both much older than Jacob. Daniel and I were friends many years ago. Later on, I got to know Jacob rather well. I must have met Caroline Johnson during that period."

Harrie said, "You wouldn't believe the weird prospects the employment agency sent us. I had given up until we interviewed Caroline. She was perfect for us, and she's available right now. My only concern is that she seems almost too good to be true."

Philip looked at the young women seated across from him. "Appearances can be deceiving."

Harrie put her cup down. "That was one of my grandmother's favorite sayings. She said it all the time."

He sat back in his chair, and looked at them with his steely gaze. "Okay, then here's another saying – If you think something seems too good to be true, it probably is."

12

Philip Lawrence took his glasses off and sat back in his chair. He vigorously rubbed his face in an attempt to wipe away the fatigue.

In the hour since Harrie and Ginger had left, he had been thinking about something they told him. He made a phone call and got right to the point. "We spoke a few days ago about you doing more work for me. I'd like to meet with you to discuss that. Could you come by my home this afternoon to go over the details?"

When the man agreed, Philip ended the call by saying, "I'll leave word at the gate that I'm expecting you."

He hoped he wasn't making a big mistake, but at this point, he had to risk stirring things up. There were facts that needed verification. He sighed heavily and went back to the safe room. He closed the door behind him, chuckled to himself and thought, *Philip, old man, you really are getting paranoid.*

When he'd started writing the book, he hadn't planned to solve the crime or even insinuate who the guilty party was. It was just a story that haunted him, one he thought needed retelling. It wasn't his intention nor was it a good idea to provoke old animosities. However, somewhere during the writing, his perspective changed. It now seemed almost dishonest to write the book and not even attempt to offer the truth about the crime. But the truth was sure to cause trouble.

He decided to resort to his old standby method to work out the kinks. He had a small tape recorder and liked to speak his thoughts into it unedited, just as they came to him. When he replayed it, he could tell if the rhythm and pacing would work. He had no interest in computers. He still had his old IBM typewriter, but found his thoughts flowed better using a yellow legal pad and his Mont Blanc pen or the tape recorder, which was almost as old as his Selectric. He spoke into the microphone.

"Ginger, today I feel like using the tape instead of typing. I hope you don't mind too much. Just transcribe it the best you can, and see what kind of sense you make of it. Okay, here goes. Today is Tuesday, April 11."

He closed his eyes, and the story came alive again in his mind.

"I'm thinking back to the time I heard about the murder of Chipper Finn. I was in Washington. When I returned to Albuquerque, the story was still on the front pages of the *Albuquerque Morning Sun,* soon to be my new employer. They assigned me to the Metro desk. I ran all over town, trailed by a young kid with a big Speed Graphic camera. The paper wanted background info on the victim, the investigation and any suspects. All I knew about the case was that Chipper had been murdered, her body found in the desert and one of her boyfriends arrested. After talking to many people, I learned that the boyfriend had been beaten and tortured by the sheriff in Ventana County and two other upstanding lawmen. For whatever reason, the sheriff needed a confession, and he needed it sooner rather than later. That intrigued me. So I talked to Chipper's friends, her mother and the people she worked with. I even tracked down her brother. I began to get a picture that was very different from what we had seen up to that point. Chipper had been portrayed as a 'party girl', someone who went out with lots of men and was pretty free with her favors. She was rumored to have had a tumultuous relationship with Manny Salinas, the boyfriend who was arrested and mistreated so badly. But according to her friends, Chipper and Manny never even dated. It seems Manny was a friend of Chipper's older brother. She had known him since she was a little girl, and she considered him more like a sibling than anything. They occasionally hung out together because Manny sometimes served as a bouncer at the club where Chipper worked at the time of her death. According to everyone I talked with, they were not an item. Not only did she not date Manny, she didn't really date at all. According to two of her girl friends, Chipper had been involved with an older man. Neither of the girls would admit to knowing who the man was. All they said was he was some big shot with lots of money. Her mother, if she knew any of this, wouldn't admit it either, and maintained that Chipper never dated anybody. But some other people told me Chipper's heart had been captured by a young man. But no one had a name. Or if they did, they weren't giving it to me.

"There was one girl I wasn't able to locate at the time. She and Chipper had become friends when both worked in Los Huevos. People said they were closer than sisters, and this girl, Becky Martinez, was the one who knew all about Chipper's older man friend. Becky disappeared just before Chipper was murdered. I talked to many people but couldn't find out where she'd gone. I decided not to mention her name in the follow-up stories I did. I had a hunch she might turn up someday and would appreciate not being speculated about in the papers. I also discovered, through sources I developed at the Albuquerque Police Department, that she was not on their radar to be interviewed. So I kept quiet. After all, I really didn't know anything solid, and it seemed she didn't want to be found. I had a gut feeling that if she had dropped out of sight, perhaps she'd better stay that way.

"Manny was acquitted. It finally came out about the beating and torture, and the sheriff and all his buddies were put on trial in federal court and convicted of violating Salinas's civil rights. The civil rights case soon became the big story. There was a state police captain, as well as a deputy, who joined old Smiley Hernandez in the federal prison at La Tuna, Texas. By the time all that was over, the young woman's murder had been all but forgotten. It would have stayed that way, too, except for what happened next."

Movement on the monitor from the camera overlooking the front porch and driveway caught Philip's attention. A car had just arrived in his driveway, and he watched the young private investigator he had called get out of a black SUV.

13

Wednesday Morning, April 12, 2000

Wednesday morning dawned gray and cloudy, but the clouds still seemed reluctant to part with any of their precious contents. Harrie grabbed a sweater and umbrella as she left her house. She felt prepared to handle whatever weather the day would bring.

The drive to the office was so familiar she did it on autopilot as she thought about the meeting with Senator Lawrence the previous day. She found his friendship with one of the Snow brothers interesting. Maybe Caroline would remember meeting him. She pondered whether he could be right about somebody watching her and Ginger. Harrie's grandmother always told her that she should 'trust her gut'.

Her mind drifted to thoughts of her Nana. As an only child, she spent many summer months with her maternal grandparents. She loved visiting her Nana and Baba and playing with their dogs and cats. They lived in a small town about an hour from Fort Worth. Nana knew all sorts of things that other people's grandmothers didn't. She always seemed to know what Harrie was thinking and how she was feeling.

The summer after Harrie's twelfth birthday, she took one last trip to her grandparents' house. She traveled on the bus alone for the first time. The prospect of seeing her grandparents pleased her, but made her melancholy at the same time. Her family was moving to Albuquerque, and she knew she wouldn't be able to see them as often. She resented her father's job for sending them to this new place. Who ever heard of Albuquerque, and why would anybody want to live in a place most people couldn't even spell? She moped around the house the first few days she was there. Even her grandfather's Golden Retriever couldn't entice Harrie out of her mood.

After three days, her grandmother suggested taking a walk. Harrie sensed Nana had something to say to her, so she walked along quietly. They sat on the bench close to the playground where birds gathered, hoping for a handout.

"You know, Harrie, having a new place to live is like unwrapping a very special present. It's special because it doesn't give you just one gift. It gives you a new gift every morning as you wake up to new experiences."

Harrie looked up at Nana, confused. "But we're moving away. I won't get to see my friends anymore. I'll have to go to a different school. I won't have my room, and . . ." her voice broke with a sob, "worst of all, I won't have you and Baba."

Nana put her arm around Harrie's shoulder and hugged her. She patted her head, letting Harrie get out the tears. "I know what you think, but you are wrong, dear. You're not unhappy because you won't get to see you friends or have your old room or any of that. You're unhappy because you're scared. You're afraid you won't make any friends, afraid you won't like your school. But you can make new friends and love your new school even better than your old one. All you have to do is let it happen. You've been thinking about this with a negative attitude." Nana laughed. "If you don't watch out, you'll make it all come true."

Harrie wanted to protest but had the strangest feeling in the middle of her stomach that they had this conversation before. Nana smiled. "Sometimes people experience a thing called '*déjà vu*'. It means you're doing something you think you've done before. Are you having that feeling right now?"

Harrie felt a little shiver. "How could you know that?"

"Sometimes people visit us in our dreams. I've visited you, your mom, and many others. Last night, you visited me."

Harrie couldn't have been more surprised if the birds at their feet had begun to recite Shakespeare. "How could I have done that? I don't remember it."

"My guess is that you were asking for my help. People do that sometimes. If they're troubled and searching for answers, they can go looking for them after they are asleep at night. Sometimes they remember a dream or part of one, and they seem to think of a solution. A lot of problem solving goes on in a person's dreams."

"But why wouldn't I remember something like that. It's so spooky!"

Nana laughed. "It's only spooky because you just heard about it for the first time. When you think about it, it's an efficient use of time. What else does your brain have to do while you're lying there in your bed?" Nana looked over at Harrie. "Does this make any sense to you?"

"Um, I guess so."

"Do you have any questions you want to ask me?"

"Yes. Can you get inside my brain anytime you want to?"

Nana laughed gently. "Not really. I only go where you invite me. It's just the stuff you're trying to figure out that I pick up on. Then I pay you a dream visit." Nana stood up, and Harrie realized it was time to start back.

"Last night I explained you're heading into what can be the best thing that ever happened to you. Everything from this point on will be the true beginning of your life. You aren't a little child anymore. You'll make the best friends you've ever had, starting now. You'll experience a new place with all its differences. You're beginning the process of leaving the nest, just like those birds back there we were feeding. Do you understand what I'm telling you?"

Harrie looked into her grandmother's eyes and felt a sense of peace she hadn't felt since she found out about the move. She grinned and took Nana's hand. "I think so."

"Good. I don't want this to sound complicated. Just remember. From now on, you can make a big difference in how your life turns out. Listen to your feelings. Trust your instincts. There are angels all around us, and they will help us if we open our minds and our hearts to hear them. There's one more thing that you have to promise me, and it's really important, so listen carefully."

Harrie struggled to take in everything her grandmother told her. This was all so new, and she felt the truth of what she heard. "I promise, Nana, I promise. What is it?"

"It's easy to let negative thoughts and attitudes take over your mind. You must learn to protect yourself from the negativity you might generate and from the negative energy of people around you. There are no guarantees for happiness, Harrie, and you'll have your share of sorrow. Everybody does. But you can rise above the negative stuff."

Harrie's mind returned to her driving as she entered the busy area around her office. She felt calmer than she had all week and sent a mental thanks to her grandmother for the wisdom she'd always tried to impart.

Caroline Johnson was already there, and Harrie wished her good morning and welcomed her to their little team.

After stashing her briefcase in her office, Harrie turned to see a man talking and laughing with Caroline and Ginger. Harrie tried to understand why the scene startled her. Then the man turned. That little stray curl was loose on his forehead again, and he flashed his white-toothed smile.

Sunglasses was back.

"This is Philip Lawrence," the senator said when the investigator answered his cell phone. "Would it be possible for you to drop by again this morning? I need to speak with you about something else, and I'd prefer it be in person."

The PI said he'd be there within the next half hour. Philip felt relieved. By taking a step toward a course of action, an enormous weight was lifted.

Almost exactly half an hour later, Philip was seated at his desk in the library when Ramona escorted the young man in. Philip explained what he needed, and the PI said he would call him when the task was completed. They agreed to meet again later in the afternoon.

He still had a few minutes before lunch. He decided to make another call. He didn't need to look up the number.

When she answered, he smiled at the sound of her voice. She had a way of cheering him up when he most needed it. They had become good friends in the last few years. They were both alone and sometimes lonely, but neither was interested in a romantic relationship. They rarely saw each other face to face, preferring the immediacy of telephone conversations.

He explained the reason for his call and was relieved she was willing to do what he asked. He wished her a good day, and promised her, in return, to take care of himself. It was an honest and uncomplicated relationship. He couldn't ask for a better friend.

Philip selected a volume from the bookcase, and went down the hall for lunch. A smile softened his face as he sat down to eat.

Maybe it would be a good day after all.

Harrie looked at her watch for perhaps the fifth time. Less than fifteen minutes had passed since she arrived and saw Sunglasses standing in the outer office, looking like he owned the place. She struggled to concentrate on the papers in front of her. She felt like such a fool. God only knew what Caroline must think right now.

Instead of going out to help Ginger get Caroline acclimated, Harrie had sequestered herself in her office. She didn't understand why. When Ginger poked her head in a few moments later, Harrie mumbled an excuse about needing to finish something. Ginger sounded annoyed and said they could use her help when she had a minute. Then she closed the door, leaving Harrie to her busy work. But the only busy work Harrie had consisted of regaining control of her unexpected runaway emotions.

The reception area was surrounded by three offices, a conference room and a tiny kitchen. Because it originally held a savings and loan branch office, there was a small vault at the back that now housed filing cabinets and storage shelves. The offices and conference room had windows facing the reception area. Vertical blinds afforded privacy when needed. Harrie had quickly availed herself of that privacy and had thus cut off her normal view. When she peeked out and saw Sunglasses had left, she took a deep breath, gathered her wits and opened her office door to see Caroline and Ginger bent over something on Ginger's desk. She joined them and saw they were examining catalogues from office furniture stores and a brochure from a local computer company.

Ginger looked up and gathered the catalogues. "Let's takes this stuff to the conference room so we can spread it out and decide what we need."

Harrie felt gratitude for the reprieve but knew she would have to deal with her strange behavior and smooth things over with Ginger. They picked out the furniture for Caroline then turned their attention to the computer brochure.

"Do you both have PCs in your offices?" Caroline asked.

Ginger sighed. "Well, I guess you could call it that. It's a laptop I got from one of my sons when he needed a new one. He said it was too slow, and it couldn't remember stuff, whatever that means."

Harrie couldn't stifle her giggle. "Memory, Ginger. The computer's memory needs to be upgraded."

"Whatever. I just know that about half the time the screen turns this blue color and everything stops."

Caroline handed the brochure to Ginger. "This is the computer company we used at the law firm. They're local, reasonable and dependable. If you'd like, I'll call them and ask for a quote."

Caroline looked at Harrie. "What about you? Are you in the market for a new computer?"

"Heavens, no. I just bought myself a new laptop. It has all the latest bells and whistles, and it'll do me fine for the next few years."

"I'd like to have our computers networked," said Caroline.

Harrie and Ginger nodded uncertainly.

"Good," said Caroline, "I'll make an appointment with Duane, their PC Manager. He'll see what needs to be done."

Ginger looked at Harrie blankly.

Harrie said, "We've been talking about upgrading our Internet connection. If we network, it will be more cost effective, and it will make our lives so much easier. You'll love it."

"Does this mean I have to learn how to email?"

Caroline's eyes widened. "You mean you don't already use email? How do you manage without it?"

"Well, see, I do this weird thing called 'writing letters.' You guys should try it sometime. It's quite satisfying, and people actually keep them in boxes and take them out and reread them."

Harrie laughed aloud. "Don't pay any attention to her, Caroline. She's used email for years. She just doesn't like it."

Caroline looked relieved. "You had me going. For a minute there, I thought I'd have to train you."

Then she said to Harrie, "I found a message for you on the answering machine just before you arrived today. It came in sometime last night."

Harrie took the note from her without looking at it and slipped it into her pocket. "Thanks. We'll set up some kind of message box so you can get them off your desk, and we'll be responsible for retrieving them."

"I'll add that to my list of supplies. In fact, I'll run on over to the office supply store right now, if that's okay with you."

Harrie looked over at Ginger's office and saw her on the phone in an animated conversation. Harrie decided she would return the phone call from the message in her pocket and give Ginger a chance to finish. There would still be time to discuss this morning's episode.

She picked up the phone and reached into her pocket for the pink slip. The phone number didn't look familiar. She looked at the name of the caller. *This can't be right.* She looked again.

Harrie was holding the pink slip in one hand and the telephone in the other when Ginger asked, "What's up?"

Harrie handed her the phone message without speaking. Ginger looked at the paper and let out a squeak.

"Why the hell is Nick Constantine calling you?"

Harrie drank the last of the water and thought about switching to coffee, but her nerves were already jangled, and she didn't need more stimulation. She walked over to look out the east window. Normally she loved to watch the way the morning sun lit up the cables of the Sandia Peak tram that draped in two wide swaths up the face of the mountain. When the light was just right, it looked like a gossamer spider web instead of the heavy steel cable it actually was.

But today she didn't even notice. The muscles in the back of her neck felt tight. When the phone on Harrie's desk rang, she jumped so violently her neck made a little popping sound. Ginger came back in the room just as Harrie grabbed the receiver.

"Southwest Editorial Services," she said in a strained voice.

"Hey Kiddo, it's Steve." Harrie nodded to Ginger and pressed the button to put the call on speakerphone.

"I'm putting you on speaker, Steve. Ginger's here with me, and we both need to know what you found out."

"Not much, I'm afraid. I called the number you gave me and got an answering service. I told them I needed to contact Nick Constantine, and they said he was out of town until tonight and couldn't be reached. I left my name, cell and home numbers, and asked that he call me as soon as he gets back. They hung up before I could ask for more information, not that it would have done any good. I'm sorry, Harrie. I can't think of anything else we can do until he calls me back."

Harrie's shoulders slumped. "That's okay, Steve. You tried. Thanks for agreeing to take this unpleasant task off my plate. I just hope he calls you back rather than calling me again. I'm not going to talk to him. Not without knowing what's going on."

"Look. If he's out of town until tonight, and he can't be reached by phone, it's unlikely he'll call back until then. Does he have your home number?"

"I can't think of any way he could possibly know my home number."

Steve thought a moment. "You know, there's someone else I can contact to see if Nick's been in touch. I'll try to locate this guy and see if he knows anything. Let's not worry until we know what's going on, okay? Just make sure someone else answers the phone the rest of the day. Then, tonight after work, why don't you come to our house for dinner? I can pick up some hamburgers or something. If he calls me back, you'll be right there, and we can make a plan. In fact you could stay with us tonight."

"Thanks, Steve," Harrie said. "I don't think tonight will be a problem. I feel much better just knowing you're dealing with this instead of me. And thanks for the dinner invitation. Next time maybe I'll cook for you."

They laughed, and Harrie ended the call. Ginger sat down and looked at Harrie.

"Okay, now that we have Nick under control for the time being, let's discuss something else. Do you want to tell me why you went all Greta Garbo on us earlier?"

Harrie leaned back in her chair. How to explain the unexplainable? "I've been thinking about what Philip said to us yesterday. He gave you those keys and went on about us possibly being in danger. All this talk about black SUVs and watching out for strangers, and then I walked in this morning and the first thing I see is Sunglasses standing in our offices making himself right at home. It was freaky. Why was he here, and why did you and Caroline act like you knew him?"

"Well, it's really funny when you think about it. I mean, what are the odds he would turn up again after the conversation we had about him and the possibility of you two going on a date."

"Yeah, it's hysterical. Is that why he was here?"

"No, he just happened to arrive, saw Caroline unloading the boxes from her car, and he offered to help a lady in need."

"Yes, but why did he arrive *here*, at our office?"

"He never said. He just happened to park next to Caroline and saw she needed help."

"But it looked like both you and Caroline knew him. You were being pretty chummy with him."

"It turns out that he's the son of a friend of Caroline's or something like that. So, naturally, when he recognized her in the parking lot struggling with those boxes, he offered to carry them. He seems very nice. I would have introduced you to him if you had joined us. But no, you ran away and hid."

Harrie protested, "I wasn't hiding—exactly. It just threw me, seeing him standing there like that."

"Well if you're really nice to me, maybe I'll introduce you to DJ next time."

"DJ? What kind of name is DJ? And what do you mean 'next time'?"

"That's what they call him, DJ – DJ Scott. He seems like a very respectable person. Anyway, Caroline has known him since he was a baby, so he must be okay."

"If you don't mind, I'll wait before I pick out my silver pattern. Honestly, you really are the limit. You're ready to set me up with this guy, and all you know about him is that he was once a baby, and he's kind to his mother's friends. I'll bet Ted Bundy was occasionally nice to his mom's friends, too."

They heard the front door open and close. Caroline stuck her head into Harrie's office and said, "I've returned, and I'm happy to report success. The office furniture and equipment will be delivered tomorrow and so will the computer. Duane from the computer company will come after the delivery to do the network installation." She gave them a jaunty salute and went back to her temporary station.

Harrie spent the rest of the morning going over the senator's manuscript and making editing suggestions. At four o'clock, Caroline gently tapped on Harrie's open door. "Excuse me. If you would like me to open up in the mornings, I'm going to need a key. Do you have an extra one?"

Harrie marked her place in the document and thought for a moment. "You know, I'm not sure we do, but I can certainly run over to Lowe's and have one made."

After checking with Ginger to make sure she didn't have a spare key, Harrie headed for Lowes, telling Ginger that she would be back before closing time.

As soon as she pulled into the afternoon traffic on Wyoming Boulevard, she knew her timetable might have been optimistic. She turned up her music on the CD player and resigned herself to a city dweller's worst nightmare – rush hour traffic. Even so, she drove into the parking lot at Lowe's only fifteen minutes later. Her luck held when she discovered the guy who made the keys wasn't busy, and she was soon back in her car. She decided on what she thought might be a quicker route back and was congratulating herself on the good time she was making when she caught the red light at Eubank and Academy. She looked at her watch and saw she had only ten minutes to make it back to the office before five. She tapped her fingers impatiently on the steering wheel as she watched the red light, willing it to turn green. The driver of the car immediately in front of her caught her attention because he seemed to be watching her in his side mirror. As she averted her eyes, something stirred in her subconscious. She turned her head ever so slightly trying to get a better view of his face in his mirror, hoping her dark glasses hid the fact that she was staring. There was something unsettling about those eyes looking back at her, and they were definitely looking at her. She felt a rush of adrenaline.

When she returned her attention to the traffic light, the left arrow had just turned green, and the line of cars started up. The peeping driver moved his vehicle through the intersection and maneuvered his way through the westbound traffic until he was several car lengths ahead of her. Was it someone she knew? Why did she feel so creepy about the driver? Then she realized he was in a black SUV.

17

Wednesday Evening, April 12, 2000

Philip leaned back in his leather chair, eyes closed, lost in Rachmaninov's *Variation Eighteen* of *Rhapsody on a Theme of Paganini*. The swelling music as the orchestra reached for the final burst before the gentle, calm climax was almost erotic. In the silence that followed the last note, he opened his eyes, feeling calm and relaxed.

It was time to get back to his dictation. In the kitchen, Ramona prepared dinner for him, but he knew it would take at least another hour. She always set it out in the dining room and tapped softly on the door to let him know she was leaving. He had grown accustomed to this routine over the years and looked forward to it each evening.

He went back to the hidden room and activated the monitors. He picked up the microphone and thought about his visit with the private investigator that morning. Philip had used him several times recently and was pleased with the result. He wanted part of the story about Chipper Finn checked out, and he was concerned for Ginger and Harrie. It was possible they were mistaken about a mysterious stalker, but he didn't think so. Philip described that situation to his visitor and asked him to find out if the women were being followed. Then he then asked him to check something at the New Mexico Department of Public Health. The detective had worked quickly, delivering his report that very afternoon.

Philip switched on the recorder and dictated for the next forty-five minutes. When he was done, he unlocked the bottom drawer of his desk and placed the cassette in a box with others like it. He removed a large document folder from the drawer. He selected some documents from the folder and transferred them to a brown 9 by 12 envelope. He sealed it and stared at it, wondering again if this was the right thing to do.

He thought about the people who had been involved and those who might still be affected by his decision. But only one course of action satisfied his conscience. He knew at least one person wanted to stop him. Maybe more than one, but he would not be swayed by fear. He picked up his pen and wrote across the sealed flap, "To Be Opened In The Event Of My Death."

There were several photographs on the walls of his sanctuary, mostly scenes of landmarks such as the Capitol and the Lincoln Memorial and of the Senator shaking hands with well-known figures, including Presidents Nixon, Carter, Reagan and the first President Bush. He removed one picture and loosened its back. He slipped the brown envelope between the photo and its backing.

He exited the safe room, secured it and sat at his big walnut desk. As he wrote a note for Ginger, Ramona knocked softly on the library door. "I'm leaving now, Senator. Your dinner is on the table. Have a pleasant evening."

He called back, "Come in, Ramona. I'd like you to do something for me."

He clipped the note to another item, put them in a stamped envelope and handed it to Ramona. "Would you mind dropping this off at the post office for me on your way home?"

"Of course, Sir. No trouble at all. Will there be anything else?"

"No, thank you, Ramona. I'll see you in the morning."

18

Harrie drained her wine glass. Steve refilled it.

"Whoa there," said Harrie. "I still have to drive home, you know!"

"We could always drive you instead," he shot back jovially.

Ginger shook her head. "I think my husband is trying to render you incapable of driving so you'll be forced to stay with us tonight."

Steve raised his eyebrows in mock astonishment. Then his smile faded, and he became serious. "I think it's a good idea for you to change your routine a bit, Harrie. What would it hurt if you stayed here tonight?"

Harrie looked puzzled. "I can't stay here tonight. I have to get home and feed Tuptim."

Steve sighed. "I'm worried about you." He shifted his gaze to include Ginger and said, "I'm worried about both of you. This thing with Nick calling today is more than a little strange, and the timing is odd, don't you think?"

Harrie looked at Ginger, who shrugged, and then back at Steve. "Well, I definitely think it's odd for Nick to call but I don't get what you mean about the timing." Harrie had told them about her trip back from Lowe's that afternoon and the man who seemed to be watching her in his side mirror. She didn't see any connection.

"Look, all I'm saying is that you've seen a suspicious automobile several times in the last few days. Now, after – what, ten years? twelve? – Nick calls you."

Harrie held up a hand. "It's been thirteen years, but who's counting?"

"My point is you got the divorce by default. He never even responded to the notification. He literally dropped out of sight. So suddenly, it's urgent for him to speak with you? Call me cynical if you want, but it's too much of a coincidence. And I haven't been able to find out anything about why he would be back."

Ginger sat quietly, listening to the conversation. Harrie hoped her friend would join her protest against Steve's unfounded concern. But Ginger said, "I wasn't going to tell you this. It seemed silly to get you all upset for nothing. Except now . . ."

A chill crept up Harrie's spine. An image flashed into her mind, the figure in the hooded jacket. The person from her dream two nights ago turned slowly toward her and pushed back the hood. Only now, instead of being faceless, there was a person with features.

Harrie gasped. She reached for her wine, but her hands were trembling so much that she stopped short of grasping it.

"Harrie," Ginger stammered, "what happened? What's wrong?"

Steve knelt down beside Harrie and took her hands in his. "Your hands are like ice and you look like you've seen a ghost. What's going on?"

"It's the dream," she whispered. "The man in the dream—I told you about him Tuesday, remember, on the way to Philips' house?"

Ginger knelt down on the other side of Harrie. "But Sweetie, you said you couldn't see a face—that you couldn't tell who it was. What's gotten you so upset?"

Harrie took deep, steadying breaths and closed her eyes. When she opened them again, she said, "Something fell into place as I listened to you. My brain dumped the dream back into my mind, and I saw his face. I've never had anything like that happen before." A sense of wonder and curiosity now replaced her fear. "I have no idea if my mind made up things to fill in the gaps, or if I really did dream it, but the person I told you about pushed back the hood, and I clearly saw his face for the first time." She looked from Steve to Ginger and back again.

"The man in my dream was Nick."

Steve looked skeptical, and a stunned expression covered Ginger's face. She stood up and sputtered, "You mean you just now saw Nick's face as the man from the dream, and you didn't see that part before? How is that possible?"

Harrie shook her head. "I have no idea. You started to tell me something, and you hesitated. That's when the dream popped back into my head, and I saw Nick. Please, tell me what you started to say."

"Okay. I might as well tell you. It can't be any worse than what you've already seen. A week ago I found a message on our answering machine. It was a man, and he sounded vaguely familiar, but I couldn't place the voice. He didn't leave a number. Said he'd call back when his plans were firmed up." She slumped in the chair and shook her head. "I forgot all about it until today."

Steve looked puzzled. "What made you remember now?"

"When Harrie showed me the message that Nick had called, it hit me maybe that's why the voice sounded familiar. Don't you see? He could have been in town all week. He could be the one who's been hanging around in the black SUV."

"Are you saying Nick was the voice on the answering machine?"

"It's been a long time since I've heard his voice. But when I found out he had called Harrie, I thought the first call might also have been Nick. The more I think about it, the more convinced I am."

"Why didn't you say something this morning after he called? I couldn't imagine why he would be in town, much less calling me, and why in God's name would he have become a stalker? I still can't believe there's any connection," Harrie folded her arms in front of her chest, a look of defiance on her face.

"Like I say, I wasn't sure. And you were already so jumpy from Sunglasses showing up. That's why I suggested we have Steve return the call. I figured he could find out what was going on, and maybe you wouldn't have to talk to Nick at all. Also, if he had been the one who left the message last week, he'd tell Steve, and the mystery would be solved."

Harrie's face relaxed into a smile. "You're right. I was having a bad day even before I got the phone message." She patted her friend's hand. "You did the right thing."

They were exchanging theories about why Nick would be coming through town and what he could possibly want when Ginger interrupted. "I bought a chocolate fudge cake. It hasn't been cut yet. Come help me."

When the phone rang, Steve took the call in the den.

When he returned, Ginger and Harrie were setting out desert plates with slices of the cake. Ginger looked at him, a teasing remark on her lips, but she stopped when she saw his face. "Steve, what's wrong?"

He stared at her. "The call was from Presbyterian Hospital. Nick's been in an automobile accident. My business card was in his pocket so they called me. They don't know if he's going to make it."

19

Harrie watched the hands on the waiting room clock reach ten o'clock. Two hours, she thought. How much longer could this go on? Ginger also watched the clock as if her stern attention could make time move faster.

"How much longer do you think Steve will be in there? He's been gone forever." Harrie didn't really expect an answer. She said it just to keep from jumping up and running out of the building.

When they'd arrived, Steve insisted he be allowed to speak to Nick's doctors. He hadn't made much headway until he mentioned he was an attorney. After that, the nurse admitted him to the inner sanctum of the Emergency Room. They had seen him only briefly since then. Steve's business card they had found in Nick's wallet had a notation that Steve was to be notified in case of emergency. Harrie and Ginger had chewed over that bit of news ever since Steve dropped it on them during his brief return at about eight-thirty. He'd gone back inside before they could question him further, and with nothing else to go on, they ran out of ideas about how Nick came to list Steve as his emergency contact. It all seemed so unlikely and out of character.

Ginger looked back at the wall clock. "If he doesn't come back within the next half hour, I'll go see for myself."

As if on cue, the heavy door opened with a mechanical hiss, and Steve emerged. Before either woman could question him, he stopped them. "He's still in surgery. There were some problems because he lost so much blood. One of the doctors came out just a few minutes ago to tell me we might as well go home. They promised me they'll call the house when they know something. They brought in a neurosurgeon. That's really all I know about his condition."

"But what about the other thing," Ginger pressed. "Why did he name you as his emergency contact?"

Steve gave his wife a tired smile. "Think about it, my love. If the man is unconscious, how exactly would I find out why he did that?"

"Oh. Right." Ginger grinned sheepishly. "It took that steel trap mind of yours to set me straight, as usual." She put her arm around her husband and gently massaged his back. "Okay," she said. "Let's all go back to our house and see if we can get some sleep. Harrie, before you say anything, I propose we stop by your house on the way, pick up Tuptim and some of your clothes, and you stay with us. It'll be a lot easier if we are all in one place."

Too tired to argue, Harrie headed to the car with them. "Steve, were you able to get in touch with your friend at APD?" Steve had tried earlier in the evening to contact Lieutenant Bob Swanson who might be able to get details about the accident.

"Yeah," Steve said. He looked over his shoulder as he steered out of the parking lot. "He called me on my cell phone while I was in the surgery waiting room. He said he would contact the responding officers and get whatever information they had. They were still at the scene of the accident and hadn't finished their reports yet, so it'll probably be morning before he can get back to me."

"So, we still don't know what caused this accident, why Nick was in Albuquerque, why he wanted to see us, or why he called Harrie," Ginger ticked off on her fingers each unanswered question. "Do we even know what kind of car he was driving?"

"As a matter of fact, we do. It was a late model Cadillac Escalade."

Harrie furrowed her brow as she tried to picture that automobile. "Isn't that a big old SUV?"

Steve looked at her in the rear view mirror and raised an eyebrow. "The lady gets the prize. Congratulations. It is, indeed, a 'big old SUV,' as you say. Would you care to guess what color it is?"

20

Thursday Morning, April 13, 2000

Harrie pushed her way through the fog of sleep. Tuptim was pawing at her head under the blanket. It slid off, and she saw the headboard of a bed she didn't recognize. "What the—"

Ginger stuck her head in with a bright and altogether too cheery, "Good morning, sleepyhead!"

Tuptim streaked through the opening, and disappeared down the hall. Harrie surveyed the wreck she had made of the bed linens and grumped, "Please, have some respect for the dead!"

Ginger brought in a steaming cup of coffee, placed it on the bedside table and sat down on the rumpled bedding. "Somebody looks like they had a restless night."

Harrie said, "What time is it? Why do you serve coffee in the middle of the night?"

Ginger laughed as she retrieved Harrie's robe from the chair. "It's already seven. If we intend to get to the office at a decent hour, I suggest you drink some coffee and rejoin the living. I'm making bacon and eggs and you have 15 minutes to get your butt to the kitchen." She tossed the robe to Harrie and bustled out.

"You know you sound just like my Mother, don't you," Harrie shouted at the receding figure.

By nine they were in the office. Steve had insisted they carry on as usual while he went back to the hospital alone. Except for one phone call from the doctor about two in the morning, there had been no further word. Nick was out of surgery, but still in critical condition. Steve said he would call if anything changed.

They drove to the office together in Ginger's car. When they arrived, Caroline had already been there an hour, and she had accomplished quite a bit. Things were put away, and supplies were stacked neatly in the file room. Her new computer purred, and files were organized and labeled. In Harrie's opinion, it was nothing short of a miracle.

Of all the things Harrie would have expected from Nick, returning to Albuquerque was the next to last. The very last was that he would stalk her.

But based on his having a black SUV, he evidently had done exactly that. But why? And what about the dreams? Were those connected to Senator Lawrence and his book? If that was true, was Nick's part of the Senator's story? As she thought more about it, her list of questions grew longer and her list of answers remained at zero.

She set aside the editing and opened her laptop. Maybe it would help to make a list of all the questions and the facts. Perhaps something would jump out at her.

A few minutes after four, Ginger dropped into the chair in front of Harrie's desk. "Steve just called. He's on his way over here." Ginger took a deep breath. "It's over. They tried their best, but there was too much damage. He died half an hour ago."

Harrie stared at Ginger as though someone had just slapped her. She couldn't speak, and she didn't understand her reaction. Her throat felt like she had swallowed a large rock. She felt the tears start, and tried unsuccessfully to hold them back. She shook her head and finally found her voice.

"I don't understand. I didn't even like the man, much less love him. In fact, I would be more inclined to say I actively hated him. So why am I all teary-eyed over a louse who walked out on me and took not only my savings but also my dignity?"

Ginger went to Harrie and put her arms around her. "You're a loving, gentle person. In spite of all he did to hurt you, there's something sad about the fact he'll never have the chance to become a better person. Maybe you feel grief for the loss of all the hopes you had before you married him." She smiled. "Maybe it's that you never got a chance to tell him what a jerk he was."

Harrie returned the smile. Then she said, "Maybe it's frustration at knowing we'll never be able to figure out why he was here, what he was doing, and why he was trying to contact me. I guess I'll just have to live with the fact that my curiosity will never be satisfied, and it's all because of a stupid traffic accident."

Ginger looked up, startled. "Oh, God, I didn't have a chance to tell you. I got sidetracked by your crying. Steve assumed the head injury was caused by the crash, but the police report said he had his seat belt on. The air bag deployed and would have cushioned him from such a bad head injury. It wasn't the accident that killed him. The doctors . . ." Ginger trailed off.

Harrie's knuckles were white as she gripped the edge of the desk. "Are you going to tell me what you're talking about, or do I have to wait until Steve gets here?"

"The doctors found a bullet in his brain."

21

Friday Morning, April 14, 2000

Ramona Sanchez's daily routine since her employment by Senator Philip Lawrence twenty years ago was essentially the same. After preparing his dinner, she filled the coffee maker with water and freshly ground coffee and set it to turn on at six. She arrived each morning by seven and prepared the senator's breakfast first thing upon arriving. She could always tell how the day was going for him by how much coffee was missing. An empty pot meant he had been up early and was already hard at work. On those days, she needed to get breakfast ready in a hurry. Other times, the coffee would be only partially consumed, and she knew she could take more time to prepare the morning meal. On this day, the coffee was untouched.

Ramona looked around the kitchen, searching for other signs that her employer had been up and about. Perhaps he had already run out of coffee and made another pot for himself. She checked the coffee grinder for signs of use. Nothing. It was just as clean as she had left it the night before. In the sink were the dishes from his dinner the previous evening. They were rinsed and stacked as usual.

She checked the magnetic message board beside the refrigerator for a note or special instructions. The board was wiped clean, and there were no scraps of paper beneath the three carefully lined-up magnets. She wasn't concerned. Ramona Sanchez was not a woman given to hysteria.

She had raised three boys to adulthood. Each had been a challenge in his own way, especially Pablito, her wayward youngest son. She learned a long time ago you had to keep your head about you until you had all the facts. If you remained calm, you could always find a reasonable explanation for what seemed to be unexplainable. She reminded herself of this as she swung open the door between the kitchen and the rest of the house.

The drapes in the living room were still closed. That's odd, she thought. Even before he got his coffee, the senator opened those drapes first thing each morning so he could look out at his flower garden. He often told her it was his source of peace and calm.

Mrs. Sanchez mulled over the possibilities. Maybe he became ill during the night? Perhaps he fell? After all, he is an old man. She shook her head. She refused to make any assumptions until she had more information.

She tapped softly on the bedroom door and waited. Her tension mounted, and she strained to hear a response from within. She tapped again, loudly this time. Still no response. Taking a deep breath, she opened the door as she called out, "Senator Lawrence, are you all right?"

Even in the dim light, she could see the bed had not been slept in. The bedspread and pillows were still smoothly in place. The door to the adjoining bathroom stood open and proved to be as unoccupied as the bedroom.

She went down the hall to the library and discovered to her puzzlement that the door moved slightly under her knock. Her alarm set in. This door was never left open. She pushed it fully open and saw him on the floor, a pool of blood surrounding his head. She heard the sound of a hysterical woman screaming.

It took a few seconds before she realized she was that woman.

22

Harrie looked at the bedside clock. Six-thirty. She hadn't slept much Thursday night. Her eyes felt like they had gravel in them. Crying always did that to her. That was another thing she couldn't understand. Why had she cried? Maybe she did feel sad because she'd never be able to tell him off. Maybe she was just a bitter female who was all screwed up emotionally because she didn't trust men. Who knew?

Might as well get up and stick my head under the hot shower. She laughed. *Or in the oven if I don't get a grip.*

Harrie felt better after the shower. She dressed quickly and surveyed her long auburn hair in the mirror. Not much she could do with it now. Brushing would have to be enough for today. She was surprised when she found Steve and Ginger sitting at the kitchen table, talking quietly and sipping coffee.

"Did I wake you guys up when I turned on the shower?"

Ginger shook her head. "We've been up since five. Just couldn't sleep anymore. How about you?"

"I know I slept for a little while, but I kept waking up all night. For once, I hoped I would dream, and maybe get some answers."

Steve's cell phone rang. After he hung up, he said, "That was the mortuary. They wondered if I could come in today and make arrangements."

"What about Nick's family? Will you try to reach his grandfather," Harrie asked.

Steve said, "I thought I told you last night. I finally reached the law firm that used to handle Dimitri Despotides' affairs. They told me the old man died two years ago. As for Nick's father, they never knew what happened to him, so unless we initiate a search for him, he's not a consideration. In any event, I doubt seriously that a guy who was paid to marry a wealthy heiress, produce an heir, and then took a big settlement payment to get lost would be interested in financing a funeral for a son he hasn't seen since birth. Nick's mother died when he was sixteen, and she was an only child. The upshot is, there's no one left in the family. Nick was the last surviving member of the Despotides dynasty."

Harrie frowned. "So where does that leave you? Are you supposed to take care of everything?"

"I guess so. I haven't seen the will, of course, but if the note they found in Nick's pocket is really what he wished, then I'm it. I'll have to go down to the law firm first thing this morning and find the guy Nick conned into doing his will years ago. We need to push things through so I can legally act as his representative for the funeral arrangements. I presume he had enough money to pay for a decent burial, but with Nick, I'm not going to count on it."

"We should get to the office early," Ginger said. "Yesterday was a total loss as far as getting any work done."

Harrie nodded in agreement. "I'll take Tuptim home first and change into some fresh clothes. I love being your guest, but next time, remind me to pack more than one outfit."

When Harrie unlocked her front door, Tuptim jumped from her arms and went in search of her very own cat box. Harrie changing her clothes, gathered her briefcase and sweater and headed for the office.

As she drove, she thought about Nick. She could imagine all sorts of reasons why someone would want to kill him—she herself had thought of it more than once if only as an exercise in fantasy. Of course, except for the knowledge she had gained being married to Mark, she didn't have any experience with murder. With that thought, she realized the irony. Murder had also taken Mark from her. A violent felon had killed him when he was simply doing his job, and now someone had murdered her first husband, too. It was one more reason not to get involved in a relationship again. Maybe she somehow caused the death of men who dared marry her. She almost laughed as she realized how conceited that sounded, even to her. *Come on, Harrie, nice try. You definitely are not a femme fatale.*

She pulled her car into the parking lot next to the black SUV. As she expected, the office door was already unlocked and she could see Caroline standing beside her desk, talking to a man. Harrie spoke as she cleared the door.

"Okay, who belongs to that black SUV out front?"

"I do," said the man as he turned toward Harrie.

She stood perfectly still. The man smiling at her, bright white teeth sparkling and blue eyes twinkling, was none other than DJ Scott, aka Sunglasses.

23

A torrent of emotions and thoughts engulfed her. Something inside her took over, put a smile on her tight face, and caused her feet to walk forward. She watched from outside herself as she acknowledged the man she'd been trying to avoid and greeted him with a warm smile.

"You must be the DJ Scott I've heard so much about from Ginger and Caroline. It's good to finally meet you. I'm Harrie McKenzie."

Good grief! Have I completely lost my mind?

"Yes, Mrs. McKenzie, I learned your name during my last visit. How are you today?"

It wasn't what she expected. "Please," she said, "call me Harrie."

He smiled and said, "Harrie it is, then."

An awkward moment of silence ensued before she retrieved her briefcase from the floor where she had deposited it. "If you'll excuse me, I have some calls to make. It was nice to meet you."

As she turned to go to her office he said, "I'd like to speak to you privately if you have a few minutes. Perhaps when you've finished your calls, we could talk in your office?" It almost sounded like a question, but not really. Far from being flirtatious and friendly as she'd expected, he was very businesslike.

She said the only thing that came into her head. "Of course. I'll just be a moment."

She realized she didn't have any calls to make. It had been an excuse. She tried to be clinical about her reaction to the man. Why did he affect her this way? He was attractive, but that was no reason for her to go all breathless and fluttery. She was not interested in having a man in her life—even a gorgeous one. Been there; done that. But here she was, acting like a high school girl with her first crush.

She got out her day planner and stared blankly at the calendar. Today was Friday, the end of the Week from Hell. Nick was dead. What was her most pressing task for today? She had many pages of editing to do, and she and Ginger needed to confer with Senator Lawrence at some point this afternoon. Steve was arranging a funeral. A black SUV was parked right outside her office, and it belonged to DJ Scott. He wanted to talk to her. About what? Who was he, really? What could he possibly have to talk to her about? Why had someone murdered Nick? She shook her head. If she kept this up, they would take her away in one of those weird white jackets.

After deciding she'd stalled long enough, she invited DJ to her office. Her level of apprehension ratcheted up a notch when he closed the door before he sat in one of the chairs in front of her desk. He reached inside his suit jacket and flipped open a leather folder to reveal a badge and photo ID.

"FBI?" Harrie gazed at the case and looked back at DJ. Her confusion must have been apparent. "You're with the FBI?"

This time his smile was more like the one she saw when he helped her to her feet in the parking lot.

"Guilty. I'm Special Agent DJ Scott."

"Nobody said anything about your being with the FBI. What could you possibly have to talk to me about?"

"I would have mentioned it to you when I was here on Wednesday, but you disappeared, and I had to leave soon after."

He smiled, and she studied that face. He was uncomfortably good looking. A very bad sign, she thought.

She raised her hand in a dismissive gesture. "Don't worry about it. You still haven't told me why you need to talk to me."

"Your name came up during an investigation, so I need to ask you a few questions. Would that be all right?"

What could she say but, "Certainly."

"You were married to a Nicos Constantine from 1986 until 1987, is that correct?"

"It would appear you already know the answer to that. Why do you want to know?"

DJ sat back in the chair and studied her. "As I said, we're conducting an investigation, and one of the individuals of interest is a Nicos Constantine. We have information that you were married to him during a part of the time his activities brought him into contact with the subjects of our investigation. I don't mean to be cryptic, but could you please verify the dates of your marriage to Mr. Constantine?"

Harrie felt the heat of anger rise up from her chest, flooding her neck and most likely her face as well. "Have you been following me?"

"Why would you think I've been following you?"

"Well, this is just a little too coincidental, don't you think? I find you lurking outside my office on Tuesday morning. You disappear, only to reappear Wednesday morning. Ever since Monday, a mysterious black SUV has popped up wherever we happen to be. Now here you are again on Friday morning, black SUV parked, nice as you please, just outside our door, and you ask me if I was married to Nick Constantine, even though you apparently already know damn well that I was." She crossed her arms in front of her chest and glared, defying him to dispute her logic. "Well?" she demanded.

Before DJ could recover, Ginger barged into the office, breathless and very pale. "I'm sorry to interrupt. I just got a call from Ramona Sanchez. Something's happened to Philip. He's being taken to Presbyterian downtown. You've got to take me down there. I'm too upset to drive. Steve's cell phone is turned off. I can't reach him." She looked panicked and not very steady on her feet.

Harrie grabbed her purse and put her arm around Ginger. She turned to DJ. "Your questions will have to wait. As you can see, I have something more pressing that needs my attention."

DJ shook his head. "No, let me drive you both." He ushered them into the reception room where Caroline waited, looking slightly alarmed. "I'm going to drive them to the hospital to see about their friend," he said to Caroline. "You can call my cell phone if you need anything before we return." He didn't wait for a reply and hurried them out to the black SUV.

24

For someone who hated being inside a hospital, Harrie had certainly seen too much of this particular one in the last few days. They were seated in one of the waiting areas scattered around the facility. Construction was ongoing, and Harrie could hear a jackhammer, rata-tat-tatting away close by.

Ginger paced a short distance away, her cell phone to her ear, still trying to reach Steve. DJ had spoken with the ER gatekeeper and had been admitted after showing his credentials. Things were eerily similar to Wednesday night.

"I've left five voicemail messages on Steve's phone," Ginger said as she dropped down in the chair beside Harrie. "I suppose all I can do is wait. I called my mom and she got hysterical, of course. Thank God my dad was there to calm her down. I promised I'd call them back when we know anything." She sighed and leaned her head back against the wall. "Is it just me or is the world going crazy?"

"I don't know about the rest of the world but I can tell you our own little corner of it is."

"Ramona tried to call me after she found him on the floor," Ginger said. "If only I'd had my cell phone turned on when I left home."

Harrie hugged her friend. "There's nothing you could have done. And it's better that you didn't go tearing off by yourself. I'm glad I was there to help. Well, to be more accurate, I guess I'm glad DJ was there to help. Although why he thought I wasn't capable of driving you down here is beyond me."

"Speak of the Devil," Ginger whispered. "Here comes your Knight in Shining Armor."

Ginger's cell phone chirped. "It's Steve. Thank God! Go talk to DJ while I fill my poor husband in on what's happening."

Ginger walked over to a quiet corner, leaving Harrie waiting for DJ and feeling tongue tied-again.

"The news is both good and bad," he said. "The bad news is they have to operate. He was shot in the upper torso and they need to remove the bullet. Then when he fell, he hit his head, so they also must assess possible damage to his brain. He's been unconscious since Mrs. Sanchez found him.

So here's the good news. At this point, they don't think it's life threatening. But the surgery will take several hours. He really is going to be okay."

Ginger walked up just as he finished the last part. "Did I hear you say he's going to be okay? When can I see him? I have to talk to him. We need to know who did this." She started for the entrance to the emergency room.

DJ grabbed her arm. "Whoa. You can't go in there. Anyway, he's not in emergency. They've already taken him up to surgery." DJ nudged her gently toward the chairs again. "Come back and sit down."

DJ told her what he'd already explained to Harrie. "There's nothing we can do here at the moment. Let me take you back to your office. I left them my cell number, your cell number, and your office number. They promised to notify you as soon as the surgery is over."

Ginger leaned back and closed her eyes. "Okay. If you're sure they'll call us immediately. I guess I should go back to the office, pick up my car, and go to my parents' house. They're the ones I'm worried about now."

"Good," DJ said. "That sounds like something productive. Meanwhile," he turned toward Harrie, "I still need to talk to you, and I'd like to do that at your office."

"Yeah, sure, why not? Let's get it over with."

When they arrived at the office, Ginger walked out the door, and Harrie motioned DJ into her office. She sat behind her desk, and motioned him to be seated. "Okay, can we get on with this interrogation please?"

"Let me apologize again for the awkward way this interview started, and that's what it is, by the way, an interview—not an interrogation." He looked at his notes. "I believe you were going to verify the period of time you were married to Nicos Constantine."

"I seem to remember you were going to tell me why the FBI cares."

"Mrs. McKenzie," he began, and at her raised eyebrow corrected himself. "Harrie," he said, "because of the nature of this investigation and the stage that it's in, I can't answer your questions. I will tell you that you are not under suspicion. Your only connection, as far as we know at this time, is that you were married to Constantine. It was during that period of his life we believe he became involved with some of the people in the case I'm working. At the conclusion of our investigation, I might be in a better position to explain further. Much depends on what you are able to verify and whether the United States Attorney decides he has a case to prosecute.

So for now, I'll ask you to simply answer my questions. I'll explain what I can as we go along. Can I count on your cooperation?"

"Well, since you put it that way, I can't very well refuse. Not that I'd have any reason to. It's just so creepy, this happening right now. I mean, the timing is really remarkable, don't you think?"

DJ frowned. "I don't get your meaning. What timing? Are you talking about the senator's assault?"

"No, that's not what I meant, although come to think of it, that's pretty strange too. I'm talking about the fact that you appear here to ask me questions about a period of my life I've tried to put out of my mind for thirteen years. But I can't seem to escape it, no matter what I do." Harrie shook her head and looked up at DJ. "How far does this go? Do you also need to know about my second husband?"

He ignored her sarcasm. "No, as I said, our interest in you is strictly during the period of your marriage to Nicos Constantine, and you say that ended thirteen years ago?"

Harrie sighed. "We married in 1986, as you said earlier today, and we divorced less than a year later in 1987, but he left even before that. Everything was done through our lawyers. Steve handled my end of the divorce, and Nick had his own lawyer. I never saw or heard from him again. Not until this past week."

DJ looked up and stopped writing. "You saw him this week?"

"No, I didn't see him. At least I don't think I saw him, even though there was this man in an SUV at a traffic light . . ."

DJ held up his hand as he interrupted her. "Let's go at this a different way, okay? Let me ask you some questions, and you answer them. Try to focus only on what I'm asking. Now, about this week, did you see him or not?"

Harrie drew herself up, lifting her chin to a defiant tilt. "Like I said, as far as I know, I didn't see him, but I did receive a phone call from him."

DJ looked up, eyebrows raised, "What did you talk about?"

"Nothing. I was out, and he left a number for me to call."

"And what day was this?"

Harrie went over the past few days in her mind, finally pinpointing the day. "It was Wednesday morning. In fact, I received the message right after you left."

"So did you?"

"Did I what?"

"Did you return the call?"

"No, I asked Steve to do it. He's Ginger's husband."

"Did Steve talk to him?"

"Steve talked to his answering service. They said he was out of town and wouldn't be back until that evening. So we went to Steve and Ginger's house, had dinner and waited for him to call when he returned."

"What time was that?"

"Well, we had dinner about six o'clock, and—

DJ stopped her again, warding off yet another detour. "Let's just cut to the main issue. What time did you or Steve finally talk to him?"

Harrie frowned. "We never did talk to him. That was when we got the call he'd been in an accident and was at Presbyterian Hospital."

DJ's voice took on a sharpness Harrie hadn't heard before. "So Nicos Constantine is in the hospital?"

She realized he didn't know. "I'm sorry. I assumed you must have known. In fact, I assumed that was why you chose today to grill me. Nick died Thursday afternoon."

DJ's eyes narrowed and he leaned forward. "What happened to him?"

"At first, we thought it was just a traffic accident. His SUV crashed into a retaining wall on I-25, but after they got him in surgery, they discovered a bullet in his brain. I'm afraid someone beat you to him. I thought you FBI types would have known this stuff. Aren't you supposed to be investigating him?" She was being bitchy, but she didn't care. She was tired, and she hated this conversation.

DJ sat very still for a moment, looking off to his right. Harrie turned to see what was holding his interest, but all she saw was Caroline working at her desk. He stood abruptly, like a man on a mission.

"Thank you for your time. This obviously changes things quite a bit. I'll need to talk to you later, but I must get back to my office for now." When he reached the door, he stopped and turned to her. "Please be careful. If someone was watching you before, there's even more reason to think they'll be back."

Harrie felt her heart thud sharply against her ribs. "Why would you think that?"

"I guess you weren't too far off track with that remark you made earlier about the odd timing. I doubt it's a coincidence that two people you know have been shot in the last two days."

The cold feeling she knew so well started its crawl up her arms and the back of her neck. "What do you mean?" She didn't really want to know, but she couldn't keep from asking.

"I was going to tell you this later, but . . ." He looked down at the floor, appeared to make a decision and faced her again. "We have reason to believe that Nick Constantine was working for Senator Philip Lawrence."

25

Friday Evening, April 14, 2000

Caroline Johnson was tired. It had been a busy week. Between furniture delivery, network setups and the general chaos of the day, her head throbbed. She liked being busy, though. It kept her mind off things that were best left alone. This was exactly the kind of job she needed. She felt comfortable in her ability to bring organization to the office of her new employers, and she knew how to help them get their work done.

She worried about them a little. So much bad news in such a short time. At first, she'd been more concerned about Harrie. Ginger seemed to have a more levelheaded approach to things. But this morning, when Ginger found out about the attack on Senator Lawrence, it looked like Harrie was the calming one. Obviously, they were devoted to each other. It was good to have close friends.

Caroline had brought home a banker box full of folders to sort through over the weekend. In view of all the disruption at the office, Harrie and Ginger had not been able to get much done today. Caroline was glad she could help them out.

She quickly prepared dinner from some leftover roasted chicken. She retrieved the box from the dining room, took out some of the folders from the box and sat down to eat and proofread. She read through the first time looking for obvious typographical errors. The second time, she read for content.

As she reached for another folder, she noticed a brown clasp envelope wedged in between the pages. Curious, she removed it and several other pieces of mail that she didn't remember seeing earlier when she gathered up the materials. Now that she thought about it, she didn't remember seeing the postman when he made his delivery that afternoon. He must have dropped the pile on her already stacked desk. First thing Monday she would establish a mail delivery receptacle. Things were likely to get lost if there wasn't a proper place for them.

She set aside the other mail and examined the brown envelope. There was no return address, but it didn't look like junk mail. Still, you could never tell these days. Marketing companies were always coming up with new ways to make their ads look official and important. This one was handwritten and addressed to Ginger. In the lower left corner, the words "Personal and Confidential" were written in the same cramped handwriting.

Caroline hesitated. Something about that writing seemed vaguely familiar. It looked rather old-fashioned. She sighed and dropped it back in the banker box. Better not take the chance, she thought. I don't want to open something that really is personal.

She worked for the next two hours and finished all the folders. With a sense of accomplishment, she returned the corrected material to the box and took it back into her dining room. As she turned out the light, she thought about the brown envelope again.

Maybe I'll call Ginger at home in the morning. If she thinks it's important, I'll take it to her. Otherwise, I can take it back with the rest of the stuff on Monday morning. That's probably soon enough. How important can a plain brown envelope be, anyway?

26

As they finished the last few dinner dishes in the O'Leary's kitchen, Harrie and Ginger heard a cell phone ringing. Ginger rushed into the dining room to retrieve her purse and the beckoning phone.

"This is Ginger Vaughn. Yes, yes, I understand." She listened intently, but asked no questions.

When she finished the call, she stood with the phone open in her hand. Harrie, impatient as always, had followed her into the dining room.

"What did they say? That was the hospital, wasn't it? Is he awake? Is he all right? Say something!"

Right then, Steve and the O'Learys rushed in, also demanding answers. "Who was that? Was it about Philip? Can we see him now?"

Ginger held up her hands to halt the torrent of questions. "Hold on a minute. Give me a chance." She swallowed hard before she continued.

"Yes, that was the hospital, and Philip is back in his room. The surgery to remove the bullet was successful, but there was swelling in his brain from the blow to the head when he fell. They had to induce a coma. He'll need to be kept that way until the swelling goes down."

Mrs. O'Leary leaned her head against her husband's shoulder and cried soundlessly. Don O'Leary put his arm around her and stroked her hair.

Harrie tried to sort out the jumble of emotions. Something was wrong, something besides the attack on the senator. There hadn't been time to think about much except that. If only she could clear her head, maybe she could figure out what was eating at the edges of her consciousness.

Steve said, "I'm going to make a pot of coffee. We need to strategize how we're going to deal with the next few days."

"I need to call Ramona Sanchez," Ginger said. "The poor woman called me four times today, and each time I had to tell her I didn't have any new information. She must be worried sick by now."

Ginger left the room to phone Ramona, and Harrie joined Steve at the kitchen counter. "Tell me what happened today with the arrangements about Nick."

Steve filled the brewing chamber with water. "Well, the first thing I did was locate the attorney who did Nick's will. I was right. It was that idiot who worked at our firm around the time Ginger and I got married. A copy of the will was still in my firm's employee files. Nick took advantage of a little perk we used to provide which allowed any lawyer to have one of his fellow attorneys draw up a standard will at no charge. I had to go down to the basement file room in the vault, but I finally located it."

"So what did it have to say about any final arrangements? Or was Nick that forward thinking in those days?"

"Oh, yeah, it's all there. That was one of the requirements to get the free will prepared. They had to follow a certain format and provide information the firm deemed essential to have on hand for all employees. The format included information about arrangements for a funeral or disposal of a body, and you're not going to believe this. I was absolutely dumbfounded."

"Don't tell me. He wanted an elaborate, expensive funeral, right?"

"No, quite the contrary. He arranged to have his body donated to the UNM School of Medicine. Afterward, he's to be cremated with no funeral, no memorial, no nothing."

Harrie looked at Steve, disbelief showing in her wide-eyed, open-mouthed face. "Are you certain you found the right will? You're sure these were the last wishes of Nicos Constantine?"

Steve nodded. "Absolutely. I checked it all out. I even tracked down the moronic attorney. Teddy Krylach is just as dumb as I remembered him. He's in private practice now in a little hole-in-the-wall office downtown, close to police headquarters. Good thing, too. It seems Nick kept in touch with him over the years and had recently provided a codicil to the will."

"Did that express the intent that you become his legal representative?"

"Yes, it did. Of course, Krylach didn't see the need to inform me of my new status, even though Nick attached a letter with the codicil asking him to do just that. The dumb ass just filed everything away with a copy of the will. When I showed up, he was only too happy to rid himself of the obligation to deal with it. He gave me the entire file. Said it was my problem now. So, I'm it, and I'm supposed to file the will for probate and make sure his last wishes are carried out."

Harrie got out coffee mugs. "Why didn't Nick didn't just get in touch with you in the first place instead of tracking down Krylach? It doesn't make sense."

"It does if he didn't want me to know he was back in Albuquerque and had been for a well over a year."

Harrie's voice went to a high-pitched squeak. "But—but why? How—?"

Ginger returned to the kitchen. "What wrong with her?" she asked her husband.

He shrugged and Harrie said, "I knew it! I just knew it! That's why I've been having those awful dreams. It was Nick who's been stalking us, and now I have proof!"

"Hold on a minute. We don't have any proof. The fact he was living here doesn't mean he stalked you."

Ginger looked from her husband to her friend. "Will you guys tell me what's going on, and will you please keep it down," she whispered. "I don't want to disturb Mom and Dad."

Harrie was instantly remorseful. She lowered her voice and calmed herself. "I'm sorry. Steve just told me Nick's been back in Albuquerque for over a year."

"What?" Ginger yelled. Steve put his finger to his lips and closed the door between the kitchen and the rest of the house. He filled her in on their conversation. Ginger shook her head in disbelief.

"Why did he come back to Albuquerque, and why the secrecy?"

Steve shrugged. "I don't know, but now I have something solid to go on. The hospital gave me his belongings today, along with his address and the key to his apartment."

"You say we're not expected to provide a funeral or anything like that?"

"Nope. Nothing. The medical school took possession of the body and when they're finished, the cremated remains will be returned to us."

"Wait a minute," Harrie protested. "Why do 'we' have to take the ashes? And by the way, who is this 'we' you're talking about, Kemo Sabe? Do you have a mouse in your pocket?"

A small hint of a grin played on Steve's mouth. "I'm using the 'we' simply to help explain the next little bit of information. You see, the codicil he left concerns his final wishes, and it states that you and I, my dear Harrie, are to dispose of his ashes."

Harrie blew air through her lips. "Oh, yeah. Now that's a good one. Why, pray tell, would he want me involved with the disposal of his ashes. That's crazy!"

"Well, crazy or not, he specifically asked that you and I take his ashes up to Sandia Crest and scatter them."

Ginger was speechless and Harrie was too stunned to respond.

Finally, Ginger managed, "The guy must have been a mental case, Steve. Harrie is the last person he should ask to do anything"

"Mental case or not, unless Harrie refuses to do it, she and I are designated." Steve turned to Harrie. "I'll do it alone if you would rather not be involved."

Harrie sighed and shook her head. "It's not fair that you take on everything. Whatever he did to me is in the past. He's dead now and can never hurt me again. Maybe it would be fitting that I help spread him to the four winds and let nature take him where she wants."

Ginger raised an eyebrow. "Well, be sure you wear one of those filter masks when you do the deed. The wind might shift and blow him back into your life and your lungs."

27

Saturday Morning, April 15, 2000

Harrie poured herself another cup of coffee and sat down with the newspaper. She wished she felt as bright and perky as the morning sun pouring in her kitchen window.

Another night of wild dreams had left her groggy. The news of Nick's strange request was on her mind as she had gone to sleep. Another interesting tidbit from Steve was that Nick died with quite a bit of money, leaving bequests for several scholarships and charities.

Shortly before they were married, Nick had told her about his grandfather disinheriting him. The old man had set up criteria Nick had to fulfill to get back in the will. One of the requirements was to use his law degree and actually practice law. Another was to marry a Greek girl. Harrie had laughed when Nick said they must prove to his grandfather that she was Greek. She was in fact half Greek, her father being born to Greek immigrants. But they changed their name to Drake when they became American citizens, and short of obtaining copies of her grandparents' naturalization papers, she didn't see how she would prove to anyone she was even half Greek. She told Nick all this, but he seemed undeterred.

She decided his grandfather must have had a change of heart, or Nick changed enough to convince the old man. How else did he end up leaving a small fortune behind?

Then she remembered the shady dealings he'd been involved in. Maybe the money he had left was tainted.

She also thought about the connection between Nick and Senator Lawrence. No matter what DJ Scott said, that simply didn't make sense.

When the telephone rang, she thought it was Steve or Ginger and answered with, "Hey, what's up?"

There was a brief silence before a deep voice responded. "Harrie, is that you?"

She sucked in her breath. "DJ! How did you get my number?"

He sounded businesslike. "It was with the information about Nick Constantine. I've been trying to interview you, remember?"

"Oh, I'm not likely to forget. But it wasn't me who ended the session yesterday afternoon."

"I apologize for that, but your information was startling. As you can imagine, it changes our inquiry rather dramatically."

"I might agree with you if I knew exactly what your inquiry had been in the first place. Are you ready to share that with me yet?"

He laughed briefly. "You are a persistent woman, aren't you?"

"I am. But you didn't call me for small talk, did you?"

"No, I didn't. Could we meet this morning to finish our conversation? I'm handing over the investigation to one of our other agents."

Harrie felt a wave of disappointment she would never have expected. "Oh, is the investigation concluded?"

"No. I requested that my ASAC assign the matter to another agent, and he agreed. I need to complete all the paperwork this weekend so that I can hand over my reports to the other investigator on Monday."

"What's an a-sack?"

"Actually, it's A-S-A-C. It stands for Assistant Special Agent in Charge. So, how about it? Can we meet for breakfast or something?"

Harrie looked down at the old, baggy T-shirt she had slept in. *Great! How quickly can I turn from a bag lady into a sparkling young woman?*

"Uh, sure. I have a couple of errands, but I could meet you in an hour."

"Great," he said. "How about the IHOP on Paseo del Norte at nine thirty?"

Immediately after agreeing to the meeting, she regretted it. It was a detour she didn't need. She wanted to call Ginger and find out what she could do to help the O'Learys. They were like a second set of parents to her. She decided to make the breakfast quick, be out by ten-thirty.

Exactly forty-eight minutes later, she was threading through the Saturday morning traffic. If there were awards for such things, Harrie would surely receive one for getting herself put together in record time. She glanced in the visor mirror as she waited at the traffic light at Wyoming and Montgomery. Yep, everything was in place, including her head. Apparently miracles were possible after all.

28

She pulled into the parking lot at IHOP and immediately spotted three black SUVs. She wondered why it is that once a particular type of car is in your mind, you see them everywhere.

As she locked her door, she sensed someone behind her. She whirled to see DJ and jumped. "You must like sneaking up on people. They teach you that at the Academy?"

He raised his arms in mock surrender. Instead of the usual business suit, he was in jeans and a tee shirt with a casual jacket. He filled everything out nicely. "Hey, I come in peace," he said. "I just walked over here from my car." He pointed to a little red sports car.

"Where's your big SUV?"

"That's a bureau car. I don't drive it when I'm on my own time."

The waitress brought coffee, and Harrie noticed with a twinge that DJ added a generous splash of cream to his.

"Can I ask my questions before our order arrives? It would be nice to get this out of the way so we could enjoy breakfast."

"By all means," she said.

"Can you could tell me anything about any friends of Nick you might have met."

"This probably sounds strange, but I don't think he had any friends, other than Steve, of course."

"You're talking about Steve Vaughn, Ginger's husband?"

"Yes. Steve and Nick graduated in the same class at Harvard Law. Then they worked at the same law firm for a short time. Perhaps Steve could tell you about other friends he might have had."

Harrie tried to read what DJ wrote, but she wasn't good at reading upside down. As if he could read her mind and without looking up, he said, "I'm just making some notes for the next agent"

"Why are you giving the case to someone else? Why not finish what you started?"

"Sometimes, several agents work a case and are assigned different people or groups of people to interview. Then they write up their reports, and they all go into the case file for that particular investigation. In situations like that, with multiple agents involved, the ASAC will pull all the information together to present to the U.S. Attorney. So it's not like I'm turning over a case assigned specifically to me. I was just working on one small piece of the puzzle. Believe me. I have plenty of other cases that need my attention."

"But it sounded like you wanted to be taken off this case for some reason. Forgive me for sounding nosey, but why do you want to be replaced?"

"Let me ask you a few more questions, and then I promise I'll answer yours. Fair enough?"

Harrie smiled. "Okay, that's fair. Ask away."

DJ's questions were: Did Nick do a lot of traveling during their marriage? Yes, he did. Did he seem unusually secretive about where he was going? Yes, he did seem reluctant to give her much information about where he would be. Did he spend large sums of money that he couldn't explain away? Yes, he had a gambling problem.

DJ nodded. "We know about Nick's gambling problem. But there may have been another explanation. We have reason to believe he may have been involved in money-laundering activities in Nevada."

Harrie shook her head. "It just keeps getting better and better, doesn't it? Are you also going to tell me now that he wasn't a womanizing jerk?"

DJ smiled. "Well, I wouldn't want to take away all your fond memories of your ex-husband. He might have been a womanizing jerk, but we don't have evidence of that."

"So, this is the investigation you people are doing? You're looking at money laundering in Nevada?"

"That's only one small aspect of it. It also includes public corruption, illegal real estate transactions, smuggling, and violations of the Mann Act."

"The Mann Act?"

"That's the legislation that made it illegal to transport women or girls across state lines for purposes of prostitution. It's also sometimes called the 'White Slave Traffic Act'."

"And you think Nick was involved in that?"

"We've been trying to determine if he worked with some men who we do know were involved. His death makes that more difficult."

After their order arrived, they ate quietly until Harrie put her fork down and said, "Okay, I have to know. What made the FBI interested in Nick? I mean, what brought him to their attention in the first place?"

"How good are you at keeping your mouth shut?"

"Who would I tell? As I said, Nick had no friends. All his family is gone now. Who else would care?"

"Well, for starters, how about your friend Ginger and her husband? They both knew Nick. Steve and Nick were friends. You're very close to them. Wouldn't you think it natural to share what we've talked about with them?"

Harrie chewed that over. "You have a point. It never occurred to me not to tell Ginger and Steve Especially considering what we found out yesterday."

DJ nodded. "Yeah, that's what I thought." He stopped, as though he had just registered the rest of her comment. "Wait a minute. What did you find out yesterday?"

"Quite frankly, I don't think it's true anyway. It's really the most unlikely thing you could imagine. According to Steve, Nick was worth several million dollars."

"Okay, I need to talk with Steve. How about you invite him to your place, and we can all talk there?" He picked up the check and started for the cashier. "I'll follow you," he said.

When they reached his car, she grabbed his arm. "What's going on that I should know about?"

DJ studied the ground before he spoke. "You asked me back there what brought Nick to the attention of the FBI. Well, I'm going to tell you, but you have to promise me to not say anything to anybody. Agreed?"

She nodded and let go of him. The warmth of the bright morning sun couldn't keep the chill away.

"Nick came to our attention from an informant."

"Do you know this informant or does it work like that?"

His smile was one of resignation instead of humor. "Yes, I know this informant quite well. It's someone who knew the people Nick worked for and knew there were bad things going on. And I'm afraid that person, as well as you and your friends, might be in danger."

29

When she was eight, Harrie had a pet hamster named Gigi who spent most of her waking hours running inside a wheel. Harrie was now beginning to feel like Gigi.

She had been living peacefully and uneventfully. Now she was being followed (maybe), her ex husband had been murdered (certainly), and another man she knew less well had been attacked (definitely). And to top it off, an irritatingly attractive FBI agent was following her home in his car because she was in extreme danger (according to him).

Everything seemed to come back to Senator Lawrence and his book about a murder that happened long before she was born. But that didn't explain a thing about why Nick had been killed or why she and Ginger would be in jeopardy by association. Before, she had been content to drift along, editing the book and learning a bit of history about people long dead. No more. This was getting personal, and nobody had any answers.

She pulled into the garage of her townhouse. DJ drove past her house and parked down the street. He waited until there were no other cars on the street before exiting his car and walking quickly into her garage. She hit the button on the wall, closing them safely inside.

"Why all the intrigue?"

"Just normal precaution," he replied.

"Sit down, and I'll make a fresh pot of coffee. What should I say to Steve to get him here?"

"Does he ever help you out with repairs and stuff? Maybe you could tell him you need a light bulb changed or something."

Harrie rolled her eyes. "Oh, pul-leeze! Where do you get your information about women? Romance novels?"

"Hey, no offense intended. I figured you must need help sometimes with things around the house. Or do you also specialize in home repairs?"

"I do most things on my own. For the rest I call my faithful handyman."

"A handyman? How do you know this guy? We need to think about who has access to you, and be sure they are who they say they are."

"Relax," Harrie said. "He's about seventy and I've known him since I was twelve years old." She got out two mugs and opened the refrigerator. "I noticed you use cream. Unfortunately, I don't have any. I take mine black, and I haven't kept cream in the house since—" she stopped. "Um, what I mean is, would plain milk be okay?"

"Milk is fine. It's better for me anyway. I love cream in my coffee, but I don't keep it in my own refrigerator. Too much fat, and it spoils before it's all gone. I only use it when I'm at a restaurant because it's available. Bad habit."

Harrie poured some milk into her rarely used creamer.

"I have to tell you this is all so overwhelming and confusing. Yesterday, you said Nick was working for Senator Lawrence. Are you absolutely sure about that? What would he have been doing for him? Surely Senator Lawrence isn't involved in white slavery!"

"Nick's working for Senator Lawrence hasn't been verified. But I can tell you this. The people we are investigating are a very nasty bunch. Nick knew some of them, that much is sure. We don't know if he was involved in their activities. The fact that he was murdered is a strong indication he was. Beyond that, I can't say any more."

"Are you aware of the book Senator Lawrence is writing?"

"Sure. I read the newspapers, too. As of last Sunday, everyone knows he's writing about the murder of Chipper Finn."

"Does that have anything to do with the stuff you think Nick was involved in?"

"Good question. Our investigation covers a lot of territory. These people are part of a group who've been around New Mexico for a long time. It's possible there's some connection. The Senator knows a lot of politicians and people in high places. Apparently, his book will speak about some of them. Most of those people from fifty years ago are dead, but there could still be some around who have good reasons for not wanting certain information to come to light. There is no statute of limitation on murder."

She shuddered. "I know the FBI was involved in the Chipper Finn case. There must be something in your files about it. The senator wrote about that in the book. Couldn't you look it up, and see if any of the same people are part of this mysterious group you speak about?"

"The FBI wasn't involved in the murder case. Chipper Finn's murder wasn't a federal crime. What the Bureau investigated was the violation Manny Salinas' civil rights."

"Are you telling me you can't get your hands on information relating to that murder because it wasn't a federal crime? I thought the FBI had access to a huge data base of information about crimes all over the country."

"I didn't say I couldn't get information. I'm just trying to explain it wasn't our case. Technically, we have no reason to investigate it."

"Why do I sense you're sidestepping this issue for some reason? Do you think there's more to it?"

"Look," DJ shifted uncomfortably in his chair, "could we just call Steve and get him over here. We could play Twenty Questions all day, but it wouldn't get us anywhere. Let's just stick to the things I do know."

"Okay." As Harrie went to the phone, the doorbell rang.

DJ put his hand on her arm, stopping her. "Don't answer that until you verify who it is," he whispered.

She nodded and started toward the entryway. DJ followed closely and stood to the side of the door. She put her eye to the peephole and started laughing.

Standing there, looking at her with concern, were Steve and Ginger. "Where have you been? We've been calling all morning and you didn't answer, not even your cell phone." Ginger stopped abruptly as DJ stepped into sight.

"Come in," he said. "I've been wanting to speak to you."

30

Steve studied DJ with the look of one guy sizing up another. "What do you mean you've been wanting to speak to us?"

Harrie stepped up to greet her friends. "Steve, I don't believe you've met Special Agent DJ Scott." She turned to her companion. "DJ, this is Steve Vaughn. Why don't we all go into the kitchen and talk?"

When they walked into the kitchen, Harrie saw Ginger look at the table, note the two coffee cups and lift her eyebrow in a quizzical 'what's going on here?' gesture.

Harrie smiled. "DJ called this morning and asked to continue our interview so he could make a report this weekend."

DJ added, "I had just asked her to call and see if you could come over and talk to me."

Steve and Ginger sat in the two vacant chairs, and Harrie placed a mug of hot coffee in front of each of them. Steve asked, "What could you possibly have to talk to me about?"

DJ pulled the leather case from his jacket, and opened it to show Steve his badge and ID. He explained about the investigation involving Nick Constantine, and his need to ask Steve some questions. "Would it be okay with you if we did that now?"

Steve seemed to relax a bit. "How long will it take? We have several errands this morning."

"Not long." He turned to Harrie. "Would you mind going into the other room with Ginger while Steve and I talk?"

Harrie and Ginger's eyes met, an unspoken communication transpired between them, and they both shook their heads. "I don't think so," Ginger said. "Harrie and I have no secrets, and I think I have a right to know what you think you're going to learn from my husband. If Steve has no objections, I think it's time we were all brought up to speed together." When she leaned back and crossed her arms, the message was obvious.

DJ's jaw tightened, but he nodded. "Is that all right with you, Steve?"

Steve stifled a grin. "I wouldn't think of objecting, not when they both gang up on me."

For the next twenty minutes, DJ asked questions, and Steve answered as best he could. He was able to name some of the other attorneys he and Nick worked with back in 1985. He verified that Nick didn't seem to have any real friends apart from him. He told DJ what he knew about Nick's family, how his grandfather had sent him on his way to make it on his own, and how he had been disinherited.

"That brings up another question I need to ask," said DJ. "I understand Nick's will indicates he had quite a bit of money. Where do you think it came from?"

Steve shook his head. "I'll have to wait until Monday to get that information. I only found out about the contents of the will late Friday. It appears he had financial advisors in New York, but it was after five on the east coast when I learned all this."

"Do you think he legitimately earned a substantial amount of money in the fourteen years since you've seen him, or do you think he got involved in something illegal?"

Steve shrugged. "Nick never struck me as all that industrious. By that, I mean making an effort to attract good clients, putting in extra time to bring in more billable hours, that sort of thing. So, if I had to guess, I'd say either he managed to sweet talk his grandfather into putting him back in the will, or he was mixed up in something that involved a lot of easy money. Knowing what I did about his grandfather, I'd be more inclined to say it was the latter."

DJ looked at Ginger. "Do you have anything else to add?"

"Only that when he left town back in 1987, he left a pile of bills and emptied his and Harrie's joint bank account. I can't imagine him changing enough to become a hard-working, honest guy. I guess that's a mean thing to say, considering the guy's dead, but that's my gut reaction."

Harrie said, "Could you possibly share with them some of the things you were telling me earlier at breakfast?" At that statement, Ginger turned and openly stared at Harrie, a little smile playing across her face. She mouthed the word, 'breakfast?' at Harrie, and received in return a frown that clearly said, 'stop that!' Thankfully, DJ was occupied with his notes and seemed not to notice, although Steve was thoroughly enjoying the exchange between his wife and her best friend.

When he looked up at them, DJ seemed to have made a decision. "I told Harrie earlier today that I have reason to believe that whoever killed Nick might come after her or the two of you. I'm also quite concerned about a confidential informant of mine, who might now be compromised.

Ordinarily I wouldn't share this kind of information, but your safety could depend on it. Can you give me your word that what I tell you will never leave this room?"

The other three looked from one to the other and nodded solemnly.

DJ continued. "Harrie asked me what possible connection there could be with Nick's death and the attack on Senator Lawrence. We have reason to believe that Nick was trying to find out exactly what the senator was going to say in his book about the murder of Chipper Finn."

Ginger and Harrie were stunned. Steve maintained the watchful air of the attorney gathering information and asked, "What would have been Nick's purpose in having that information?"

"Nick probably couldn't have cared any less, personally, but he racked up some debts in the late eighties with people who had strong motives for wanting to know. We believe that those people may have offered to waive those debts if Nick got them that information. Do any of you know if the senator had experienced a break-in to his home recently?"

Harrie looked at Ginger, but Ginger just shook her head. "He never said anything about a break-in. And I can't imagine a break-in crook getting into Canyon Estates. In any event, he has a safe place where he keeps all his notes and information."

Ginger's cell phone chirped. "Excuse me. I'll take it in the living room."

Harrie looked at DJ. "What else do you know that you're not telling us?"

"Only something my informant told me. Perhaps it was the fear of a break-in, rather than an actual one. Senator Lawrence seemed to be concerned about his notes and papers getting into the wrong hands."

"How, exactly, would your informant know anything about Senator Lawrence?"

"We call them confidential informants for a reason. We don't tell people how they get their information."

"Then how can you be sure it's reliable?" Harrie persisted. Ginger returned to the kitchen.

"That was Caroline. She took some work home with her last night, and while she was going through it, she discovered some mail that was delivered Friday afternoon."

"Is it something important?"

"It's a brown 9 x 12 envelope, addressed to me, marked 'Personal and Confidential' in the bottom corner. She wants to bring it to me, so I gave her directions and told her to come on over."

"Great," said Harrie. "The more, the merrier."

"Not so great," said DJ.

Harrie frowned. "What's wrong now? Do you have a problem with Caroline Johnson?"

"No," he admitted. "I don't have a problem with Caroline Johnson. I just want to make sure everyone stays safe until we get to the bottom of this."

Harrie threw up her hands in exasperation. "Then what's wrong with our assistant coming over to my house?"

"Because," DJ sighed, "your assistant is my confidential informant."

31

"Why do I get the feeling that isn't something you intended to tell us?" Harrie's defiance had been replaced with amazement.

"No shit, Sherlock," Ginger said under her breath. Steve raised his eyebrows. Ginger returned his look. "Well, he obviously had no intention of telling us. Don't look at me like that."

"Okay, okay," DJ said. "Let me explain. I planned to tell you if it became absolutely necessary. I just hoped it wouldn't, that's all."

Harrie said, "That's why you were hanging around our office on Tuesday, wasn't it? And I'll bet that's why you came back on Wednesday. You wanted to check with your spy."

"An informant is not a spy," DJ said rather more forcefully than he intended to. "She had information that came into her possession, and she thought it was important to bring it to the attention of the FBI. She's not spying on you, or your business. Now, before she gets here, let me explain what happened. You know that Caroline was Jacob Snow's administrative assistant, and that Daniel Snow is his older brother. For many years, Caroline worked with Jacob very closely, keeping his calendar, handling all his correspondence and attending meetings with him. She had access to all his files and personal correspondence and even maintained a cabinet in her office for some of it. In the old days, Daniel had been the managing partner, but he decided to run for District Attorney in the late forties, so Peter, their brother-in-law, who was also with the firm, took over. However, he didn't have the head or the temperament for administrative functions, and in late 1949, Jacob became head of the firm.

"Caroline worked there almost thirty years. Then Jacob suffered a stroke. He died six months later having never regained consciousness. During that period, Caroline kept the office together. She knew everything there was to know about the practice, and the other attorneys depended on her knowledge and management skills.

"A few weeks before Jacob died, Caroline took some files home to work on. Since they were personal files, she didn't see any problem about violating confidentiality. After all, she had been Jacob's personal assistant all those years.

"Later that evening as she sorted through files, she noticed a large folder that was taped shut unlike all the rest of the folders. She didn't remember ever seeing it before. There was nothing written on the outside and nothing indicating what it contained. It occurred to her it might be something Jacob put together as final instructions in the event of his death. She decided to unseal it and look inside.

"What she found was a collection of old newspaper clippings, some letters, a few photographs and a sealed brown envelope. The clippings were all related to the murder of Chipper Finn in 1950. There were many references to Daniel Snow as the prosecutor in the trial that followed. After the trial, the news stories were all about Daniel's campaign for New Mexico Attorney General and eventually about his career in the U.S. House of Representatives.

"The letters were not in envelopes, and there weren't any signatures. Several appeared to be from the same person. The tone became more threatening in each letter. There was no salutation so she couldn't be sure they were meant for Jacob. Maybe he had obtained them some someone else."

Steve interrupted. "What do you mean by 'threatening'?"

"The writer of the letter indicated he would turn over certain information about the death of a cocktail waitress to some other business associates that both the letter writer and the letter receiver had in common."

"That sounds ominous," Harrie said.

"Right," DJ replied. "The person writing the letter obviously knew, or thought he knew, who was responsible for Chipper Finn's death. And Mr. Letter Writer was telling Mr. Letter Receiver that he knew."

"Did it ever mention who the killer was?" Ginger asked.

"No, but it was clear that Mr. Letter Receiver also knew who the murderer was and did not want it to become known."

Harrie spoke up. "Could Caroline tell who had written the letters?"

DJ shook his head. "They were typewritten."

Ginger said, "Well that has to be a clue. How many people, especially guys, knew how to type before the computer came along?"

Steve raised an eyebrow. "I took typing in high school, I'll have you know."

"What about the photographs?" Harrie asked, focusing again on DJ. "Did she recognize any people in the pictures?"

"As far as she could tell, the photographs had nothing to do with the letters or the clippings. They were just pictures showing Jacob's brother, his sister and her husband. There was one photo of a young man and woman, but Caroline couldn't tell who they were. The photo was old and creased, like someone had carried it in a billfold for a long time."

Steve said, "You mentioned a sealed envelope. What about that?"

DJ nodded. "That piece turned out to be a real mystery. It was one of those big 9 x 12 brown envelops, and it had a typed label on the front. The back was sealed with old-fashioned sealing wax—the kind they used back in the 1800s. The label said, 'Upon my death, deliver this envelope, unopened, to Senator Philip Lawrence.' Caroline was surprised at this. She thought the senator was a friend of *Daniel* not Jacob. Of course Jacob knew Philip, but Caroline didn't think they were that close, so she didn't understand why such an important document would be addressed to Philip Lawrence."

Harrie felt a mixture of excitement and apprehension. "What did she do with it?"

"She set it aside and put the rest of the items in a box. She decided she would wait a while to see if Jacob's condition improved. On Monday, she took the sealed envelope back to the office and put it in Jacob's drawer, behind all the other file folders. She hid the box of clippings, photographs, and letters in her guest room.

"Jacob died two weeks later. The office closed the day of the funeral, and after the burial, there was a reception at the family home. After the reception, Caroline decided to go to the office and retrieve the envelope. But when she opered the bottom file drawer where she'd left it, everything was gone."

"You mean the envelope was gone?" Harrie asked.

"No, I mean everything—the envelope, all the files that had been in the drawer, everything. It had been completely cleaned out. She looked in the other drawers. They were all empty. There was nothing there anymore that belonged to Jacob."

"What did she do then?" Steve asked.

"She was scared. She didn't know what to think. There was no sign of anything else being disturbed. Obviously, whoever cleaned out the desk had a key and knew his way around. The only conclusion she could make was that somebody who worked there went in and took everything. She immediately went into her own office and found her file cabinet open. Her own files, pertaining to other staff members or things not involving Jacob were still there. But anything she'd done for Jacob was gone."

"What about the box of stuff she had at her house?" Harrie asked.

"That was exactly her next thought. She rushed home, opened the door, and found her house had been ransacked. She backed out and immediately called the police. After they'd checked to make sure no one was in the house, they let her go in to see what was missing. Without calling attention to what she was doing, she went through each room and opened closet doors. Nothing had been taken, just pulled out and dumped all over the place. When she got to the guest room, she checked her hiding place and was relieved to see the box was still there."

"Did she tell the police about the box?" Steve looked worried now.

"No," DJ said. "After they left, she called me."

In the silence that followed, Harrie, Ginger, and Steve looked at each other, then back again at DJ.

Ginger broke the silence. "When did all this take place?"

"About eighteen months ago," DJ replied.

"Okay people," Harrie said. "Are we going to ignore the big elephant in the corner?"

Steve looked at her with a puzzled stare, "What elephant?"

Harrie laughed mirthlessly, "The one our friend just planted over there. The one concerning why Caroline Johnson called him about that box of goodies rather than turn them over to the police."

Ginger spoke up. "Don't you remember, Harrie? I told you. Caroline and DJ's mother are friends. She probably called him because she figured he'd know what to do, being an FBI agent and all. Isn't that right, DJ?"

The doorbell interrupted, and Ginger went to open the front door.

Caroline Johnson greeted Ginger and said, "I'm so sorry to disturb you on the weekend. I hope I didn't overreact about this silly envelope." She handed her the envelope in question.

"Not a problem," Ginger said. "Come on in. We were just talking about you."

They walked into the kitchen, and Ginger stashed the envelope beside her purse. Caroline stopped when she saw the group around the table. "I seem to be interrupting something," she said. "My goodness, DJ, what are you doing here?"

"I came to talk to Harrie, Ginger and Steve. I was just telling them about your experience at the firm after Jacob died."

"Oh, my," Caroline said. "Why did you feel it necessary to tell them about that, dear?"

Harrie's ears perked up. Why is she calling him Dear?

DJ stood up, and came around the table to stand beside Caroline. "I'm going to need their help, that's why. They needed some background on this situation."

Harrie tilted her head and studied the pair standing before her. "It seems there's some background we're still missing. You want to tell us what else we don't know?"

DJ smiled at her, the lock of hair once again in the middle of his forehead. "You're very astute you know." He looked around at the group, "Somehow, you've all been under the impression that Caroline and my mother are good friends."

Ginger said, "That's what I thought you told me that first morning we met."

"Ah," he said, holding up his forefinger to make a point. "That's not actually what I said. I believe I said Caroline has known me since I was a baby."

Ginger looked confused. "Well, okay, what's the difference?"

DJ put his arm around Caroline's shoulder while she looked at him with an adoring smile. "The difference is that Caroline is not my mother's friend. Caroline is my mother."

32

Now that she knew, Harrie was surprised she hadn't seen the resemblance earlier. DJ had to be at least six feet four inches. Seeing the statuesque Caroline standing beside her son, gazing at him with pride, it should have been obvious. Both were slim, blue eyed and attractive. Except for the fact that DJ's hair was dark and Caroline's was blonde, they looked remarkably alike.

Harrie broke the lengthy silence. "Let me ask you something, Caroline. Before you came to work for us, did you know I had been married to Nick Constantine?"

"Heavens no!" Caroline said, bristling at the suggestion.

"Okay, tell me this. Did you know we were editing Senator Lawrence's book?"

Caroline's shoulders slumped. "I hoped you were, but I didn't know until you told me during the interview. When I spoke with Steve at the retirement luncheon, he mentioned you and Ginger were working on a big project. I asked Steve what type of work you did at Southwest Editorial Services, and he said you specialized in editing and transcription services. Then I read the article in Sunday's paper about the senator's book." She looked from Ginger to Harrie, her eyes pleading. "Please believe me. I never intended to deceive you. I had no idea David was investigating your ex-husband until Wednesday. I wanted to tell you about everything, but he asked me to wait."

Harrie said, "Excuse me. Who's David?"

Caroline put her hand to her mouth. "Sorry. I'm not supposed to call him that. His full name is David James Scott, but they call him DJ at the Bureau. I'm always forgetting."

DJ interrupted. "Okay, Mom, I'm sure they're not interested in my personal history." He turned to Harrie. "Look, I assure you, my mother didn't know, and even I didn't know the connection until last Wednesday. I didn't get the assignment to investigate Constantine until that morning. Now, could we get back to the problem at hand? There's a situation here that's getting worse by the day."

That got Steve's attention. "You keep alluding to our being in danger. Can we talk about that, please?"

DJ looked at Harrie. "Could we go sit in your living room? This may take awhile."

Harrie said, "Of course."

When everyone else was seated, DJ still paced a small area in front of the fireplace. "First, I need to apologize to you all. This situation got out of hand, and it's my fault. I should have insisted my mother leave town months ago. If she had, she would be safe now, and you would be, too."

Ginger said, "You don't know that. You couldn't control Philip writing the book, and you certainly couldn't have stopped Harrie and me from editing it, so you have no need to apologize to us." She thought a minute. "Of course your mom might have been better off."

"She's right, DJ," Harrie said. "I still don't see why Ginger, Steve, and I are in danger because of the book. That's just crazy!"

DJ sat in the armchair opposite them and leaned in. "Don't you see? Your connection is Nick Constantine. This is just speculation but I think I know what happened to that brown envelope we were just talking about. Someone went to the office during Jacob's funeral. Using a key provided by a member of the firm, that someone took the envelope. I think that someone was supposed to turn the envelope over to the person who supplied the key, and then the thief would be paid for his troubles. But said thief saw an opportunity to make a better deal, and took off with the envelope."

"Are you implying that Nick is the person who spirited away the brown envelope?" Harrie's face was a mix of disbelief and anger.

"I don't know if he's the one who took it, but I'm almost certain he ended up with it."

"Why do you think that?" Steve asked.

DJ looked at him. "You've heard the term, 'follow the money'?"

Steve stood up, shaking his head. "You're saying the fortune Nick left is the result of blackmail?"

DJ shrugged. "Think about it. Somebody went to a great deal of trouble to obtain that envelope, only to have it slip from their grasp. We believe it contained the name of the person who murdered Chipper Finn. But in addition, we think it had information about the political corruption activities that gripped New Mexico at the time. If Nick got his hands on the envelope, he could have set his own price, and any number of individuals would be willing to pay big."

Harrie was skeptical. "But still, I can't imagine any one person coming up with the kind of money Nick apparently had. I think it makes more sense that he reconciled with his grandfather and was put back in the will."

"Think about this," DJ said. "Suppose Nick made copies of what was inside. What if he collected money from not just one person, but from multiple interested people?"

Harrie picked up the thread DJ was spinning. "So, you think several people paid Nick a lot of money, and each of them received a copy of the envelope's contents. Then, what? They compared notes, and found out they'd all paid for the same thing?"

"Why not?" DJ asked.

Caroline had been quiet until now. "I phoned Elizabeth Snow from the office that day as soon as I discovered the envelope missing. She told me, and I'll quote, 'Don't worry about it. I'll take care of everything'. Doesn't that sound like maybe she already knew who took it?"

Everyone paused to think over that possibility. Harrie was the first to speak. She turned to Caroline. "You obviously knew Jacob Snow very well. Do you think he could have been involved in the sort of criminal activity we're talking about here?"

"No. In fact, I think Jacob stopped whatever was going on during the time Daniel ran the firm. Daniel was always the 'wheeler dealer' type. Their brother-in-law, Peter, wasn't as smart as Daniel, and he was lazy. From what I understand, Peter would do just about anything Daniel told him to do, and that included handing out bribes and calling in favors. Daniel also had a son named Eric, who was a handful, according to Jacob. He told me that Eric was in one scrape after another when he was a teenager, and that Daniel was always sending Peter in to take care of things and clean up after Eric.

"One night, about two years before Jacob had his stroke, we were working late on a particularly complicated brief. We had food delivered in so we could keep working, but Jacob seemed very tired, so we ate dinner and talked instead. He told me the reason Eric had not gone into law and joined the firm was because of a girl he was involved with in the late forties. Eric fell in love with her, but Daniel didn't approve. Peter was sent in to arrange a European tour for Eric about that time. He had graduated from high school that summer, and it was his parents' gift to him. When he got back in the fall, he was supposed to enroll at the University, and then go on to law school. But when he returned from Europe, he tried to find the girl."

Harrie asked, "Do you know who she was?"

Caroline nodded. "It was Kathleen Finn. But he didn't find her then because she was gone for about six months, When she showed up again in February of 1950, Jacob heard she had learned that Eric's father and uncle were involved with the illegal gambling going on in Los Huevos and the bribery of many of the state's highest officials."

"How would she know all that?" Ginger asked.

"Some people thought she had used Eric to gain information about his family."

Harrie asked, "So obviously Eric Snow knew about his father's illegal activities?"

"Jacob was sure he did. Around the same time Chipper turned up dead, Eric and his father had a huge fight. Within days, Eric was sent back to Europe. Jacob was told much later that Eric was furious when he found out Chipper was threatening to expose the family secrets. It seems she was blackmailing them."

Harrie felt chilled. "Are you saying Eric Snow killed Chipper Finn?"

Caroline shook her head. "I can't say that for sure. Jacob wouldn't go so far as to commit himself, but that was the feeling I got."

Steve spoke up. "What happened to Eric? I don't think I ever heard anything about him."

"He returned to New Mexico about five years later and, according to Jacob, convinced his father to buy him a piece of land in Alaska. He went up there and became a bush pilot, taking hunters and other people up into the high country. He's supposed to have died many years ago in a plane crash. But I found something after Jacob had his stroke that made me wonder about that story."

"What did you find?" Harrie asked.

"I discovered a checking account I'd never seen before. It was an old account, opened in 1955. I noticed that four times a year, a check was sent to a post office box in Tucson, Arizona. Apart from that, there were no other withdrawals."

Harrie said, "Who were the checks made out to?"

"They were made out to a place called Serenity Hills. I did some snooping. It's a private sanitarium for the mentally ill."

33

Saturday Afternoon, April 15, 2000

Jonathan Templeton opened the Albuquerque Evening Star and examined the headline: *Senator's Condition Stable but Grave.*

He read the first few paragraphs and confirmed what he already knew. Philip Lawrence was down, but not out of the game. Jonathan did not consider this good news. He hoped his uncle would not be too upset.

He quickly checked the other sections of the paper, looking for a reference of some kind about the fate of another individual. Hell, it might not even be considered 'newsworthy'. There were so damn many traffic deaths in this state that they didn't even publicize all of them. He was about to give up his search when a small article caught his eye: *Unidentified Man Crashes on Interstate 25.*

Jonathan thought about removing Section B before taking the paper to his uncle, but sure as hell, today would be the day the old man wanted to read the entire thing from front to back. Better not risk it, he thought.

Jonathan smiled to himself. The more he thought about it, the more he became convinced he had nothing to worry about. Even if his Uncle Daniel saw the article, why should it mean anything to him? He put the paper back together carefully, making sure all the pages looked undisturbed.

When he reached Daniel Snow's study, he tapped softly on the door. No sound came from within. He gently opened the door and tiptoed inside. As usual, his uncle was leaning back in his leather executive chair. The old man's eyes were closed, and he snored softly through his open mouth. Jonathan quietly approached the desk and put the newspaper in the center on top of the blotter, opened and ready to read. Then he backed out of the room just as quietly and eased the door shut as he left.

Daniel slowly opened his eyes and scanned the room to make sure he was alone. His wrinkled face took on more creases as he smiled. *Fooled him again, the gullible, smug little bastard! Takes me for a doddering old fart he can outthink and outmaneuver. One of these days, his cockiness will be his undoing.*

Daniel opened the paper and read the story accompanying the headlines. Not good news. He hated the thought of his old friend lying in a hospital, unconscious and in pain. He wondered if his own end of life would be less traumatic. If he could hang on a little longer, he thought he might regain some control over his destiny. The key was to lay low. But this thing with Philip was just the sort of problem he'd been trying to avoid.

In Section B, another small item caught his attention. He had a good idea what it meant. He read the rest of the paper, formulating a plan as he went. He made some of his best plans while reading the daily papers.

He unlocked the top drawer of his desk and brought out a worn address book. He needed a job done. After completing the call, he replaced the address book and locked the drawer. When he heard someone coming, he leaned back in his chair, closed his eyes, and assumed the position of the aged old man everyone expected.

When those around you assumed you were senile, you could get away with a lot.

34

Harrie shook out two capsules of Ibuprofen and noted the container was almost empty. She blamed the week of headaches on the turmoil they'd been through. She decided a quick shower would do wonders for her aching head and befuddled mind.

As the hot spray pounded her back, she thought about the morning's revelations. She felt odd about DJ and Caroline. Though she accepted DJ's explanation about why he had not mentioned that Caroline was his mother, part of her still wondered if there was more to it. She understood DJ wanted to protect his mother, and she understood Caroline's fear that Ginger and Harrie would misunderstand her interest in working for them. But she couldn't help wondering about the connections between these events and Caroline's past.

She thought about how much DJ annoyed her. But she couldn't deny her attraction to him. *How weird is that?*

Harrie dressed in record time and was out the door, pulling into the O'Leary's driveway with time to spare.

The pungent scent of steaks cooking over hickory infused charcoal filled the air. Harrie realized she hadn't eaten since breakfast and she was hungry. She grabbed a knife and joined Ginger at the counter. They worked side-by-side, chopping vegetables for salad.

"How's your mom?" Harrie asked.

"Much better. She's really a strong lady, you know. Once she got over the initial shock, she buzzed around, taking care of things. She's been in almost constant contact with Ramona Sanchez. The security people at Canyon Estates patrol Philip's street more frequently, and the Albuquerque Police will also drive by."

"Do they know if anything is missing?"

"I don't know. I wonder if the police know about the special room. I haven't even mentioned it to Mom and Dad because I don't know if they are the other two people Philip told about his secret. What do you think I should do?"

Harrie shrugged. "Well, it seems to me if your parents were the other two people who knew about the room, Philip would simply have told you. Or, maybe he was just being cautious. I think you and I should go over there and see if anything's out of place. After all, we've been there twice this week. Your folks haven't been there recently, have they?"

"Not as far as I know. In fact, I'd bet they haven't been there in at least six months. But do you think I should tell them? Do you think we should tell DJ?"

Harrie stopped chopping and looked over at Ginger. "I don't think we should tell anybody, especially DJ, until we've checked it out ourselves. Which brings up another question? Who sent the envelope that Caroline brought over today?"

"It's from Philip. But it doesn't make any sense."

"Why, what's in it?"

"It was a photograph of my parents, Philip, my brothers, and me, taken years ago. I couldn't have been more than fourteen. It was at the Doc Long picnic grounds in the Sandias. We used to go up there on summer afternoons. Whenever Philip was in town, he enjoyed going with us."

"Wasn't there anything else?"

"Just a note from Philip. But it didn't seem to have anything at all to do with the photo. And yet, he had it clipped to the picture. I'll show it to you when I finish here. Doesn't say anything, really. I can't imagine why he mailed it, much less why he marked it Personal and Confidential."

They finished preparations just as the steaks came off the grill, sizzling and exuding their tantalizing aroma. The warm afternoon made the outside table the perfect place to enjoy their meal. When they finished, Mrs. O'Leary helped clear away the dishes, but Ginger took over when everything was back in the kitchen.

"Mom, you go on ahead. I know you and Dad wanted to visit the hospital this evening. Harrie and I will take care of this."

Casey O'Leary kissed her daughter on the cheek and hugged Harrie. "You girls are the sweetest things. You've both always been such a help to me." She left them to clean up and went in search of her husband and Steve.

Harrie whispered to Ginger. "Quick, show me the note."

Ginger retrieved the brown envelope from her purse and handed it to Harrie. "If Mom comes back, put it away. I don't want to show it to her yet. She'll just get all weepy."

Harrie took out the photograph and the note. The picture was as Ginger had described it. No hidden meanings that she could see. She turned her attention to the note.

"My dearest goddaughter. I was rummaging in my old desk today, and I ran across this photo of the trip we took to California that summer in 1980. Do you recall the fun we had in the desert? Don't ever forget those DEATH VALLEY DAYS! Love, Philip"

Harrie turned the note over to see if there was anything on the other side. It was blank. She looked at the back of the photograph. It had 'June 76' and everybody's name printed on it.

"The dates don't agree," Harrie said.

"What dates?"

"Look at the note. It mentions 1980, but the date on the photo is 1976."

Ginger looked where Harrie was pointing. "You're right. I didn't look at the back of the photo. I wonder what that's about."

"Did you and your folks ever take a trip to Death Valley with Philip?"

"I don't remember taking any trips with Philip. Maybe my parents did before I was born."

Harrie's face lit up. "Ginger, 1980 is the year we graduated from high school. You went with me to Texas in June to visit my grandparents, remember? Then we were busy getting ready for college after that. I know you didn't take any other trips that summer."

"What are you girls looking at," Casey O'Leary asked as she came into the kitchen.

Harrie slipped the photo and note into her purse. "Oh, it's just a picture one of my relatives sent me recently. It's a group of cousins I don't even know. I'll send it on to my mother." She smiled brightly, and Ginger hastened to her mother's side.

"Now remember, you can't stay too long. They'll probably kick you out after twenty minutes. That's what they did to me and Steve this afternoon."

Mrs. O'Leary, now successfully distracted from further interest in the photo, kissed her daughter on the cheek and joined her husband.

"That was close. I suppose the sensible thing would be to just ask my folks about the dumb picture instead of hiding it from them."

"Let's wait a few days until we have a chance to check things out in the hidden room. Then if we don't solve the puzzle, we'll ask them. Wait a minute," Harrie looked at her watch. "It's still early. Why don't we go over there now?"

Steve walked in with the last of the utensils from the grill. "Where are we going?"

Ginger signaled Harrie with a look. "Nowhere, Dear. We were just talking."

"Don't give me that innocent act," he said. "You two are up to something. I can always tell."

Harrie jumped in. "It's me, Steve. I was just contemplating a trip to the office. I thought I'd try to get some work done tonight."

"Bad idea, Harrie," Steve said. "It's not wise for you two to be at the office alone at night—not until we get to the bottom of all this."

"I don't care what DJ says. I still have a hard time believing we are in danger," Harrie said.

"Maybe this will change your mind," said Steve. "DJ called me on my cell phone a few minutes ago when I was cleaning the grill. I had given him Swannie's name because he wanted to talk with someone from the APD. Swannie told him something, and DJ passed it along to me."

Harrie narrowed her eyes. "Do we have to guess, or will you tell us?"

He became very serious. "They got the results back from the ballistics test on the bullet they took from Philip. It matches the one the surgeons removed from Nick's brain."

35

Sunday Morning, April 16, 2000

Harrie opened her eyes, snapped them shut again, and moaned. *Note to self: three glasses of wine late in the evening is a bad idea.*

The dream from last night was stranger than usual. She found herself observing the old west in the late 1800s. She saw a wagon train of pioneers slogging their way through mountains, deserts, and wilderness on their way to California. At one point, she observed Philip Lawrence, looking haggard, dressed in boots and dusty clothes. He was the leader of the wagon train, and it was his job to deliver the pioneers safely to the trail's end. A terrible storm came up. The wagons huddled together in a circle, and the rain beat down on them with fury. Lightning flashed all around, and the weary travelers were frightened. Suddenly an old man, white-haired and stooped, appeared out of the raging tempest. He stood in the middle of the circle of wagons, and lightening came from a staff he held high above his head. Philip Lawrence went out to face the man, and a bolt from the staff struck him down. A younger man broke from the crowd of watchers and ran to Philip, picked him up from the ground, and carried him back to the safety of the wagons. When he turned to face the wizened foe, Harrie recognized the young warrior as DJ Scott. She woke up then.

Thank God for coffee.

She grabbed her purse, cell phone and sunglasses. "Guard the house, Tuptim. I'll be back soon," she called to the sleeping cat.

She backed out of the driveway and froze. A black SUV was parked at the end of the block. Heart pounding, she shoved the car in drive and tore off in the opposite direction.

She fumbled in her purse for her cell phone. *Damn! Which pocket did I put it in?*

She took turns watching the traffic in front of her and checking the mirror. So far, no black SUV in sight. This was getting old! Why should she still be worried about black SUVs anyway? Hadn't she already decided it was Nick following her last week? If that were true, she had nothing to worry about. Except DJ kept harping about the danger they were in from whoever killed Nick and attacked Senator Lawrence. So, maybe it hadn't been Nick's black SUV after all. Maybe it was the one parked down the street from her house. And maybe she was just a paranoid, hysterical female.

She decided to see if she could flush out anyone who might be following her. She slowed down, and turned into the shopping center at Wyoming and Montgomery. She parked by Hastings Book Store and waited. It didn't take long. Two minutes later, a black SUV turned into the same parking lot. She pretended to look for something in her purse, all the while watching in her side and rear mirrors. The SUV parked in the row behind her, several cars over. Now what?

No one exited the SUV. She couldn't just sit there in her parked car. She took a deep breath and got out. She walked as nonchalantly as she could. She felt eyes staring at her back as she walked, but at last she reached her goal and stepped into the vestibule of the Hastings.

The anti-glare film on the windows not only kept the sunlight out, it also allowed those inside to observe without being seen from the outside. She watched intently for movement from the SUV. The seconds turned into minutes. She perked up when she saw the driver's side door to the SUV slowly open. She watched intently as a figure emerged. She felt a tap on her shoulder, and a deep masculine voice said, "Waiting for someone?"

She caught herself before a shriek escaped her throat. She whirled around, and found herself facing none other than the man from her dream – Special Agent DJ Scott.

36

"If I have a heart attack anytime soon, I'll make sure everyone knows you're to blame," Harrie's voice quivered. DJ flashed his gorgeous smile, and she felt her insides melt like warm Jell-O.

"What are you doing here today?" he asked. "I thought you'd be hard at work, making up for lost time."

"I am. I'm on my way to the office right now."

He looked at her. "Gee, it looks to me like you're standing here, waiting for someone."

Harrie debated with herself about whether to mention the black SUV. "No, I just stopped here to—" she shook her head. "Okay, I give up. I was watching that black SUV out there. I thought it might have followed me from my house. I pulled in here to see if it turned in, too."

DJ's jaw tightened, his face became all business. "Where is it?"

Harrie turned around to point it out, but the SUV was no longer there. "It's gone," she said.

"Are you sure it was the same car?"

She shook her head. "No, I can't tell one from the other. It looks like all the others I've seen this past week. I see them everywhere I go now."

"Okay, I have a suggestion. Let's use my car to go to your office. You do what you have to do with the manuscript, and then I'll take you to lunch. I can bring you back later to pick up your car. How's that?"

She looked at him, her expression one of caution and suspicion. "What's this all about? Why the lunch invitation? Come to think of it, why are you even here?"

"Well," he said, "I enjoy browsing through bookstores, and I didn't have anything better to do on a lazy Sunday afternoon." He watched her reaction. The look on her face said she wasn't buying it.

He tried again, "Okay, here it is. I'm worried about you. I was on my way to check on you. I spoke to a police lieutenant friend of Steve's yesterday."

Harrie interrupted, "Don't tell me. You're talking about Bob Swanson."

DJ nodded, "Yeah, that's right. Anyway, Swannie was interested in what I could tell him about Nick's activities that brought him to the attention of the Bureau. In return for that, he offered to help me out."

Harrie didn't say anything and waited for him to get to the point. DJ took a deep breath and continued. "So when I told him about the possibility you and Ginger had a stalker, he immediately suggested placing a couple of unmarked cars in your neighborhoods. You know, just to be on the safe side."

Harrie couldn't believe this. "You have the police tailing me?"

"No. They just drive by occasionally and check things out. Sometimes, they park across the street and watch awhile, but they aren't following you." Then he added, "At least I don't think they are."

Harrie sputtered. There were so many words vying to come out of her mouth, she couldn't organize them. "You . . . I'm not . . . This isn't . . ." she looked up at him, gesturing wildly with her hands in the absence of coherent speech.

DJ took hold of both her arms, and held them down by her side. "Calm down. I had planned to tell you about it over lunch. You don't need to get all excited. It's just routine."

Two young men, pants dangerously low on their hips, shuffled into the store. They stared at the tall man and the short, energetic woman engaged in heated conversation. They snickered and muttered something Harrie couldn't hear, but she had an idea it wasn't flattering.

Her anger melted. She looked at DJ and laughed. "I'm sorry," she said. "I know I must seem like a mental case to you. I'm normally very calm and reasonable. I think you bring out the worst in me."

"Oh, I hope not," he said.

"Okay, I accept your invitation. Frankly, I feel a little nervous about going to the office alone today."

They got in DJs car and pulled out of the parking lot. Harrie said, "You were going to tell me what you were doing at Hastings this morning."

"I told you, I like to browse for books."

"Yes, you did, and that's lame."

"Okay," he said, a small smile playing across his lips. "Yesterday, I found out about a book written a few years ago. It has to do with the sheriff of Ventana County. You must know about the man they arrested and tried for the murder of Chipper Finn. He was beaten and tortured by the sheriff and a couple of his cronies from Los Huevos."

"Yes. Ginger and I saw the newspaper clippings from those days. They had a lot of information about Sheriff Smiley Hernandez and his questionable ethics. How did you find out about this book?"

"I went back to the office yesterday afternoon to finish my report. It occurred to me there had to be other people who had written about this incident. After all, it was a major event in the course of New Mexico politics. I asked Swannie if he knew of any, and he said he heard of one but didn't know the name of it. So I did an internet search to see if I could find the book and who wrote it."

Harrie said. "I never heard about any of this until we started working on Senator Lawrence's book. So you obviously found someone. Who was it?"

"Good question. There's a book, all right, but the author used a pseudonym. I thought if I could get the book and read it, I might learn something. Maybe I could even figure out who wrote it."

"So did you? Find the book, I mean."

"They didn't have it, but they ordered it for me. It should be here by next week."

Harried mulled this over as they drove along. "Why use a pseudonym? If somebody like Senator Lawrence is writing a book on the subject and he's willing to publish it under his real name, why should someone else be so shy?"

They stopped at the light at Wyoming and Academy, and DJ turned to look at her. "When you think about it, doesn't it seem like a prudent precaution? In view of what's happened to the senator, he probably wishes he'd chosen to do the same."

"Wait a minute," Harrie sat up straight, brimming with excitement. "What if that's it?"

The light changed to green, and DJ glanced at her quickly before turning his attention back to traffic. "What do you mean?"

Harrie said, "What if the person who wrote the book used a phony name, not because he was afraid of the bad guys, but because he *is* the bad guy?"

DJ pulled the car into the space in front of Harrie's office and turned to stare at her. "You know, I'm beginning to worry about myself."

Harrie looked confused. "Why?"

"Because," he said, "you're beginning to make sense, and that scares me."

37

Sunday Noon, April 16, 2000

After DJ made a call from the phone in the reception area, he walked into Harries' office.

She looked up from her work and said, "You look like my cat when she's snagged a forbidden treat. What's up?"

"It finally occurred to me I had an available resource I hadn't considered until now."

"A resource for what?"

"Everything to do with books," he said. "Did you know my mother used to own a bookstore?"

Harrie nodded. "She told us about that during her interview. Does she remember anything about a book on the subject of Sheriff Smiley Hernandez?"

"Not only does she remember, she just happens to have a copy of it." His face beamed.

"Now that's creepy! What are the odds your mother would just happen to have a book you were searching for today?"

"Actually, I'd be surprised if she *didn't* have it. She worked for the Snows for thirty years, and the Chipper Finn murder had a profound effect on them as Jacob explained to her. And you know she loves books. Once she has one, she keeps it."

"That's sounds reasonable, but it still seems amazing."

"Yeah, I guess so. Are you ready for some lunch?"

After lunch at a cozy café, Harrie felt relaxed, her headache gone. In fact, she couldn't remember the last time she'd felt this good. They had just settled back into DJ's car. He looked at her and said, "You look pretty happy about something."

"Yep, I guess I do. This is the most peaceful day I've had all month."

"Do you mind if we stop by my mom's and see if she's located that book yet?"

"No problem for me, but why don't you just take me back to my car? You don't have to chauffeur me around all day."

DJ smiled, almost shyly. "I like being with you. It doesn't feel like I'm your chauffeur. It feels like we're spending time getting to know each other better."

Harrie laughed nervously. "Is that allowed?" She corrected herself. "What I mean is, can you get to be friends with somebody you're investigating?"

"I told you before, no one's investigating you. Anyway," he looked at her, "I've turned this case over to someone else, remember?"

Harrie felt her skin grow warm. *My God, I'm blushing! What's next? Swooning?* "Oh, right, you said that yesterday." She hesitated, and then looked at him. "So it's okay for us to be friends?"

"Friends?" he said, raising an eyebrow. "Sure, we can be friends. That's always a good start, don't you think?"

Harrie didn't trust herself to respond. Instead, she smiled and chatted aimlessly about the weather, the traffic, and any other damn thing she could think of to avoid the topic he'd introduced.

They turned into the driveway of a brick house, and Harrie admired the well-manicured lawn and rose bushes just beginning to leaf out. "What a lovely home. Has Caroline lived here long?"

"About ten years. She bought it after her husband died."

Harrie looked at DJ, surprised. "Her husband? Are you saying her husband wasn't your father?" Then she caught herself. "I'm sorry. That was rude."

He shook his head. "Not at all. Anyway, didn't you wonder why we don't have the same last name?"

"I hadn't really given it any thought."

"My father died before I was born. He and my mother were just kids. They ran away and got married after Dad was drafted into the Army. He was shipped to Vietnam a month later. By the time she found out I was coming along, Dad had been killed."

As they got out of the car and walked toward the front porch, Harrie felt sadness she wouldn't have imagined feeling for someone she barely knew. "I'm so sorry. How awful for your poor mother."

"Yeah, it was hard on her. Especially since her parents had forbidden her to marry him in the first place. They were rather strict. You see, she had just turned fifteen, and my Dad was eighteen. She had no choice so she swallowed her pride and went back home. But enough of my sad story for now. We have plenty of time to get into all that later." He rang the doorbell.

Caroline greeted them warmly. "I've just taken a pie out of the oven. It's your favorite, dear – apple. After it cools a bit, I'll serve it."

She escorted them to the kitchen. There were bookcases in every room they passed on the way. The smell of cinnamon and tangy apples spiced the air. Caroline got out coffee cups while they sat down at the table.

Harrie looked around the room. "I love your home, Caroline. It's so warm and friendly. You have a wonderful touch with decorating."

They sat and talked for a while, sipping coffee, and Harrie felt comfortable being with them. After a few minutes, Caroline said, "I found the book." She left the room and when she returned, she carried a hardback book with a colorful dust jacket. DJ looked at the cover: *The Lie That Killed A Town*, by Francis Black. "Intriguing title. Have you read it?"

"Oh, yes," she said. "I skimmed through it again this afternoon after you called. This 'Francis Black' seems to think there was a terrible miscarriage of justice. He blames the FBI for destroying the careers of some of the upstanding citizens there. It doesn't exactly correspond to what I'd always heard about that era."

DJ leafed through the book for a few minutes. "It doesn't say all that much about the murder does it?"

Caroline shook her head. "No, it doesn't. He focuses instead on the theory that somebody high up had a vendetta to destroy the political leaders in New Mexico at that time. He paints the picture of a bunch of good old boys who were badly misunderstood."

"Who's the 'high-up' person he thinks was targeting these poor guys?" Harrie asked.

DJ chuckled. "Who else? J. Edgar Hoover. Ever since he died in 1971, he's been painted as the bad guy for everything that ever happened in law enforcement. People who had the most to hide had a field day after his death. They thought all their dirty little secrets had died with the man, and they felt free to disparage him without fear of reprisal."

"So, what does the book say about the murderer?"

"That's interesting," Caroline said. "He doesn't come right out and name the person, but he insinuates it was Eric Snow."

"So this guy confirms what your boss said. Do you think he had inside information?" Harrie asked.

"Well if so, it doesn't follow the same line Jacob took."

DJ looked up at his mother. "What's different about it?"

Caroline sat down at the end of the table. "Remember I told you Jacob was convinced Chipper Finn got information about Eric's father and uncle? That they were behind the gambling, bribery and payoff schemes? He thought Eric killed her to keep her from revealing that information to the authorities."

"Yeah, sure. You said he wanted to protect his family."

"According to Mr. Francis Black, that wasn't anywhere near the truth. Daniel Snow and Peter Templeton are painted as the heroes of the piece. Daniel tried valiantly to see that Chipper Finn's murderer was convicted of her death, and then, when he failed to do that, he resigned as District Attorney. He went on a crusade to bring about reform in New Mexico politics and clean out the pockets of illegal gambling. That's what got him elected as New Mexico's Attorney General."

"Okay," Harrie said, "I'm confused. Why would Eric kill her if it wasn't to protect his family from the scandal?"

"Ah, that's where it gets interesting," Caroline replied. "I'd forgotten about this part, though why, I can't imagine. It's really the most interesting theory in the book. According to the author, Chipper gave birth to Eric Snow's child, and he killed her because she tried to blackmail his family."

38

Sunday Afternoon, April 16, 2000

"Who else besides Nick do you think was in a position to steal that envelope from Jacob Snow's office two years ago?"

They were on their way back to the parking lot at Hastings to retrieve Harrie's car. They had been discussing the case all afternoon and still had many unanswered questions.

"I don't know," DJ said. "We don't yet have enough information about Nick's activities in the past eighteen months."

"It seemed you had a lot of information earlier this week. You were convinced he did work for Senator Lawrence and that he owed a big debt to a bunch of money launderers."

"That was before I found out about the will, and the apparent fortune he possessed. If it all proves to be on the up and up, we might have to look at the information we have in a different light."

Harrie watched the passing scenery as she thought about other possibilities. "What type of work did Nick do for the senator?"

DJ pulled into the parking lot, killed the engine and turned toward her. "We know Nick obtained a New Mexico private investigator license right after he arrived back in town, eighteen months ago. We know he met with Philip Lawrence at least twice in the last two weeks. Then on Monday, he was spotted entering the estate of Daniel Snow. We don't know for sure who he visited, but Daniel doesn't see many people these days, so it might have been his nephew, Jonathan."

"Wouldn't it make more sense if he worked for the Snows? If there's something fishy going on, they would seem to be the more likely employer."

"I thought of that, and of course it's entirely possible. But he had already made inquiries and according to the reports he filed, he did that on behalf of Senator Philip Lawrence."

Harrie rummaged in her purse for her car keys, but stopped at that remark. "How could you possibly know Nick filed a report? Where did he file it?"

"He filed it with the PI firm he worked for."

"Nick worked for a firm? Why would he do that if his work was shady? And it doesn't sound like Nick. He was a loner."

"It's easier and quicker to get a license through an established firm which can provide the surety bond, proof of a physical location in New Mexico where records are maintained and made available for inspection by the State, licensing fee, background check and all the other things the state requires for a PI license."

"But wouldn't working for a firm hamper his ability to keep what he was doing secret?"

"Depends on the firm. I spoke to their manager Friday after I found out Nick died. He said they use an automated machine to take phone-in reports. Who knows if they check up on what their operatives report. The manager told me Nick's last report was Wednesday evening."

Harrie swallowed hard, fighting the sudden formation of a lump in her throat. "That must have been just before someone killed him."

DJ put his hand on her arm. "Are you okay? I forget this is probably a little hard for you to hear right now."

She shook her head. "I'm okay. I just have a hard time getting my mind to accept all that's happened. I'm not used to having people I know attacked and killed." The moment the words left her lips, she realized the terrible irony of that statement. *My God, have I already forgotten about Mark?*

She reached for the door handle. "I've got to get home. Thank you for lunch and for going with me to the office."

"Wait," he said and touched her arm. "Where are you headed now?"

She looked at his hand on her wrist. A small surge of electricity coursed through her. She disengaged herself from his grasp and pushed the warm thoughts from her mind. "I have things to do at home. I'm a working girl, you know, and weekends are when I normally do laundry and all that inconvenient stuff."

His look grew serious. "Promise me you'll stay home with the doors locked."

"I'm not going anywhere. Besides, wouldn't your patrol cars follow me?" Her smile softened the words into gentle banter.

"Okay, I'll call you later on, just to make sure. Keep your cell phone with you."

Harrie made up for lost time as soon as she got home, sorting clothes, loading the washer and cleaning up the clutter. She had her favorite CD on as she danced around the living room, pushing the vacuum and singing.

Tuptim jumped onto the back of the recliner and set up a howling that only a Siamese can manage. Harrie turned off the vacuum and heard the phone ringing. "Why thank you, my faithful watch cat. What would I do without you?" Harrie grabbed the phone.

"What are you doing right this minute?" Ginger sounded excited.

"I'm cleaning. Why?"

Ginger's voice was barely above a whisper. "Can you come get me?"

Harrie felt a shiver of apprehension. "Sure, but where are you?"

"I'm at Mom and Dad's. We need to talk. Alone. Steve's in the living room with them right now."

Harrie thought about her promise to DJ. "What's going on? Why all the mystery?"

"Ramona came by earlier and told my parents there's some sort of emergency with one of her sons. She'll be gone a couple of days and thought she should tell someone. She can't tell the senator so she told my parents."

"So?"

"So if she isn't going to be there to clean and keep an eye on the place, I thought we might want to check up on things."

"You have a devious mind, you know that? I love it. But do you really think Steve's going to let you and me go check on the senator's house without him?"

Ginger's voice dropped another notch. "He doesn't have to know. Nobody knows I have the key."

Apprehension settled around Harrie's shoulders like a heavy woolen shawl. "But what excuse will you use to get out of the house and keep Steve from coming with you?"

"I'll tell him you're going shopping for a new dress and want my opinion."

Harrie took a long breath. "I have a bad feeling about this." She hesitated, weighing her options. "Okay. Give me ten minutes to get out of my grubbies and drive over."

"Trust me, this will be worth it. Ramona told me Philip had been dictating into his tape recorder a lot recently. He told her it was a personal history he wanted me to have someday."

"And you think this is significant and urgent now?"

"Yes I do. He told her about it 'right after that nice young man' came to see him."

"What nice young man?" Harrie asked, knowing what she would hear but dreading it anyway.

"That handsome private investigator, Nick Constantine."

39

Sunday Evening, April 16, 2000

Harrie saw nothing that looked like an unmarked patrol cars as she headed for the O'Learys. Ginger must have been watching out the window, because she rushed outside as Harrie drove up.

"Do I need to go inside and tell them I want your fashion advice?" Harrie asked sarcastically.

"Just drive," said Ginger. "Somebody out there who tried to kill my godfather, and I just know something in that safe room will help us figure it out."

Harrie gave her a sideways glance. "You're the one who always keeps me from going off half-cocked. I don't like this role reversal." She grinned. "Who are you, and what have you done with the real Ginger?"

Ginger smiled and said, "Well don't get used to it. I'm no more comfortable with this than you are. But with this new information, I feel like we need to act now."

"You mean what you told me about Ramona seeing Nick?"

"Yes, and something else. I overheard Mom say to Dad, 'I've told Philip for years that woman would be his downfall, and now it's happened'."

"What did your father say?"

"Nothing. He saw me coming and clammed up."

Harrie frowned. "Is there a woman in the senator's life we didn't know about?"

Ginger shook her head, "The only woman connected to Philip I ever knew about was his wife."

"He has a wife?"

"He did have. She died years ago. As far as I know, he's never been involved with another woman. Margo was my mother's best friend in college. That's how she and my father met Philip. Margo meant everything to him. They were only married about ten years before she died of cancer. He was so grief-stricken he just buried himself in his career. I don't think he even dated a woman after her death."

"Then what could your mother have meant? What woman could possibly cause his downfall?"

"That's what I have to find out," Ginger said. "I've always had the feeling Philip had some secret in his life. Something he needed to protect. I can't explain it. I just saw sadness in his eyes, even before Margo died."

"So, you're saying Philip has a big, dark secret, and your mom and dad knew about it."

"Yes, and I think they blame this woman for Philip being attacked."

"How's that possible? Whoever shot Philip also shot Nick. I thought we'd pretty much decided the connection had something to do with Philip's book."

Ginger reached up and rubbed the back of her neck, her voice filled with weariness. "I know, I know. On the surface there doesn't seem to be any logical connection. I lay awake half the night thinking about it. That's why I need to get in that room and see if we can figure it out. I need your help. You've always been good with puzzles. This is right up your alley."

"I still don't feel good about this. Especially going there in the dark. Maybe we should wait until tomorrow."

"And what would we tell Caroline when we leave work?"

"Tell her the truth."

"No. She might feel compelled to tell her handsome son about our little caper."

Harrie groaned. "You aren't going to let go of that, are you?"

"Hey," Ginger said. "When I see something developing between my best friend and a handsome guy, I'll do everything I can to encourage it. You know how us little old matchmakers are."

Harrie grinned and sighed. "Okay, okay. You win. I'll make you a deal. I'll put up with your matchmaking and you agree to delay investigating the safe room until in the morning."

"Okay. But before you leave, let me tell you another idea that popped into my head."

"Which is?"

"Don't laugh, but I wonder if Philip might have actually known Chipper Finn?"

40

Monday Morning, April 17, 2000

Harrie drove away from her house Monday morning under a clear, blue sky. That would probably change by afternoon, but for now, she simply enjoyed the soaring New Mexico sky.

She thought about the day ahead and imagined that a jewel thief might feel like this just before a heist. Her stomach fluttered and her blood pressure was probably sky high. *Why yes, doctor. My vital signs are always like this when I'm going to be breaking and entering before lunch.*

Thankfully, DJ had waited until her return last night before he called. She truthfully told him she was getting ready for bed and had been busy cleaning all afternoon. He didn't directly ask if she'd gone anywhere, but she didn't volunteer anything either. She didn't actually lie, and it could have been a lot worse if Ginger's wild plan had been carried out.

Harrie thought about Ginger's idea. Could Philip really have known Chipper Finn? If so, it would have been when he was in Albuquerque in the service. It would also explain his interest in the case, and why he'd been following it even before he moved back from Washington.

Harrie tried to remember the things Philip told them last Monday when they went to his house the first time. She remembered he told them the first time he read about the Chipper Finn murder was in the Albuquerque Morning Sun, delivered to him in Washington. What did he say first caught his attention? Something about Chipper looking familiar. Why would she look familiar? Could he have been a patron of the Los Huevos gambling establishments?

Harrie parked under a tree, and gathered up her purse and briefcase. She turned to walk into the building, and caught sight of a black SUV parked several spaces down. Her heart skipped a beat, and then caught up with a double thud. Is it DJ? She looked around the parking lot. She didn't see either Ginger's or Caroline's car. If the SUV belonged to DJ, he would have gotten out when she arrived. She fumbled through her keys, looking for the one she needed. When she found it, she let herself in and quickly relocked the door. She punched in the code on the alarm keypad and hurried into her office. She'd been holding her breath the entire time and let it out in one big 'whoosh.' She waited for a knock at the door, but none came. Where was Ginger? And for that matter, where was Caroline?

She jumped when the phone rang. She calmed her voice when she greeted the caller. No one responded. She looked at the caller ID display and saw "Unavailable." Again she said, "Good morning, Southwest Editing Services, how may I help you?

Still no answer. Harrie thought she heard someone breathing on the other end of the phone. "Who is this, please?" This was creepy.

The distinct click of a disconnect ended the call. Harrie dropped the receiver back on its cradle like it had suddenly become a snake. She reached for her cell phone and speed dialed Ginger. It went to voicemail.

"Damn!" she muttered, and snapped the phone shut again. She sat down at her desk and searched through the stack of business cards she'd collected. It had to be here somewhere. "There it is," she said out loud. *Great! Now I'm talking to myself!* She started to dial then stopped. What would she say if he answered? *Oh DJ, I'm scared! There's a black SUV parked in front of our office, and I just answered the phone and heard heavy breathing. Please come save me!*

Laughter bubbled up inside her. Her tension slid off like water from her morning shower. She didn't hear the door open.

"Harrie! What's wrong?" Ginger's silent entrance caught Harrie by surprise, and that, coupled with the laughing jag, triggered a hiccupping attack.

Ginger rushed around the desk to kneel beside Harrie. "What happened?"

Harrie waved a hand at Ginger as she went into another fit of laughter, interspersed with hiccups. When she was able to speak, she told Ginger about the SUV and the breather. By the time she finished recounting her imaginary conversation with DJ, Ginger was also laughing.

"Wait a minute," Ginger said. "Why are we laughing? This could be something serious."

"Oh, come on," Harrie scoffed. "I'm just being a nervous twit, and you know it. We get wrong number calls all the time, and we never think they're sinister. Admit it. This is a little over the top, even for me."

Ginger turned serious. "In view of all the things that happened this past week, I don't think either one of us should be that blasé. I think we should call DJ. This is exactly the kind of thing he'd want to know about."

"Maybe," she said over her shoulder. "But let me at least see if the SUV is still there before I make a fool of myself." She peered through the glass. There were a few more cars now, including Caroline's who had just arrived, but none were black SUVs.

"See, it's nothing. There's no SUV, no suspicious characters hanging around, and Caroline is just arriving with a box of stuff. Let's forget it for now, okay?"

Ginger raised her left eyebrow. "Okay, but if any more funny stuff happens, I'm calling DJ myself, so get ready for it."

Caroline walked in to find her two employers standing, one on each side of the door, in an apparent face-off. She looked from one to the other. "Am I interrupting something?"

"Not really," Ginger said. "I'm just whipping my little friend here into shape. She's altogether too casual about the danger DJ said we should watch for. We need to keep an eye on her."

Caroline put the box down and grinned. "Oh, don't worry. I'm really good at that. DJ was quite a handful when he was little. I've had lots of practice watching out for reckless kids." She turned to Harrie with a serious look. "Has something happened?"

Once again, Harrie described the events of the morning. "It's just me being more jumpy than normal. Usually it's only bugs and spiders that get to me that much. Well, okay, maybe snakes and lizards, too. But as a rule, I'm not so nervous about other stuff unless I've had a dream." Harrie instantly regretted her slip of tongue.

Caroline's eyes lit up. "What's this about dreams?"

"Nothing, really. Sometimes I have dreams that leave me jumpy. As I said, I'm not generally that easily spooked. Just lately."

"I wish I'd been here," Caroline said. "Maybe it was the same car I saw last Monday when I came for my interview. Could you see the driver?"

"No. Does everybody but me have tinted windows these days?"

They laughed, then Ginger said, "We'd better get going, my weak-kneed friend. We have an appointment, remember?"

Harrie went for her purse while Ginger spun a yarn to Caroline about visiting a new client. When Harrie came out of the office, she held up her keys and pointed to the vault. Ginger nodded and went back to the key cabinet to retrieve the set of keys Philip had given them last Monday.

When they were in Ginger's car, Harrie said, "Did you give both our cell numbers to Caroline so she can reach us?"

"I did that last Wednesday when she first got here."

"Would that have been when you also gave my number to DJ?"

Ginger pulled back in mock horror. "Do you think I would be so underhanded?"

Harrie smiled. "Yes, I do. Yesterday I discovered he had my cell number, and I had never given it to him."

Ginger's eyes glittered with interest. "Did something happen yesterday? What are you holding back?"

Harrie sighed and described her entire day, including the impromptu meeting at Hasting, the trip to the office, lunch, and the stop at his mother's house. When Harrie got to the part about the book Caroline had, Ginger's interested shifted from the personal to the on-going mystery.

"Wow, why didn't you tell me all this last night?"

"We were concentrating on this little scheme we're pulling off today."

Ginger nodded. "That's true. Anyway, how hard will it be for DJ to find out who the author really is?"

"I have no idea. We got off the subject when he told me about Nick's visits to Philip and one to the Snow residence. Did I tell you Nick dictated a report to an automated machine at the PI office where he worked? DJ spoke to the manager, who told him Nick had done some work for Philip. The last report covered that investigation."

"How do we get our hands on that report," Ginger asked, gripping the steering wheel tightly.

Harrie said. "What makes you think we could get our hands on it? They're not going to turn over the results of a private investigation to a couple of amateur sleuths."

"Ah, but I know something that could change all that. I found out another little tidbit after you left last night."

"Oh, I can't wait for this," Harrie said.

Ginger gave her a smug smile. "My dad just happens to have been appointed by Philip as his agent of record in case of emergency. He drew up a Durable Power of Attorney and named my Dad to take over all his affairs if something happened to him. It turns out Philip's current status automatically activates that Power of Attorney."

When they arrived at Canyon Estates, Ginger told the guard they needed to speak to the security supervisor, and he directed them to a building around the corner.

Ramona Sanchez had already alerted the supervisor that Ginger and Harrie would be coming and going at Senator Lawrence's home while he was ill. They showed their driver's licenses, filled out a form and received temporary passes for each of their cars.

"Okay, the first hurdle is done," Ginger said when they returned to the car. "Now all we have to do is remember how to get into that room."

Ginger worked the key in the lock and felt it release. "Well, here we go. Keep your eyes open for anything unusual."

The house seemed dark and forbidding with all the draperies closed and no sound of human presence. Apprehension settled over Harrie like a mist. "Could we look around before we go into the library?"

Ginger rubbed her arms and shivered. "Good idea. Let's see if we can get a little heat in here, too." She turned the thermostat up, and they heard the sound of the heater coming to life.

Harrie thought it odd how the lack of someone's presence could be felt almost as strongly as having them there.

Ginger flipped the light switch in the library. "My God! I wasn't expecting this!" She looked at the dark stain on the floor.

Harrie said, "Maybe we could clean it up."

"I don't think we should touch it," Ginger said. "We can check with the police later and see if it's okay."

Harrie nodded and turned her attention to the bookcases. "Do you remember which book he used to access the hidden door?"

Ginger nodded and reached behind the correct book. They heard a soft hiss as the bookcase swung away from the wall. Ginger took the combination from her pocket and tapped numbers into the keypad.

The door slid noiselessly into the wall. She snapped on the light switch.

"Should we turn on the monitor?" Harrie asked.

Ginger shrugged. "I have no idea how that thing works. If you want to give it a try, be my guest."

Harrie pressed the switch marked 'monitor' and the screen came to life.

She turned and grinned at Ginger. "Aren't you glad I'm geekier than you?"

Ginger laughed. "Yes I am."

Harrie looked at the photographs on the wall. "I didn't pay much attention to these before," she said as she walked from one photo to the other. "I was so entranced with the whole 'secret room' thing I couldn't take it all in at the time." She examined each photo, admiring the extent of Philip's accomplishments. "This is a gorgeous photo of Albuquerque from the air, and I love this view of the Capitol." She paused in front of one. "Oh, look! Here he is with President Reagan."

"That's right after Reagan won the presidency," Ginger said. "Philip spent a huge portion of the summer of 1980 helping with the campaign. He was very proud of that."

Ginger examined the two keys on the ring Philip had pressed into her hand only last week. She sighed, "I never thought we'd be using these." She opened the side drawer and picked up the big folder of clippings they'd looked at last week.

"We need to take these with us. He was very clear about not leaving them around if something happened to him." Beneath the folder was a metal box with a label on the lid. Ginger set the box up on the desk.

Harrie glanced at the label. "For Ginger's Memory Book." She frowned. "You have a memory book?"

Ginger ran her fingers over the top of the old, scratched box. "No. I don't even know what a 'memory book' is." She pushed on the metal lever. It didn't move.

"Great," said Harrie. "Now what?"

Ginger pushed the latch a few times, then looked up at Harrie and grinned. She removed the key ring from the desk lock and examined the smaller key. When she fitted it into the lock, it turned easily, and she lifted the lid.

"Cassette tapes?" Harrie reached over and picked up one of the small plastic cases. "I thought there'd be pictures and letters or something." Disappointment tinged her voice.

Ginger examined another cassette. "They're labeled with dates. They don't look the same as the manuscript cassettes he sends us with a chapter number and a heading." She examined several more. "This seems to be the latest one. It's dated last Wednesday."

Harrie tossed her tape back into the box, "Maybe the label is a clue. We can listen to these and find out which memories are so important and whether Nick's visit here had anything to do with all this."

Ginger slumped back into the desk chair. "I gave Caroline the office machine to use at her desk. Do you have another tape player? I'd rather listen to this without her knowing about it."

"I think there's one in the back of my closet. It's old though, and I haven't used it much since compact discs."

Ginger put the cassettes back in the box and closed and locked the lid. "Let's go back to the office. We probably shouldn't stay here too long."

Harrie looked at her watch. "It's almost ten. You want to swing by my house and see if I can find that player?"

Ginger smiled as she looked back in the drawer where the metal box had been. "Or," she said, as she reached in and pulled out a small, black rectangular unit. "We could just use this." It was an ancient-looking cassette recorder. "He must have had this thing at least twenty years."

They gathered up the box, the recorder and the clippings folder. Ginger locked the desk, and Harrie turned toward the monitoring system. The current view on the monitor showed the front of the house. Ginger's car sat in the driveway, but there was something else.

"Oh, please, not again!"

Ginger looked up as Harrie fiddled frantically with the controls on the panel, searching for the view she'd been watching seconds before. "What's wrong?" Ginger asked.

Harrie didn't speak as she pushed buttons and twirled knobs. The monitor again displayed the view of the driveway.

Ginger came and stood beside her. "Did you see something? It looks the same as it did when we came in."

Harrie slapped her hand against the control panel in frustration. "It is now! But that's not the way it looked a minute ago." She pointed to the screen. "Right there, in front of that house across the street, I saw a black SUV."

42

They hurried through the hall and into the kitchen, turning down the thermostat and shutting off the coffee maker. Harrie opened the front door and looked up and down the street. No SUV, black or otherwise.

"You know," Ginger said when they were safely in the car, "lots of people have SUVs."

"I know—that's what I keep reminding myself. I wish I knew whether to trust this spooky feeling I have. I'm so gun-shy, everything looks like the bogeyman."

On the way back to the office, Ginger repeatedly glanced in the rear-view mirror, and Harrie periodically looked over her shoulder. The normally talkative friends said little.

When Harrie's cell phone broke the silence, she almost jumped out of her seat. "Hello," she said in a voice wound too tight.

"Harrie, are you all right?" DJs reassuring tone washed over her.

"Hi." She said brightly. She covered the microphone and said in an aside to Ginger, "It's DJ." Ginger rolled her eyes.

"What can I do for you?" Her effort to sound normal and cheery sounded almost credible, and if it had been anyone else, it might have succeeded.

"Where are you?" DJ asked in a calm but forceful manner. "Somewhere you shouldn't be?"

Harrie looked at Ginger with wide-eyed shock, shaking her head and pointing at the phone. When she spoke again, she took on the air of a falsely accused, indignant female. "Why would you ask something like that? You make it sound like we need to be watched all the time."

"Well, don't you?" His voice was almost playful.

Ginger made the turn into the parking lot at their office and they both got out. Harrie leaned back in, gathering up the items she needed. She held the cell phone with one hand. "Look," she said, "I can't talk right now. I've got another call coming in. I'll get back to you later." As she turned around and closed the car door, an SUV pulled alongside and stopped in the space next to Ginger's car. DJ still held his cell phone as he watched Harrie through the open window. He smiled and waved.

Harrie snapped her phone shut and glared at him. "Where did you come from?"

He closed his own phone and got out of the car. He stepped up to help her carry the awkward bundle of clippings and tape recorder.

"Funny you should ask. I just came from Canyon Estates, and I could swear I saw you two drive away from Senator Lawrence's home."

43

When the three of them walked in the office, Ginger went in search of Caroline.

DJ followed Harrie into the conference room, where they deposited the folder and tape recorder on the table. She looked at DJ. "Tell me again why you're here?"

"As I said, I'm taking a short vacation beginning tomorrow. I have some days I needed to use or lose."

"Yeah, I know." Harrie pressed. "That's what you said outside, but it doesn't explain what you're doing here at our office on this sunny Monday morning. I'd think you'd be too busy packing, or cleaning out your inbox or something."

"Well," he grinned. "I'm not actually going anywhere. I'm just not working for the next few days." His smile faded. "I'm meeting with my supervisor later today and handing over my case file on Nick Constantine."

Ginger walked in while they were talking and said, "Do you have more questions for us, or are you just curious about what we're doing?"

"Actually, I *am* curious about your activities, especially this morning's little trip to Canyon Estates."

Harrie and Ginger exchanged glances, then Harrie said, "Ginger's dad has power of attorney for Philip, and we checked on the house for him. He's handling Senator Lawrence's affairs until he's ready to take over again."

"I see," said DJ, looking pointedly at the fat folder of yellowed papers. "And what did you find there besides those newspaper clippings?"

Harrie sat abruptly. "That's about it, really." She avoided eye contact with DJ. "We went through these clippings last week here at the office. We knew they're important to the senator, so we brought them back for safekeeping while he's in the hospital. They belong in our vault."

He nodded. "So you both drove over there first thing this morning, not to pick up any accumulated mail or important papers Mr. O'Leary might need, but to retrieve some old newspaper articles? And that process took you over an hour?"

"How . . . " Harrie stammered, "I mean, what makes you think it took us that long?"

Ginger laughed. "Give it up, friend. It seems we've been caught by the long arm of the law."

DJ held up both hands in a gesture of surrender. "Hey, I'm just trying to help you out here. You're both pretty bad liars, you know. Why not just level with me and tell me what you're up to?"

Harrie frowned at him. "You followed us, didn't you?"

"No, but the plainclothes guys did. They got here just as the two of you left, and they decided to see where you were headed. They checked with security at Canyon Estates and found out you both received temporary permits for your cars. Then they called me and waited for you to leave."

Harrie looked up, surprised. "Wait, I'm confused. Since when does the Albuquerque Police Department report to the FBI?"

DJ said, "Remember I told you yesterday I talked to Bob Swanson, and he agreed to keep an eye on you for a few days? Well, that's what he's been doing. He said he'd call me if anything seemed unusual, and apparently something did."

Ginger smiled. "I suppose we should thank you for your concern." She turned to her friend and gave her a stern look. "Shouldn't we, Harrie?"

Harrie nodded. She studied DJ for a moment before she spoke. "Thank you for being concerned. But, honestly, you needn't be. Couldn't we just go back to doing our job, and you go back to catching bad guys?"

"Speaking of that, would you like to know how that's going?" DJ sat next to Harrie.

Ginger sat across the table from them. "Do you know who attacked Philip?"

"Not yet," he said. "They've been interviewing the neighbors and studying video tapes from the security cameras at both gates."

Harrie spoke up. "There's another gate? I didn't realize that."

"There's one strictly for residents. It doesn't have a guard on duty except during weekday evenings when people come home from work. The rest of the time, you need a magnetic card to get in. They're also tracking to see whose cards were swiped through that controller during the evening and early morning hours around the time of the senator's attack."

Caroline tapped on the open door. "Excuse me, Ginger. You have a call."

Ginger went to take the call, and Harrie's thoughts came back to the question that had nagged at her for days. "Is there any other way someone could get by the security guards and all those video cameras?"

"If someone is determined to break in, and they're resourceful enough, they can. Gates, fences and cameras keep out the honest or slightly dishonest citizen quite well, but the pros can find a way."

"How would someone go about doing that? Wouldn't the prospect of being caught keep them out?"

DJ smiled at her and slowly shook his head. "I can see you don't have much contact with bad guys. Some criminals get a rush out of the possibility of being caught. They consider it a challenge. What would keep them from climbing over a perimeter wall?"

Harrie pondered briefly. "Maybe they would be afraid of landing in a backyard with a big, angry dog. Or that the patrol that drives around might spot them."

"How about if they came right through the gate?" DJ said. "What if they had a legitimate reason for being there? Suppose they're a resident? Or maybe they just snuck in with somebody else? There are numerous ways it could be done."

Harrie was quiet for several seconds. "I think somebody was watching the senator's house this morning."

DJ's eyes narrowed. "Why do you think so?"

"Because we saw a black SUV parked across the street."

"Was it there when you arrived?"

"No, I saw it while we were getting the clippings folder. That's why we left. We were spooked."

"Did it follow you when you left, or did it stay put?"

Harrie squirmed in her chair. "No. I mean it disappeared before we left."

"Were you looking out a window? Did you see it drive away?"

"Not exactly," she admitted. "I saw it on a television monitor. It's one of those security systems with multiple cameras placed around the property, and the picture rotates among the cameras. By the time I got the one covering the front to display again, the SUV was gone." Harrie prayed silently he wouldn't ask her the location of the monitor.

He smiled as he stood up and pushed his chair under the table. "I wouldn't worry about it. As it happens, this time it was only me. I was checking up on the two of you."

Harrie let go of the breath she'd been holding. "Well, so much for that mystery."

Ginger came back just then and asked, "What mystery is that?"

"Oh nothing. I'll tell you later," Harrie said. She turned to DJ. "So what will you do with your days off?"

"Not much. I have some little fix-it jobs at my mother's house. I thought I might spend some time making sure the two of you don't get into trouble. Maybe I'll check some other things out on my own time." He walked to the front door and paused. "I don't think you ladies should go to the senator's house again by yourselves. If you need to go back, why don't you call me, or wait until Steve can go with you."

"Are you always this bossy?" Harrie had a soft smile on her face.

"Almost always," he responded with a wink and a smile. Then he made his exit.

After DJ left, Ginger motioned Harrie to follow and led the way into her office and closed the door.

Harrie's curiosity took over. "What's up?"

"That phone call was from my dad."

Harrie nodded encouragement. "Go on. Don't keep me in suspense."

"He called the private investigation company and explained about the power of attorney. They've agreed to give him a copy of the report Nick filed before he died."

44

"Okay," Harrie said. "What do we do first? Go for the PI report or listen to some of these tapes?"

Ginger shook her head. "You and I can't get the report. Dad has to do that and take a copy of the power of attorney. He has to prove he's Philip's appointed representative. It could take a while."

Harrie thought about that. "And it'll take time to go through all these tapes. Maybe we should wait until after five when we can do it without interruption."

"That sounds reasonable," Ginger said. "In the meantime, I'll call Steve and see what he's found out about Nick's financial situation. I hope he located someone who knows the source of that money. If Nick became involved in blackmail or money laundering, we might be looking at a whole different cast of characters as suspects in his murder."

Harrie started to her own office and turned back to Ginger. "While you have him on the phone, see if he would object if we contact Swannie. If he has more information about how the intruder gained access to Canyon Estates, I'd like to know."

Ginger nodded and dialed the number.

When Harrie returned to her desk, she decided to reread manuscript pages of the senator's book. Maybe something might now seem significant in view of all that had happened lately. When she finished, she noted that the tape of the next chapter had been delivered to their office by a messenger on Wednesday morning and transcribed and edited by Ginger.

As she read that chapter, her pulse quickened. She grabbed a spiral notebook and jotted down dates and names. She worked for almost an hour, going back over earlier pages.

She turned on her laptop and divided a blank document into columns headed "Name," "Age in 1950" and "Motive." Using her notes, she filled in the columns, using her best guesses for the one labeled "motive." By her accounting, at least six men might have had good reason to commit the murder. Of course, that hinged on certain assumptions she couldn't verify at the moment.

Ginger came in and dropped down in the visitor chair with a sigh of frustration. "Steve's letting all his calls go to voicemail. He must still be trying to get through to the financial people in New York."

"Never mind about that right now. Look what I did." Harrie gestured for Ginger to join her behind the desk and look at the document she'd just printed from her laptop.

Ginger frowned. "What's all this?"

Harrie's eyes sparkled with excitement. "Remember on Saturday when we talked to DJ and Caroline about who might have had a motive to kill Chipper? I've been digging back in the manuscript, and this is what I came up with."

Ginger studied the pages, running her finger along the columns to keep them lined up. "Why do you have these people's ages listed in 1950? What does age have to do with the motive?"

"Because," Harrie said, "Caroline indicated that Jacob thought Eric Snow murdered Chipper to keep her from spilling the beans about his family's connection to the gambling and corruption. But that book by the mysterious Francis Black pointed to Eric for a different reason."

Ginger looked puzzled. "Yeah. He said it was because Chipper became pregnant with Eric's child. So? Different motive, but same guy."

"I just read the chapter you edited for Philip last week. It's the one messengered over on Wednesday. In it, he mentions the rumors going around about Chipper after she died. People said she dated this young handsome guy but nobody knew who he was."

"Eric Snow. That coincides with what Caroline told us, and also what Francis Black said. So why all these other names?"

"Don't you remember? Philip said another girl knew about an 'older' man in Chipper's life. If we can figure out the identity of that man, maybe it will point to a different killer."

Ginger looked again at the list of names. "You've included Daniel and Jacob Snow, and Peter Templeton. That's just crazy. Daniel Snow served as the prosecutor on the case."

"If you'll notice, I've also included Sheriff Smiley Hernandez and some of his buddies."

"At least you didn't include Philip!"

"There's no way it could have been Philip," Harrie said decisively. "For one thing, the dates just don't work. He left here in 1945, right after the war. Chipper would only have been fifteen at the time."

"Lots of fifteen-year-old girls have babies out of wedlock, even back then," Ginger said. "But I see your point. That's too much of a gap in time for a motive in 1950. But I still don't see why you included the Snow brothers in here. Isn't it highly unlikely they would have been involved with Chipper?"

Harrie shook her head. "That's the beauty of this theory. They were the most unlikely suspects at the time, so no one would have looked at them. Someone with a connection could have a reason for preventing the publication of Philip's book."

Ginger's eyes opened wide with understanding. "That would mean old Daniel Snow could have fathered Chipper's child. But he has to be ancient by now. Would he be capable of carrying off these attacks?"

"No, but he's rich enough to hire the deed out."

"We have to tell someone," Ginger said. "We need to call Swannie ourselves. To hell with waiting for Steve's permission."

"Hold on," said Harrie. "We don't have any proof. Swannie will laugh us out of his office. We need something other than my brilliant deductions."

"So how do you propose we get this proof, my little Sherlock friend?"

Harrie's face creased with a smile. "Tonight, my dear, we go back to Philip's and find what we missed before."

"What did we miss?"

"Somewhere in his safe room, I'm convinced we'll find that brown envelope with his name on it—the one stolen eighteen months ago from Jacob Snow's office."

45

Monday Afternoon, April 17, 2000

Harrie ate yogurt, munched carrot sticks and called that a lunch.

Ginger returned from her mores substantial meal at home and said, "I have some news. Steve had a long conversation with Swannie this morning."

Harrie was standing with her arms high above her head. Hunching over the computer for long periods played havoc with her shoulder muscles. When Ginger saw Harrie reaching toward the ceiling, she said, "So this is what you've been doing while I'm out gathering clues?"

"You've got clues? I thought you were eating lunch."

"Well, that too. But you wanted to know how the intruder got into Canyon Estates on Thursday night. Swannie's guys went door to door in the neighborhood. Nobody saw anyone who didn't belong in the area. No big surprise there. They also reviewed all the video tapes with the Chief of Security. They got a list of license plate numbers and the make and model of the cars. One detective is checking those out. So far, nothing jumps out, but they're not finished."

Harrie frowned. "I thought you said you had clues"

Ginger arched an eyebrow. "Patience, patience!"

"Sorry." Harrie dipped her head in a mock apology and smiled. "Do go on at your own convoluted pace."

"They dumped the records for the cards scanned at the west gate that evening. All were legitimate cards issued to current residents – with one exception."

"And?" Harrie prompted.

Ginger looked unhappy. "It was issued to Ramona Sanchez."

Harrie waited, expecting something more. "I sense you're attaching something of a sinister nature to this. Isn't there some legitimate reason Mrs. Sanchez might have been there? Perhaps she forgot something, or maybe Philip called her for some reason."

Ginger shook her head. "They checked the outgoing calls records from Philip's phone. No calls were made that evening, and before you ask, there weren't any incoming calls either."

"Do you have a number where you can reach Mrs. Sanchez?"

Ginger shook her head. "It didn't occur to me we'd have any reason to contact her."

"Why not ask your mom or dad? They must have some idea. Didn't you tell me your mom recommended Mrs. Sanchez to Philip?"

Ginger's eyes lit up, and her smile returned. "You're a genius! Why didn't I think of that?" She rushed from the room to call her mother.

She returned five minutes later, a satisfied smile on her face. "Success! I called Swannie and gave him the number. He promised he'd let me know what they find out."

Caroline left at five, and Harrie was eager to listen to the tapes. Ginger got the latest from her mother on Philip's condition. When the other phone line rang, Harrie grabbed it. It was Bob Swanson.

"Hi, Swannie. Shall I get Ginger for you?"

"No. I have some information, and I'm not sure how Ginger's going to receive it. I'll b there in ten minutes, if that's okay."

"Sure, Swannie, but can't you just tell me what it is?"

"I'd rather talk to you both in person."

Ginger frowned when Harries said, "Swannie's on his way over here. He has some information he wants to tell us in person."

In less than the promised ten minutes, Lt. Bob Swanson walked into Southwest Editorial Services, and they went into the conference room.

"Thanks for waiting. I know you must be curious so I'll get right to the point. I contacted Mrs. Sanchez, thanks to the number you supplied, and found her eager to talk. It seems she was ready to contact us anyway."

Ginger shifted in her chair and sighed. "Look, Swannie. I've known Ramona Sanchez for a long time. She's a hard worker and a very responsible person. Do you know she's raised three boys all by herself? Her husband died in a construction accident when the youngest was only four years old. She never once asked anybody for handouts. She's worked hard all her life. All I'm saying is it's not possible she had any connection with the attack on my godfather. She thought the world of him, and she's taken care of his home for years now. He depends on her and trusts her."

Swanson reached over and patted Ginger's hand. "It's okay. I know all about that. Unfortunately, she is the key to all this. The assailant gained access to the house through her."

Harrie said, "Wait. You're saying Mrs. Sanchez let the attacker into Philip's home?"

Swanson shook his head. "Not intentionally. But she has the magnetic card and a Canyon Estates sticker on her car. That's how the intruder gained access."

"Okay, so someone used her card and car to get into the community. But how did he gain access to the house? Did the senator let him in? If so, he must have known the person."

"It wouldn't have mattered if the senator knew the attacker or not. The guy had a key to the house, also courtesy of Mrs. Sanchez."

Ginger said, shaking her head and frowning. "How did this criminal get access to Mrs. Sanchez' key, automobile and entry card."

"As you said, Ramona Sanchez has raised three sons. The oldest opened a small restaurant a few years ago and is doing well. The middle boy went into the military and is currently stationed in Germany. He's also a fine, upstanding young man. The problem is the youngest, Pablo, or as his mother calls him, Pablito. He's nineteen, and he's been in trouble off and on for years. He got involved with a gang when he was twelve, and it's been a hard road for his mother to keep him out of trouble ever since. Recently, he started dealing drugs and apparently got sideways with some of the suppliers. He owed them a lot of money, and they gave him the option of discharging his entire debt by taking on a contract."

"I don't understand," Harrie said. "Why would a bunch of drug dealers want to harm Senator Lawrence? I hope you're not implying that he's mixed up in the drug trade."

"No. But the big bosses in the drug rings often have connections with people in positions of power and wealth. They do each other favors. The person or persons who wanted to suppress the senator's book about Chipped Finn may have called in a favor from the drug lords to eliminate the senator before the book saw the light of day."

Ginger frowned. "So you're saying some seemingly upstanding person of wealth and power hired this drug boss to get rid of Philip Lawrence, and the instrument of that attack was the youngest son of his housekeeper?"

Swanson nodded. "Exactly."

"And Ramona found out. Did she turn in her own son?"

"She hoped he would turn himself in. After he attacked the senator, he went to his contact to return the gun they had given him for the attack.

That's when he found out he'd been set up to take the fall for another murder that happened on Wednesday night."

Harrie shuddered. "You're talking about Nick Constantine, aren't you?"

Swanson nodded. "Our guess is the same person wanted both men dead. What's still unclear is who fired the shot that killed Constantine. We know it wasn't Pablito."

"How did Ramona learn all this?" Ginger asked.

"The kid got scared. His job was to kill the Senator, not just wound him. He figured they would be after him for botching the job. Pablito told Ramona he was going to Mexico and wanted her to drive him as far as El Paso. She knew something was wrong, but she didn't know what until after they got there. Before he got out of the car, he broke down and confessed what he'd done. He said *El Jefe* would have him killed and then prove he'd done both murders since his fingerprints were on the gun."

Harrie said, "She should have brought him back. If he told the police what happened, you could have helped him, couldn't you?"

Lt. Swanson shook his head. "His mother tried to get him to come back with her and turn himself in. But he told her he wouldn't last a day in jail because they had people in there who would kill him so that he couldn't talk. She realized he was probably right and let him walk away. The last time she saw him, he was walking across the bridge into Juarez."

"Poor Ramona," Ginger said. "As a mother, I understand how she feels. This must be so hard on her, and I'm sure she's frightened for him."

"She has good reason to be frightened." Swanson sighed. "I didn't have the heart to tell her the kid probably won't have any better chance of surviving in Mexico. The drug cartels down there have a great deal of power, and they're probably in business with *El Jefe*. I'm sure they'll be on the lookout for Pablito."

Harrie said, "Will Ramona be in trouble with the police because she helped her son escape?"

"I don't know," Swannie said as he gathered up his papers and stood to leave. "I wouldn't be in favor of charging her. I'm much more interested in getting *El Jefe*."

"Is there any chance you'll be able to do that?" Ginger asked.

"We have undercover cops in his gang. I think *El Jefe's* days are numbered."

Harrie stood and walked out with Swanson and Ginger. "Let me ask you something else before you go. Is there any way you can find out the identity of the person who contracted with *El Jefe* for the murders of Nick and the senator?"

"I can't talk about that just yet. But we have a pretty good idea who it is."

Harrie chuckled. "I'll bet you do, and I'll bet you've already shared those speculations with someone, haven't you?"

Swanson narrowed his eyes and studied her. "You have someone in particular in mind?"

"You know I do," she replied. "Be sure to give my regards to DJ Scott."

46

Monday Evening, April 17, 2000

As soon as Swannie left, Ginger retrieved the metal box they'd taken from Philip's safe room that morning. "Here," she said, "start with number thirteen. I think it's the next one in line, and I hope it's the most important."

Harrie put the cassette in the machine and pressed the button. They heard Philip clearing his throat then say, "This is Tuesday evening, April 11, 2000. It follows tape number twelve from earlier today. I'm picking up after the phrase, 'and it would have stayed that way except for what happened next'." There were noises as he adjusted the microphone. Then his voice became strong and sure.

"In 1952, about two years after the murder, I received a phone call at the newspaper from a woman. She sounded very frightened and wouldn't tell me her name. She told me not to tell anyone she had contacted me. She directed me to go to the Alvarado Hotel the next day at two, sit in the lobby and pretend to read a newspaper. Then, when I was sure no one had followed me, I was supposed to go into the bar, sit in the back booth and order a Manhattan with two cherries.

"When she said that, I was ready to dismiss the whole thing as a huge practical joke, cooked up by one of my colleagues at the paper. I almost told her to get lost, but there was something about her voice, fright tinged with desperation. So I agreed to the meeting and she thanked me profusely.

"The next afternoon, at precisely two o'clock, I walked into the Alvarado Hotel. The afternoon train from Chicago had just pulled into the station, and the place was alive with activity as passengers disembarked and greeted friends and family. I found a comfortable chair in the lobby and sat, pretending to read the newspaper I'd brought with me. I glanced up periodically, but no one seemed the least bit interested in a guy reading a paper in a hotel lobby. Ten minutes later, I made my way to the bar, found the proper booth, and sat facing the doorway so I could see her when she arrived. I ordered the Manhattan with the two cherries and sipped it as I waited.

"I don't know how, but suddenly she was there, sliding into the booth opposite me. She must have been hiding somewhere, observing me. She got down to business immediately, asking if I'd been followed. I thought of several sarcastic comebacks, but simply said 'No'.

"She wasn't a bad-looking young woman, but she wasn't very appealing either. Her casual cotton dress had seen better days. It was too big, and I imagined an older relative had passed it down to her. Her long black hair needed the attentions of a hairdresser. She carried a big straw handbag that could have doubled as a grocery sack.

"She said she had information to give somebody but was afraid. She chose me because she read my follow-up pieces on the Chipper Finn murder and thought she could trust me. We stopped talking as the waitress came up to take her order, which turned out to be a Champagne Cocktail. Her choice surprised me. It didn't seem to fit her circumstances or her personality, if things like that can be judged by one's choice of beverage. I found myself evaluating her and trying to figure her connection to Chipper Finn.

"After the drink arrived, she asked me questions about the stories I'd written. She must have read them repeatedly, because she could almost quote them back to me. I asked her name but she said, 'I'll tell you next time'. As she talked, her eyes searched the faces of the other patrons while she systematically shredded her cocktail napkin. She reminded me of a nervous rabbit, ready to run at the slightest hint of danger.

"Then she took a deep breath and seemed to relax a little. She said, 'I worked with Chipper Finn at Casa Caliente in Los Huevos. We became good friends and even shared an apartment for a while'.

"She took one more look around the room then leaned in and said, 'Chipper told me something two weeks before she died. If you want to know what she said, I want $1,000 in cash'.

"I almost got up and left right then because this felt like a scam with me the patsy. I said, 'Why I should pay for something I can't verify?'

"She reached into her purse and handed me a photograph of Chipper Finn and the woman across from me. I tossed the photo back and said, 'Okay, so you knew her well enough to have your picture made with her. That doesn't mean you know anything of value'.

"She pulled out another snapshot from her bag. This time Chipper Finn stared back at me, and she held a tiny baby in her arms. I looked at my companion and shrugged. 'So, what does this prove?'

"She said, 'That's Chipper's baby. That's why I need the money. It's for the child.' She took the picture back and returned it to her handbag.

"Turning casually, she looked toward the entrance of the bar. In one fluid motion, she got up and joined me on my side of the booth. Her voice was very low now, and I strained to hear her above the sounds of the patrons a few tables away. She continued her story, but kept surveying her surroundings, looking for . . . what, I wondered?

"Her voice cracked. 'When Chipper found out she was going to have a baby, I told her about a place in Las Cruces where unwed mothers go to have their babies. I grew up in Las Cruces, and I decided it was time to go back. I told her I could help her when the time came. She planned to give the baby up for adoption. She said she dreaded what her mother and brother would do if they found out about her pregnancy. As an unmarried woman, it would disgrace the family, and she could never let them find out. But after the birth, she just couldn't go through with it. Instead, she and the baby came to stay with me. She decided to come back to Albuquerque to talk to the baby's father. She refused to name him. She said unless he agreed to marry her, she couldn't risk telling me. So I offered to take care of the child while she went to Albuquerque. Then two weeks before she died, Chipper called me and said someone had threatened her. I asked who, but she wouldn't say. She begged me to take her child and go to El Paso until she got some money together and then she'd join us. I left with the baby the next day and found a room at a boarding house in the middle of town, but she never showed up. Then I saw in the papers that she'd been murdered, and I knew I couldn't come back. I stayed in El Paso, working whatever jobs I could get. We got by. But now the kid's sick, and I need money for a doctor. Please, you've got to help us. There's nowhere else I can turn'.

"I finished my drink as I stalled for time and sorted through my options. I thought I might be able to get the newspaper to come up with the cash if they thought we had a story here. But how did I know any of it was true? There were so many unanswered questions. I said, 'I'll see what I can do. How will I get in touch with you?'

"She said, 'I'll call you tomorrow'. Then she left as quickly as she had arrived."

The machine stopped. They sat staring at it a few seconds.

"The elusive Becky Martinez, I presume." Harrie said.

"Probably. There must be more on another tape." Ginger rummaged through the tapes in the box, then sat back, disappointed. "Maybe he stashed it some other place."

"Why would he do that?" Harrie argued. "If he went to the trouble of disguising this box to look like something else, doesn't it make sense he'd put all the tapes in it?"

The phone on the conference table interrupted further discussion.

"Hi, Honey," Ginger said. She listened for a few seconds, her expression slowly changing to one of excitement. She snapped her fingers to get Harrie's attention. Harrie stopped fiddling with the tapes and watched her friend, her own anticipation growing. Ginger picked up her pen and pantomimed the need for something to write on. Harrie tore a sheet from the notebook and handed it to her.

"Okay, thanks. I'll call her back right away. We're finished here for now. I'll see you in about twenty minutes." She hung up the phone with a triumphant flourish.

"So I take it we're not going back to Canyon Estates tonight?"

"No we're not, and here's why. We've been given a gift." Ginger fairly beamed her excitement.

"What gift? Stop teasing me." Harrie demanded.

"Steve just got off the phone with Elizabeth Snow. She left her number and wants us to call her and set up an appointment. Isn't that great?"

Harrie's mouth dropped open in astonishment. Before she regained her speech, Ginger picked up the phone again and dialed.

Without looking at Harrie, Ginger said, "Elizabeth Snow is Jacob Snow's widow. She read about the attack on Philip, and she's decided she needs to share some information with someone. She somehow knew that you and I were helping Philip with the book. She knew Steve from the days he worked at the Snow law firm and contacted him to see if we could call her."

As Ginger made arrangements to meet with Elizabeth Snow the next morning, Harrie reached over and picked up the list she'd worked on all afternoon. She ran her finger down the column until she saw what she wanted.

"Ginger," Harrie said, as soon as her friend hung up the phone. "This is just creepy. Look what I wrote this afternoon."

Ginger looked at the list where Harrie pointed, then turned back to her. "I'm beginning to believe you really are psychic. You've actually made a notation here that the first person we should contact tomorrow is Elizabeth Snow."

47

Tuesday Morning, April 18, 2000

On her way to the office, Harrie thought about what she'd learned of Elizabeth Snow during her Internet search the previous day.

At age seventy-five, Snow was still a vibrant, active woman. She worked with numerous charities in New Mexico, but the one closest to her heart was St. Anne's House, the orphanage she helped establish in Albuquerque in the early fifties. On its website, Harrie found a short biography for Elizabeth. A strong advocate for adoption, she had been an elementary school teacher before her marriage to Jacob Snow. Unable to have children of her own, she and Jacob adopted three girls.

Harrie wanted to ask for Caroline's help. After all, she knew Elizabeth and might be able to give them useful insight. Harrie wanted to know how Elizabeth felt about her brother-in-law, Daniel, and his nephew, Jonathan. If she knew anything about the dark side of the man, they could possibly find out if Daniel might be the one who'd ordered the attack on Philip.

Harrie arrived at the office at the same time Ginger got out of her car. As they walked in, Harrie suggested telling Caroline who they were meeting today.

"I agree." Ginger said. "We can involve Caroline to the degree she's willing."

Harrie stopped. "Do you think she has a reason not to be involved?"

Ginger shrugged. "I guess that would depend on the status of her relationship with Elizabeth. You know, some wives resent their husbands' secretary. That could make it awkward for Caroline. Let's just explain what we're doing and see how she feels."

Caroline look up from her desk when they walked in, and Harrie motioned for her to join them in the conference room.

Ginger explained about the pending appointment with Elizabeth, and their hope Caroline could assist them.

Caroline chewed at her bottom lip and nodded. "I understand why you might think I could do that. The truth is, I don't know how much help I can be. You see, I really liked Elizabeth, and she was always kind and pleasant to me. She's a warm, generous person. But after Jacob died, she became withdrawn. Naturally, I assumed she was reacting to the loss of her husband, and I didn't take it personally. But even after she resumed her life in the community, she still seemed reserved with me. I met her on several social occasions after that, and while she remained pleasant, her attitude toward me seemed different. I couldn't really put my finger on it. Eventually, I decided Jacob was the only bond we'd had, and his death ended it."

Ginger thought that over. "I understand why you wouldn't be eager to see her again, but that's not what we had in mind anyway. We just thought you could help us understand her relationship to the rest of the Snow family, especially in view of the things we've learned the past couple of days."

Caroline's eyebrows arched in an unspoken question. Harrie and Ginger took turns filling her in on the events of Sunday and Monday. When they related the story of Pablito, Caroline expressed her dismay.

"So," Harrie went on, "we wondered what sort of relationship Elizabeth had with her husband's family. Do you think she knew about Daniel and Peter's illegal activities?"

"Not in the beginning, but later on she did. I know there was a huge strain on family relations. Because Jacob was the youngest, even he didn't know for a long time what Daniel and Peter were doing. It was around the time Chipper Finn was murdered he found out about the gambling and the payoffs. By that time, Daniel was district attorney, and his brother-in-law Peter was managing the firm."

"Did Jacob tell Elizabeth about his brother and Peter before they were married?" Ginger asked. Caroline slowly shook her head. "Jacob married Elizabeth in June, 1950. I don't think he told her about Daniel and Peter at first. When Daniel ran for Attorney General of New Mexico in 1952 and won, Peter handled his campaign and afterwards worked in his office in Santa Fe. Daniel wanted to run for Congress, so he put Peter in charge of making that happen over the next few years. But by the end of Daniel's second term in 1956, Peter had become a problem because of his drinking. Daniel sent him back to work at the firm, and Peter resented that. One night he got very drunk and told Jacob a lot more about the family dirty laundry than Daniel would have allowed. I don't know exactly what he said, but for Jacob, it was the last straw.

"That's when he told Elizabeth everything about the gambling, the bribes, payoffs and other shady things that happened in the Forties and Fifties. I think she understood Jacob's desire to protect the family name, and she tried to avoid Daniel and Peter after that. It wasn't too difficult since Jacob had been doing that for years."

Harrie frowned. "So you're saying she never spent much time around them? Hmm. Then she probably won't be much of a source of information."

"Not so fast." Ginger said. "If Jacob told her all about the stuff Daniel and Peter did in the old days, she probably knows quite a lot."

"Good point. But what about Eric Snow? Do you think she'd know anything about him?"

"It's possible." Caroline said. "She might know when Eric went back to Europe, and when he finally returned."

Ginger said, "Well, thanks for the help." She turned to Harrie. "We better get going. We're supposed to be there in twenty minutes."

"If you think it's appropriate, give her my regards," Caroline said.

They were on their way to meet Elizabeth Snow when Ginger said, "Oh, by the way, Steve finally talked to the financial people in New York."

Harrie, who'd been deep in thought, looked momentarily confused. "Financial people? What . . . Oh! Those financial people!" She brightened up, her interest refocused.

Ginger nodded. "Believe it or not, Nick's money seems legitimate. Dimitri Despotides' left a sizable sum for his grandson. They estimate that Nick left an estate well over twenty million."

48

Elizabeth Snow answered the front door herself. They introduced themselves, and she guided them through the front hallway to a sunroom at the back of the house. She offered them something to drink, but they declined. She said, "Thank you so much for coming. I felt a bit awkward calling Steve, but he assured me you'd be open to a meeting."

Ginger said, "We appreciate your seeing us on such short notice."

"I'm glad it worked out so well." Elizabeth poured herself a cup of coffee from the silver carafe on the table beside her. "Before we get started, may I ask a question? Do you know the purpose of the book Philip Lawrence is writing?"

Ginger blinked. "I'm not sure I can answer that question. The book isn't finished. And now, with him in the hospital, we don't know when, or if it will be. From what I can tell, he felt the need to explore the case further, to perhaps shed light on some things that happened during that time."

Elizabeth nodded but didn't comment. She walked over to a cabinet and lifted a box. She brought it back and put it on the floor by her feet.

"I'd like to tell you a story. It may help you decide how to proceed when Philip wakes up." She turned to Ginger and smiled, "And he will wake up. He's much too tough to let this keep him down. Anyway, he'll verify this information. He's the one who asked me to pass it along to you."

Harrie felt the warm sun on her arm, but she felt a shiver of premonition, too. "May I ask if this has anything to do with Daniel Snow?"

Elizabeth looked at her with admiration. "My, you do get right down to it, don't you?" She smiled. "That's good. You seem like a smart young woman. As it happens, it has a great deal to do with Daniel. Have you ever met him?"

"No," Harrie said. "But I heard about him. I understand he and Philip used to be friends."

"Yes, but that's not the point of my story. In 1964, Daniel had been in Congress for several years. He'd gotten himself appointed to some important committees, and he thought it was time to make a run for the Senate. Jacob convinced him that wasn't a good idea."

"What did your husband do to convince Daniel not to run?" Harrie asked.

"You probably already know that Daniel and Rachel were quite a bit older than Jacob, Daniel thirteen years older and Rachel eleven years older. The two older siblings couldn't be bothered with a brother that much younger.

"Jacob grew up almost like an only child. His mother, being older when he was born, was much wiser and didn't spoil him the way she'd spoiled Daniel. Daniel always expected his every wish to be fulfilled. He became an aggressive leader. Their father died when Daniel was just out of law school. Their mother decided Jacob should go to a prep school back East where she'd been raised. That effectively kept him out of Daniel's way. The sister, Rachel, married Peter Templeton, who was also a lawyer, and he proved to be a man similar in every way to Daniel. The two of them became law partners. By the time Jacob got out of law school in 1945, he felt ready to return and join the family firm. As long as he stayed out of Daniel and Peter's business, they were content to have him there, doing work that kept him busy and unaware of their activities."

Elizabeth paused. "Undoubtedly you know about the gambling in Los Huevos during those days."

Ginger spoke up. "Yes. Philip told us about it as we worked on the book. He never told us who was involved in it though."

"Perhaps he hadn't gotten that far," Elizabeth said. "Would it surprise you to learn that Daniel and Peter were heavily involved in that enterprise?" When both women shook their heads, she continued.

"I think everybody else around here knew, too. Everybody except Jacob, his sister Rachel and their mother. Rachel and their mother went to their graves without knowing, and it was at least four years before Jacob learned the truth. When he did, it changed his life forever."

"How did he find out?" Harrie asked.

A sad smile passed over Elizabeth's face. Her voice was so soft they strained to hear her. "In early 1949, before he and I were dating, he became involved with a young woman, a waitress at a coffee shop in downtown Albuquerque. As it turned out, she also worked part time in Los Huevos at the Blue Heron, a popular gambling nightclub. In the course of working there, she saw and heard things. Many important politicians from all over the state came to gamble in the private rooms.

"In May, 1949, Daniel's son, Eric started hanging out at the club with his friends. He was young and cocky, and he hit on Jacob's girlfriend, but she put him off. He tried to impress her by bragging about his father and uncle being the owners of the club. She apparently learned quite a bit from Eric. Eric bragged to anyone who would listen that she was his girl and they were going to be married.

"She didn't say anything to Jacob about it. For one thing, he didn't know she worked at the Blue Heron. Then one night in June 1949, she just disappeared. When Jacob asked around about her, no one seemed to know where she'd gone."

Ginger said, "Did he ever find her?"

"Yes," Elizabeth continued, "she turned up in March, 1950. By that time, Jacob and I were engaged. He'd told me about this girl, but since she'd left without a word and never contacted him, Jacob assumed the relationship was over. Imagine his surprise the day she called, and asked if he would meet her."

Harrie asked, "Did he agree?"

Elizabeth let out a long breath. "Oh, yes. They met in Old Town Albuquerque at the old San Felipe de Neri church on the Plaza." She looked out the window, lost in her own world.

Harrie wanted to get her talking again. Softly she said, "Mrs. Snow? Are you all right?"

Elizabeth turned back to look at them. "Yes, I'm sorry. You see, he didn't tell me about that meeting for several years. I think he feared I'd be jealous. But how could I be jealous of that poor girl?"

Ginger said, "What do you mean?"

"Well, it was so sad. The reason she'd disappeared in 1949 was because Eric told everyone they were getting married. His attentions became so unwelcome she apparently felt the need to get away, and she snuck out of town."

Harrie frowned. "Where did she go?"

"Nobody knew at that time. The day Jacob met her at the church, she told him that Eric was the reason for her sudden departure. Now he understood her mysterious disappearance. She told him about Daniel's involvement in the gambling and bribery activities in Los Huevos, and one more thing. She said after she disappeared, she gave birth to a baby."

Harrie felt a growing excitement. "Did you ever learn the name of this girl?"

Sadness filled Elizabeth's eyes. "Yes, of course. I'm sure you've guessed. Her name was Kathleen Finn, also known as Chipper."

49

Harrie nodded. "Did your husband know why she was killed?"

"Based on what Chipper told him, and what he knew about the men in his family, he thought he knew what happened. It all revolved around Eric and his penchant for getting into trouble. Eric had received a trip to Europe as a graduation gift from his parents. In reality, Daniel wanted him out of town because he had heard about Eric's obsession with Chipper, and he was afraid the boy would do something stupid. Then when Chipper disappeared, they relaxed a bit. Eric returned in the fall and started classes at the university. He still frequented the clubs in Los Huevos whenever he had the chance, but he had strict orders to stay away from the Blue Heron.

"One night in late March, 1950, Eric went to the Casa Caliente Club. He saw Chipper and found out she had been working there since late February. He drank even more than usual that night and got falling-down-drunk. When he tried to talk to her, he was rough and abusive. She got frightened and called for the club bouncer. Eric became enraged and waited for her in the parking lot, but the club's bouncer forced him to leave the premises. Right after that, she made the call to Jacob and arranged the meeting at the church.

"Jacob was going to help her find a place to live outside New Mexico. He even set up a small savings account so she could get by until she found a job. The baby had been left in the care of a friend in Las Cruces, with the understanding that Chipper would join them as soon as she could. Chipper was desperate to keep the Snows from finding out about the baby. She was certain they knew about her knowledge of their gambling operations and was afraid that Eric's violence would escalate.

"How long was this before Chipper's death?" Harrie asked.

Elizabeth leaned back and closed her eyes. "It was less than a week before she died. It all happened so quickly that Jacob never got the money to her. He was furious. He went to Daniel and confronted him about Eric's attack on her. Not only did he accuse Daniel of engineering her murder, but he also said he knew about Daniel and Peter's involvement in the illegal gambling in Los Huevos. He told Daniel to get out of it immediately, or he would call in the FBI. Daniel ignored the accusation about the gambling, but denied involvement in Chipper's death and said he had information the murder had been committed by the club bouncer."

Harrie nodded. "Manny Salinas, the former prize fighter. But they found him not guilty. And I saw a book recently that said Eric actually did it, but they couldn't prove it."

"Exactly," Elizabeth said, "that's what Jacob came to believe. The day after they found the girl's body, Eric left for Europe again and didn't return for almost five years."

"What did your husband do about his suspicions then?" Ginger asked.

Elizabeth sighed and looked away. "Nothing. He felt he'd made a pact with the devil. Daniel resigned as district attorney in 1951. After that, he gained a lot of attention with his crusade to close down illegal gambling in New Mexico. The irony of that was a bitter pill for Jacob, especially since that crusade led to Daniel's next step up. In 1952 he successfully campaigned for and won the office of Attorney General of New Mexico, based in large part on his noble battle to reform politics in New Mexico."

Ginger said, "What was it that caused Daniel to abandon his pursuit of a US Senate seat? You mentioned Jacob had something to do with that."

"In 1957, a Congressional seat opened up with the death of a long-time, popular politician. The governor appointed Daniel to fill the remainder of the term. He then won the seat on his own. In 1972, he decided to run for the Senate. Jacob was, by this time, a very well respected attorney throughout New Mexico. He had been approached by the party many times to run for office. He was even asked to serve on the state supreme court, but he never wanted to hold office. He knew that Daniel's past could easily be used against the entire family.

"So Jacob had a brotherly talk with Daniel and convinced him he would not win a Senate seat because Jacob would see to it that he didn't. Daniel realized he could no longer control the family. Jacob talked Philip Lawrence into running instead, and the rest is history."

"Let's get back to Eric." Harrie pressed. "If Jacob really believed he murdered Chipper, how could he just let that go?"

"Believe me, that gnawed at him for many years, but there was nothing he could do at the time. He didn't have any proof. Daniel always maintained that Salinas had an accomplice and someday he would turn up. Jacob decided as long as no other innocent person was blamed for the crime, he would wait until he had a way to prove his theory."

Harrie frowned. "It's just so unfair Eric was never punished."

"Eric didn't get off without penalty." Elizabeth's mouth became grim. "In fact, he's possibly the only one who ended up receiving some sort of punishment.

"I don't understand," Harrie said.

"I told you Eric was whisked off to Europe immediately after the murder. When he came back five years later, his father was supposed to have bought him land in Alaska so that Eric could follow his dream of becoming a bush pilot. It was only after Peter died in 1990 that Jacob discovered the truth."

Ginger seemed to know what was coming. "Is Eric still alive?" she asked.

Elizabeth reached into the box on the floor and withdrew a ledger. "Technically, yes."

"What do you mean, technically?" Harrie asked.

Elizabeth opened the ledger. "This is a checkbook that Peter kept locked in his desk. Jacob didn't know it existed until after Peter's funeral. He discovered it as he packed up his brother-in-law's things. He noticed that a check was issued four times a year to a private sanitarium outside Tucson. The payments went back to 1955, the year Eric returned from Europe. Jacob went to Tucson and paid a visit to this facility. Eric had been there since the summer of 1955. He'd never gone to Alaska, much less become a pilot."

Harrie felt chilled. "Why was he in a sanitarium?"

"His raging alcoholism caused a severe stroke. Daniel feared Eric's condition would call attention to the boy's wild past. But more importantly, Daniel was focusing on his political career and feared the public embarrassment. So he had Peter arrange for Eric's transfer to the facility in Tucson. They told everyone Eric died in a plane crash in Alaska."

Elizabeth saw the reaction from Harrie and Ginger. "I know what you're thinking. I had the same reaction when Jacob told me. After that, my dislike for Daniel became an active hatred."

Harrie said, "Did your husband ever tell anyone about this?"

Elizabeth frowned. "In a way he did. About six months before Jacob had his stroke, he started a journal. He told me about what was in it, but I never read it. He said he described everything he knew and suspected about the murder. When he finished, he put it in a large brown envelope and used sealing wax, stamping it with his emblem. On the front he wrote a note, indicating that upon his death, it was to be delivered to Senator Philip Lawrence."

50

Harrie didn't dare look at Ginger. She controlled her tension by focusing on her breathing. She hoped her excitement wasn't apparent to Elizabeth.

"What ever became of that envelope?"

Elizabeth gave her a long, appraising look. "Your new administrative assistant is Caroline Johnson, I understand." Elizabeth picked up the box and took it back to the cabinet.

Harrie looked quickly to Ginger while Elizabeth's back was turned. Ginger nodded and took the question.

"Yes, she just started with us last week. We feel so fortunate to have her. I understand she worked for your husband many years."

Elizabeth smiled as she resumed her seat. "Yes, and Jacob depended on her all those years. She was an exceptional assistant." Elizabeth hesitated. "Has she said much about her time at the firm?"

Harrie swallowed hard. She caught herself before she made yet another futile attempt to evade the underlying question, and decided to just get it out in the open.

"Caroline is helping us get to the bottom of the attack on Senator Lawrence. We believe it's connected to the book he's writing about Chipper Finn's murder. Naturally, since Caroline worked at the Snow firm, she's tried to answer whatever questions she could."

Elizabeth nodded. "I had hoped she would. She occupied a unique position during a time when Jacob was incapacitated, and she handled it honorably and with discretion."

Harrie relaxed. "Caroline asked us to convey her best wishes to you, and tell you she hopes you're doing well. She speaks highly of you, too."

Ginger said, "Caroline told us about the episode on the day of Jacob's funeral when someone broke into his office and removed items from his desk. She was especially concerned about the envelope you just mentioned. Do you have any idea who was responsible?"

"Oh God yes. My ever-loving brother-in-law, Daniel, arranged to have Jacob's papers removed from his desk and file cabinets."

Elizabeth slipped into a delightful impersonation of the pompous Daniel. "I wanted to spare you, my dear, from the emotional wrench of dealing with Jacob's papers."

Her expression turned grim. "The only person that man ever tried to spare was himself. He didn't fool me for a minute. But as it turned out, he didn't get what he wanted."

"What do you mean?" Harrie looked puzzled.

Elizabeth smiled genuinely now. "Well, this is the good part. Caroline removed a number of items from Jacob's desk right after his stroke. She held on to some of them, but she replaced the envelope addressed to Philip. She contacted me the next day and explained about putting the envelope back, and that she'd hung on to the other papers. I thanked her and told her she did exactly the right thing.

"On the day of Jacob's funeral, Daniel took the opportunity to clean out everything in Jacob's desk. I'll admit I had expected as much." Elizabeth chuckled softly. "It probably took him months to go through the massive amount of paperwork, and it was all for nothing."

Harrie said, "I would have thought the envelope contained all the damning evidence about Daniel's activities. Wouldn't that have been the most important item?"

"I imagine he would have thought so, if he'd known for sure it existed. But fortunately he never got his hands on it."

"Wait, I'm confused. I thought Caroline put the envelope back in Jacob's desk and left it there."

Elizabeth nodded. "Yes, she did, and I'll get back to that. You see, Daniel, or his nephew, Jonathan . . . I was never sure which . . . was looking for something specific they expected to find in Jacob's desk and didn't, something they decided Caroline must have. They knew Jacob had some sort of records that would embarrass Daniel, and that's what they hoped to find."

Harrie shook her head. "That's when they ransacked Caroline's house. She told us all about that. Are you saying they actually did get some of the records she held on to?"

Elizabeth wagged her finger and shook her head. "No, no. I said this was the good part, and it is. Caroline discovered the break-in almost as soon as it happened, and called me. She said the envelope was gone, and I told her not to worry, that I'd take care of it. Then she rushed back to her house to see if the other items were safe, and thankfully they were, even though her house had been torn apart in the search."

Harrie interrupted, "But what about the envelope? We thought Daniel or Jonathan got the envelope."

"A young man came to see me about two weeks before Jacob died. He used to work at the firm, and came by to pay his respects. We chatted for a long time about a variety of things. He told me he had become a licensed private investigator, and that's when I got the idea."

"What idea was that, Mrs. Snow?" Ginger leaned forward in her chair.

"Why, my idea about how to spoil Daniel's fun." Elizabeth's smile lit up her face.

Harrie groaned. "This young man. His name wouldn't be Nick Constantine, would it?"

Elizabeth looked surprised. "Why yes. Do you know him?"

"You could say that," Harrie sighed. "So what did he do for you?"

"I gave him the key to the office and asked that he retrieve the envelope from Jacob's desk and bring it back to me. He did, and I put it in our safe, here at the house."

"Mrs. Snow," Ginger began. Her phone chose that moment to start chirping. "Uh, oh." She turned to Harrie. "It's Dad. I've got to take this." She excused herself and stepped into the hall to speak to her father.

Harrie persisted. "You didn't tell Caroline you got it back?"

Elizabeth sighed. "No, I didn't. I intended to, but . . . " she broke off and cleared her throat. "There was so much going on. Jacob was not doing well, our daughters had just arrived to see him again before . . ." She swallowed with difficulty. "I'm afraid I wasn't at my best just then. I fully intended to tell Caroline the day of the funeral, but when she called, Daniel was lurking close by, and I didn't want to explain right then."

Harrie's own throat felt tight. "Please. You needn't explain. I understand completely." She steered the conversation away from the sadness. "What happened to the envelope? Do you still have it?"

"No. I'd made up my mind to give it to Philip as soon as I could."

"And when was that?"

"I believe it was about a month after Jacob died."

Ginger returned and gave Harrie a let's-wrap-this-up look and said, "Mrs. Snow, thank you for your time."

When they were in the car, Harrie said, "You've got that look on your face. What's up?"

Ginger grinned as she backed out of Elizabeth's driveway. "My dad managed to get over to the PI office a lot sooner than he thought he would. He got that report Nick filed on Wednesday. He's going to meet us at our office so we can all look at it."

They were excited as they drove to the end of the block. They saw a city vehicle putting up orange barrels, blocking the street where they were supposed to turn. "Here we go," Ginger said. "The orange barrel brigade is at it again. Now what?"

"Turn in this driveway and go back the other direction. We can get on Indian School Road from there."

Ginger maneuvered the little VW expertly in a perfect turn around and headed back down the street. As they approached Elizabeth Snow's house, Harrie let out a little "Oh, no!"

Ginger slammed on the brake. "What!"

"Keep going, keep going."

"What's the matter with you?" Ginger demanded.

"Look in Elizabeth's driveway," Harrie said, pointing to a little red sports car, where a tall, dark-haired familiar figure had just emerged.

"What's he doing there?" Ginger said.

"Exactly my question," Harrie said. "Maybe I should call him and ask."

51

Tuesday Afternoon, April 18, 2000

By the time Harrie and Ginger got back to their office, Don O'Leary had arrived. He and Caroline chatted like old friends, and when he saw Ginger, he beamed and pointed to a sheaf of papers in his hand.

"Success!" He grinned with such boyish enthusiasm, Harrie and Ginger both laughed and gave him the "thumbs-up" sign. Although they were eager to get into the report, O'Leary had phoned in an order for pizza, and the conference became an impromptu picnic area.

Ginger insisted Caroline join them. "You should be in on this. After all, you've known about this situation longer than anybody here."

Caroline seemed pleased to be included. Ginger said since her dad was responsible for securing the report, he should have the honor of reading it to the rest of them. O'Leary wiped pizza sauce from his fingers and picked up the report.

"There's a lot of dull, procedural stuff here at the beginning," he said, as he scanned down through the first page.

He read silently for a minute or so before Ginger cleared her throat, with just a touch of reprimand. "I thought you were going to read it to the rest of us, Dad."

"Oh, yeah, sorry. I don't know if any of this is going to help you though. Have you ever heard of someone named Becky Martinez?"

Harrie and Ginger looked at each other with glee. Ginger said, "As a matter of fact, we heard her name just the other day. She was Chipper Finn's best friend, the one who took the baby and disappeared right before Chipper was murdered. What does it say about her?"

"Well," O'Leary continued, "Nick located her. That's one of the first assignments Philip gave him. He found her, and it says here he went to Philip's house on Wednesday and spoke with him about it. Nick gave Becky's address to Philip and agreed to go see her the next day, which would have been last Thursday." O'Leary stopped reading and looked up at the faces of his attentive audience. "He dictated this report that evening, and his last comment here says he'd file another report on Thursday after he spoke with the Martinez woman."

O'Leary dropped the report on the table, his previous excitement gone. "I'm sorry, girls. I guess that's not much help."

Ginger walked around the table to hug her father. "No, Dad. That's not true. It really is a big help. Don't you see? We'll just go back over to Philip's and look around the library. I'm sure he must have jotted down the address somewhere. Harrie and I will go find it this afternoon, and then we'll go see Becky Martinez ourselves."

"I don't think that's the best idea you've had, ladies." The baritone voice of DJ Scott came from the doorway behind them.

Harrie almost squealed, but stifled it into a soft little "oops."

The entire group burst into laughter and looked at the now red-in-the-face Harrie.

When the laughter had diminished to weak giggles, and Harrie had regained her dignity, she said, "Why are you always sneaking up on people? Or is it just me you like to annoy?"

DJ grinned. "I've always pictured myself in the role of The Shadow."

Caroline chimed in, "I can testify to that. One week he would be The Shadow, the next it was Batman or Superman. My son, the superhero."

"Seriously," DJ said, "You can't be rummaging around Philip's house. It's a crime scene." He turned to O'Leary. "Could I see that report, Sir?"

O'Leary looked at his daughter questioningly. Ginger said, "Dad, I don't think you've met DJ Scott. DJ, this is my dad, Don O'Leary. DJ is Caroline's son, Dad, and he's also an FBI agent who was investigating Nick."

O'Leary said, "Well, in that case, maybe you can glean more from this than I did. I'll admit I don't have any experience in the sleuthing business. But I'm a dynamite hardware store owner," he finished proudly.

Ginger groaned. "Really bad pun, Dad." Her father grinned impishly and handed the report to DJ.

As he read, a smile appeared on his face. "Well, well, what do we have here?" He held out the page to Harrie and Ginger.

Harrie's eyes widen. "Do you think that's Becky Martinez's address?"

DJ nodded. "Definitely."

Harrie's excitement bubbled. "Great! We don't have to go to Philip's. We can just go to this address and see Becky Martinez ourselves."

"Now hold on—" DJ began.

"Hold on yourself!" Harrie shot back. "If I'm not mistaken, you took yourself off this case, am I right?"

"Yes, I voluntarily—"

"And not only that," she continued with a full head of steam, "you're supposed to be taking a few days vacation. Isn't that right?"

"Yes, I am, but—"

"So why are you telling me that Ginger and I can't go pay a visit to the long-lost Becky Martinez?"

"Because, damn it, I don't want anything to happen to you, that's why!"

For that moment, the other people in the room didn't exist. Harrie stood practically toe-to-toe with DJ, her head tilted back at a ridiculous angle to look up at him. Her breathing became heavy, and heat rose to her face.

DJ's face relaxed into a smile. "Somebody has to see that you behave yourself, and I think I'm just the one who can do that." His grin was big, warm and thoroughly intoxicating.

"Earth to Harrie," Ginger said, barely able to conceal the glee in her voice. "Could the rest of us participate in this little discussion?"

52

A compromise was needed. Harrie and Ginger were adamant about talking to Becky Martinez, and DJ was equally determined that he should handle it. Caroline took a shot at diplomacy.

"Wouldn't it be nice if all three of you paid a call to Ms. Martinez? That way, Harrie and Ginger can ask the questions they need to ask, and DJ can be there to see that they're safe and don't get into legal difficulty." She smiled and waited for their agreement.

Harrie shrugged. "Okay, but we're not all going to fit in that little red sports car."

"We'll take my car," Ginger said.

When they approached the yellow VW, DJ graciously offered to sit in the back. Harrie stifled a giggle as she watched him fold his lanky frame into the car's small back seat. She climbed into the passenger's seat and turned to check on him.

With mock sympathy she said, "Sorry about the space back there. Your knees look kind of cramped."

"That's okay," he said with an exaggerated martyred tone.

"Tell you what," she replied. "On the return trip you can ride shotgun."

Becky Martinez lived in the North Valley around Candelaria and Rio Grande Boulevard in a neatly maintained stucco home with a trim lawn and wide flowerbeds. The small woman who opened the door had a pleasantly lined face. Her long silver hair was gathered in a thick braid.

"Can I help you?" She squinted at them through wire-rimmed glasses, her look guarded.

DJ introduced himself, Harrie and Ginger. When he showed the woman his FBI credentials, her eyes widened.

"Oh, dear. What have I done to bring the FBI to my door?"

DJ said, "There's no cause for alarm, Ma'am. May we come in for a few moments? We need to speak with you if you don't mind."

When they were seated in her tiny living room, DJ said, "I notice the name on your mailbox is Benavidez. We're looking for a Becky Martinez. Could you tell me how we might find Ms. Martinez?"

The old woman's face tightened. "What do you want with Becky Martinez?"

Harrie intervened. "Mrs. Benavidez, we're working on a book about the murder of a young woman named Kathleen Finn. We have information that Becky Martinez was Miss Finn's best friend. The man who is writing this book was attacked last week. We think it was because he planned to reveal who killed Kathleen. We know Kathleen had a baby shortly before her murder, and we have reason to believe Becky Martinez helped her by taking the baby away from this area to keep it safe. Becky Martinez might be the key to this mystery, and we want to speak to her so we can bring some justice to Kathleen Finn."

The old woman had been looking down at her hands while Harrie made her plea. As she looked up, there were tears sliding down her cheeks. She removed her glasses and ran the back of her hand across her face.

"I never thought this day would come," she said. "All these years, and nobody's been concerned about what happened to Chipper." She looked down at her lap again. "No one but me," she added.

"I'm Becky Martinez. I changed my name years ago."

Ginger asked, "What are you called now?"

"Dolores," she said. "Dolores Benavidez. I knew a beautiful lady when I was a little girl, a friend of my mother named Dolores. It seemed like an exotic name, so I chose it when I needed to disappear."

She smiled. "It's nice to remember Becky. She was a frightened girl with some very bad people looking for her. It was better that she just cease to exist. I lived in El Paso back then. I went across the border to Juarez to see a man I'd been told about. For one hundred dollars, he could give you a new identity. I still had some of the money Chipper had given me, so I paid him. A few hours later, I returned to his little shop, and Becky Martinez was gone forever. In her place was Dolores Aragon, with a new life and a clean start. My last name again changed when I married."

"Do you remember coming back to Albuquerque in 1952 and meeting with Philip Lawrence?" Harrie asked.

"I'll never forget it," she said. "I was so frightened when I called him at the newspaper. I was afraid he wouldn't meet me. But he did. For some reason, he took the time, and he looked past my rundown appearance. He listened to my story, and, more important, he helped me do something good for Chipper's baby."

Ginger leaned in and gently asked, "What did Philip do, Mrs. Benavidez? What happened to the baby?"

Dolores Benavidez picked up a pillow from the sofa and hugged it to her chest. "He did the best thing he could have done. He convinced me to put the baby in an orphanage so she'd have a chance to be adopted by a loving family who could take care of her. He even found the orphanage for us. He said it had a good reputation."

Ginger said, "Excuse me, Mrs. Benavidez. You said 'she.' Chipper Finn's baby was a little girl?"

"Why yes. She was a beautiful little girl. She had blue eyes, and blonde hair. Chipper's eyes were blue, too, but her hair was jet black." She sighed. "I've often wondered what became of that sweet little girl. It was the hardest thing I ever did, giving her up. I cried for months." Dolores looked down at her hands, and her shoulders sagged. "I knew it was only a matter of time before those people found us. I was afraid they would kill us both."

DJ said, "Did you ever try to find out who adopted the baby?"

Dolores shook her head. "I knew that was too dangerous for her. The only way I could protect her was to make sure no one could connect me to that baby. It would have made giving her up pointless." She looked back at Ginger. "Anyway, I couldn't bear to go through leaving her again. It was best I stayed away."

Harrie said, "Tell us about the orphanage. Did you take her there, or did Philip?"

"Oh, I took her myself. I felt I owed it to her. After all, I was the only mother she'd ever known. I'll never forget that day. It was in June, and it was so hot. I didn't have many clothes for her. There was never enough money. Up until then, I'd only waited tables. But I didn't dare do that when I took the baby and went to El Paso. They'd come looking for me, figure I was still waiting tables, and I'd be a sitting duck. So, I started cleaning houses. It was hard work, but sometimes the ladies I cleaned for would let me bring Angelina with me. That was a big help. When I couldn't take her along, the landlady at the apartment where we lived would take care of her for me.

"But that spring, Angelina had sore throats over and over. The doctor said she needed to have her tonsils removed or something bad would happen to her little heart. I didn't know how I could pay for that, so I thought maybe I could get some help from Mr. Lawrence. I hoped he would give me enough money to get the operation for Angelina. I'm afraid I misled him at first. You see, Chipper told me the name of the man who stalked her, but she never revealed the identity of the man she was in love with, the name of the baby's father. I'm sorry to say I led Mr. Lawrence to believe that I knew. I was desperate."

Harrie said, "You read the columns he wrote about Chipper. But why did you think he would help you?"

Dolores smiled at Harrie. "You should have read those things he wrote about Chipper. He sounded so kind and so determined to find out what happened. You could just tell by the way he wrote about her that he would care what happened to her baby."

Harrie pressed on. "Tell us about the orphanage where you took her. Do you remember the name of it or the address?"

Dolores Benavidez's brow furrowed as she delved into her memory. "I can't quite remember the street name, but I do remember the name of the place, though. St. Anne's House."

She smiled and said, "St. Anne is the patron saint of women in labor and young girls, you know. Anyway, it was such a lovely place, and the people were very kind. I remember this one lady from that day. I think she volunteered there. She took to Angelina right away, and I knew she'd be safe. I knew they would take care of that sweet little thing."

Harrie hardly dared to breathe as she asked, "Do you happen to remember the name of the nice lady who helped you that day?"

A big smile played across Dolores Benavidez's face. "Oh, yes. I don't think I'll ever forget her name. Anyway, I see it in the papers all the time. She's a very prominent woman, doing all kinds of charities and things. I'll bet you've seen her picture, too. Her name is Elizabeth Snow."

53

They thanked Dolores Benavidez for her time and promised to give her regards to Philip when he was better. She stood at her front door and watched them drive away.

"Are you thinking what I'm thinking?" Ginger asked Harrie.

"What are you thinking?" DJ asked.

Ginger looked over at him. "As you may or may not know, we spoke to Elizabeth Snow this morning."

Harrie had been true to her word and allowed DJ to sit in the front seat on the return trip. She, meanwhile, pulled against her seat belt in the back seat to lean as far forward as she could to hear what they were saying. She propped her arms on the back of the front seat so she could talk to both of them. She responded to Ginger's remark.

"Elizabeth helped St. Anne's House get started back in the early fifties. I read about it on their web site. She's been involved with them all these years. This is no coincidence."

"So what are you saying?" DJ asked. "You think Elizabeth Snow hid this child someplace so her brother-in-law couldn't find her?"

"I think it's a lot more than that. Did you know Elizabeth and Jacob adopted three little girls? We need to find out when they got the oldest one."

Ginger looked at Harrie in the rearview mirror. "What makes you think it has to be the oldest one? Maybe they already had a little girl and then they adopted Chipper's baby."

DJ shook his head. "No, I can't buy that. I don't think Elizabeth Snow would endanger a child that way. What if, over the course of the years, the girl grew up and looked just like Eric. You know, he was blond, too. That's one reason they named him Eric."

Harrie frowned at DJ. "No, I didn't know that. And more to the point, how did you know that?"

"Do you remember that box of stuff my mother had at her house when someone broke in Jacob Snow's office and stole the brown envelope?"

Harrie nodded, "Yes, and by the way, Elizabeth told us all about that break-in when we spoke to her this morning."

He grinned. "Yes, I know. She told me."

Harrie punched his shoulder, "When were you going to tell us that, huh? Sneaking around behind our backs!"

He held up both arms in surrender. "I didn't sneak. I was right there, in the open, in full view when you drove up the street."

Harrie sputtered. "You saw us? Why didn't you say something earlier?"

He swiveled around and looked at her, "I was waiting for one of you to come clean."

Ginger raised her voice. "Okay, you two. Could we get back to the subject? Save your little sparring rituals for later."

Harrie blushed furiously, and DJ grinned at her discomfort. "As I said, my mother found a photograph of young Eric in that bunch of pictures she rescued from Jacob's desk. It had his name printed on the back. It was a high school yearbook picture from when he graduated. When I came to pick up the box, I saw the photo, and we talked about how innocent he looked when, in reality, he was such a wild young man."

Harrie said, "I'd forgotten you took that box. What did you do with it?"

"I gave it back to Elizabeth. Mom thought she should have it and believed Jacob would prefer that Daniel not know she had it. It was easy for me to call on her and deliver it to her safely a few weeks after the funeral."

"Okay," said Harrie. "Maybe Elizabeth didn't adopt the little girl herself. But she must know who did."

"Not necessarily," DJ said. "It wouldn't have been the orphanage who handled the adoption anyway. That would have been handled by a licensed adoption agency. They would keep the information about a child's placement confidential to protect both the child and the adoptive parents. It's highly unlikely St. Anne's ever knew what happened to Angelina."

"I thought lawyers handled private adoptions all the time," said Harrie. "Why couldn't Elizabeth have gotten a lawyer she knew to find a family for the child?"

"Because that's not the way it works, especially back in those days. The rules were very strict, and a private adoption would never have happened involving a child from a state-licensed orphanage."

Harrie cocked her head to the side and studied DJ's profile. "How do you know so much about adoptions, wise guy?"

"Well, I did go to law school, you know. Anyway, I think it's an interesting subject. I have some friends who were adopted and one of them asked for my help in locating his birth parents. I learned a lot in that process."

They pulled into the parking lot at Southwest Editorial Services, and DJ went inside with them. Harrie and Ginger went to their respective offices, and DJ stood at Caroline's desk for several minutes. Harrie peeked out her window and saw they were talking.

Before DJ left, he stuck his head in Harrie's office. "I have some errands to run. Will you be here all day?"

Harrie didn't know what to say. "I—well—I don't know. We haven't planned the rest of the day. Why do you ask?"

He stepped all the way inside the door. "I hope you're not planning anymore snooping expeditions, that's all. I really do wish you'd stay put for now. I'll call you in a couple of hours."

Harrie leaned back in her chair and eyed him suspiciously. "Why? Do you plan to check up on me daily now?"

DJ grinned. "Probably. But I want to check back with you this afternoon because I'd like to take you to dinner tonight, if that's okay."

Harrie swallowed hard. "Well uh, sure, I mean, I . . ." She took a deep breath. "I imagine we'll be right here the rest of the day."

"Good. I'm counting on that."

Ginger didn't wait five seconds after DJ left before rushing into Harrie's office.

"Did he ask you out? Are you going? Come on! Give already!"

Harrie laughed. "Woman, get a grip. What is it with you married folk? You just can't stand to see single people not paired up with somebody."

"Yes! I knew it!" Ginger almost hugged herself with glee. "He asked you out didn't he?"

"We may go out to dinner. Do you mind if we get back to work now?"

Ginger finally settled down, and they got back to the list of suspicious people. Harrie felt grateful to have her friend occupied with something other than matchmaking. They discussed what they'd learned from Elizabeth and from Becky Martinez. They went to the conference room, and Harrie listed the suspects on the white board, the most suspicious in black, the next in red and the least likely in green. They worked together to compile a list of questions that needed answers. They sat and studied the two columns: suspects and unanswered questions.

Harrie finally said, "If we knew who wrote *The Lie That Killed A Town*, maybe we could talk to him. How can he be so sure that Eric is the killer?"

Ginger said, "Didn't you say DJ intended to check into that?"

Harrie said, "Yes, but I've just had a better idea." She jumped up and walked out to Caroline's desk and asked, "How does one go about finding the true identity of an author who uses a pen name?"

"Go to the publisher of the book and see if you can find out from them."

Harrie said, "Could you do that? Do you still have contacts in publishing you could call?"

Caroline smiled. "I have a few people I correspond with by email. Let me guess — you want me to find out Francis Black's real identity."

Harrie nodded. "If you could do that for us, it would really help."

Caroline said, "I think I know someone who might be able to get it for me."

Harrie rushed back to tell Ginger, who had just closed her cell phone. She looked immensely pleased with herself.

"Good news!" said Harrie.

"Me, too!" Ginger countered. "You first."

"Okay, Caroline knows someone who may be able to find out the identity of Francis Black. Isn't that great?" Harrie beamed like a chocoholic who just snagged a box of Russell Stover's Best.

"That is good news. Now you want to hear mine?" Ginger's smile was more in the nature of being smug. "I happened to think of something, and I called my dad to verify my memory."

Harrie said, "Okay, let me have it."

Ginger handed her the strange note from Philip. "I've studied this cryptic message he wrote. I've thought about it, and it just never made sense. Then I remembered something Dad said the other night. Dad said Philip always thought he had lived a previous life as a cowboy, and he loved stories about the old west. So one year, as a gag, Dad went out and bought a toy gun and holster set. He wrapped it up and gave it to Philip for Christmas. That little gun set was on display in his office in Washington as long as he was a senator."

Harrie shrugged. "That's an interesting story, but what does it have to do with anything?"

Ginger took the note back. "Right here he says, 'Don't forget those DEATH VALLEY DAYS.' See how he capitalized the whole thing?"

"And . . .?" Harrie prompted.

"That's it," Ginger said, looking at Harrie expectantly. "Don't you see? He must still have that toy gun and holster. Maybe it's a clue to find another tape, or maybe he hid the missing tape in the holster."

"All this because he capitalized the phrase 'Death Valley Days'?"

"Yes. Dad told me Death Valley Days was a TV program in the Fifties. Philip loved that program. This had to be his way of telling us to look at the gun and holster. I think I saw it on the wall in his library. If we go there, we'll probably find the missing tape."

Harrie thought for a few seconds. She opened her laptop and typed "Death Valley Days" into the search engine. She clicked on one of the entries and her eyes got bigger as she read.

"Come look at this," she instructed Ginger.

Ginger came around the desk to look over Harrie's shoulder. "Yes, that's it!" she said, excitement in her voice. "See, it's just like I said."

"Ah, but you didn't say anything about this. The host of the show during 1965-66 was the actor Ronald Reagan."

It was Ginger's turn to look puzzled. "So? What's your point?"

"I think I know where our missing tape is. And it's not in a toy holster."

54

Tuesday Evening, April 18, 2000

Harrie checked her reflection in the full-length mirror on her closet door and frowned. *Too sedate. I don't want to look like a nun.* She took off the long-sleeved, white blouse and grabbed a sheer pink top with a low-cut neckline. She pulled it over her head, looked in the mirror and groaned. *Where did I get this thing? I look like a pink lollipop.*

Ever since DJ had invited her to dinner, Harrie had refused to think of it as a date. It was just dinner—nothing more. True to his word, DJ had called just before she left the office and told her he'd made reservations at Sandiago's at the base of the Tram. The restaurant nestled up against the Sandia Mountains and afforded a spectacular view of the city. She had rushed out of the office with Ginger cheering her on. Now she faced her most difficult decision – what to wear.

Out loud, she said, "Okay, what am I trying for here, Tuptim? Am I businesslike and remote, or am I all squishy and vulnerable? What do you think?" She looked over at the cat, perched on the edge of the bed, who watched her with typical cat-like indifference.

"Yeah, that's what I think, too." Harrie said. She pulled off the pink concoction and tossed it on the bed beside the cat.

She finally settled on a slim black skirt and a soft knit top of vibrant red. The ensemble clung to her small frame. She slipped into seldom worn, black high-heeled pumps and stood back to survey her image. *Not too bad. Reserved, but feisty.*

"No wild parties, Tuptim. Remember, you're in charge until I get back."

Her nerves began to shoot out little pulses of anticipation. When the phone rang, it gave her something to concentrate on besides the looming prospect of going to dinner with DJ Scott.

When she picked it up, she heard DJ's voice, talking to someone in the background. She said "Hello" twice before he responded.

"Harrie, I'm sorry. I have a slight problem. I got called into the office for a meeting this afternoon. It's taking longer than we anticipated. I've had to change the reservations to eight o'clock. Will that be a problem for you?"

"No, of course not. I'm in no hurry."

"Good. I hope to leave here within the hour, so should be there to pick you up no later than seven-forty. I really apologize for the delay."

"Don't worry about it. Really. I have work to do in the meantime. But listen. I have an idea. Why don't I just meet you there? It would save time. You could just zip on out I-25 and not have to deal with the extra traffic to pick me up."

"I'd rather you not be out alone. It's not a problem to pick you up." Harrie heard someone in the background saying, "Scott, we need you back in here, now!"

"DJ, go. I'll meet you there. Just go." She hung up the phone before he could object further.

She thought about her unexpected added time. There were many things she could do until time to leave for the restaurant. She still pondered the question when the phone rang again.

She picked it up and said, "DJ, get off the phone and go back to your meeting!"

Ginger responded on the other end of the line. "I'm not DJ, and stop ordering me around."

"Oh, sorry, Ginger."

"I take it there's a problem with the date tonight?"

"Not really. He's just running late and had to postpone the reservations. He insisted on picking me up, and I told him it would save time if I just met him there. He wasn't thrilled about that."

Ginger chuckled. "Of course he wasn't. If this is a real date, and it sure sounds that way to me, then he wants it to be boy-picks-up-girl and then boy-takes-girl-home. At which point, boy might get to know girl better."

"Oh, give it up!" Harrie said. "Anyway, why did you call?"

"Just to tell you that Steve took the boys out for pizza tonight with the soccer team. So . . . " she paused, impishly, "I'm going over to Philip's to see if I can locate that missing tape."

"Oh, no you're not!" Harrie couldn't believe her ears. "You're not going there without me. I'm the one who figured it out!"

"We don't know that yet. I could still be right. Anyway, this is a perfect opportunity for me to go over there without any interference from Steve. And since you're going to have DJ tied up all evening, I won't have to worry about him, either."

"I don't think so lady. I'll meet you there. It's more than an hour until the dinner reservation. We can go through things and find the tape. I'll be closer to the base of the mountain than I am now, and I can leave about ten minutes before I have to be there. It'll save you time so you can be home long before Steve and the boys get back. And I'll make it to the restaurant about the same time as DJ. It's perfect."

Ginger sighed. "Why do I listen to you? DJ's going to find out, and he's going to blame me, I just know it."

"Just get going, and he never has to know anything about it. I'm leaving now, and I'll see you in ten minutes at Philip's house."

When Harrie pulled up to the gate of Canyon Estates, she smiled brightly at the guard and pointed to the sticker on her windshield. He smiled and waved her through. She looked in the mirror and noted he still took down her license plate number before he returned to the guardhouse.

A huge full moon was just edging up over the Sandia Mountains, the clouds playing hide and seek with it. Ginger waited at the open front door. She grabbed Harrie's arm and pulled her inside.

"What's going on?" Harrie demanded. "Is somebody watching?"

"Who knows," said Ginger. "I figure we should play it safe, that's all. Come on. Let's get this over with."

They walked down the hall and Harrie said, "Why don't you turn on some lights? We're going to trip on something."

"No." Ginger said, rather sharply Harrie thought. "We'll turn on lights once we get to the library. There aren't any windows in there, so nobody can see the lights from the street."

The beam of a flashlight suddenly illuminated the hall. Harrie jumped. "Blast it, Ginger! Warn me next time you're packin' a flashlight! My God! Where did you get that thing? It's huge!"

"Sshh," Ginger warned. "Keep it down. Somebody could hear you."

Harrie whispered hoarsely, "Just who do you think will hear us inside the house? If you tell me somebody else is in here, I'm leaving!"

"Sorry," Ginger said, in a low but otherwise normal voice. "I'm just a little spooked. I thought I saw someone between the houses when I drove up."

"Oh, great," Harrie said. "Now you've got me spooked."

They entered the library and switched on the light. Ginger pointed to a frame on the wall above the sofa. "Look. That's the toy gun and holster I told you about."

Ginger took the display down and pulled at the toy gun. It wouldn't budge. "Wonderful," she said. "It's been glued in. Why would anybody do a dumb thing like that?"

Harrie chuckled. "Probably because he didn't want the little gun to fall out of the little holster. When you plan to turn something like that into a display, you have to make sure the pieces don't get separated."

"I guess you're right. Well, so much for my idea. Let's see if your hunch turns out any better." She returned the frame to its place on the wall and opened the safe room.

"See there," Harrie said, "Philip is shaking hands with President Reagan." She reached up and removed the frame from its hook and turned the picture over. Four tiny metal latches held the corrugated backing. She released the latches and used her fingernails to pry up the backing. Behind the photograph was a brown 9 x 12 envelope.

Ginger leaned over and removed the envelope. "This must be what we're looking for." She handed it to Harrie and returned the photo to the wall.

Harrie held the envelope like it was a snake. "This doesn't look like the brown envelope Caroline and Elizabeth spoke about. Look. There's no sealing wax, just some writing."

Ginger took the envelope and studied the back. "Oh, my God. It's Philip's handwriting. It says 'To Be Opened In The Event Of My Death'." Ginger looked at Harrie. "We shouldn't open it. What if it's something that doesn't have anything to do with the murder? What if it's something personal like his will?"

"He wouldn't hide his will. Think about it. His attorney must have a copy. Besides, he mailed you that photograph and cryptic note the day before he was attacked. There must be a connection. We have to open it."

Ginger hesitated. "Maybe I should give it to my dad. He's Philip's official representative now. He should be the one to open it."

"If he'd wanted your dad to have it, he would have sent him the note and photo instead of you. We have to open it. He's depending on us to figure this out."

Ginger sighed. "Okay, I guess you're right." She slid her finger under the flap. There were two documents. She pulled out the first one.

"It's a birth certificate" Ginger said and read it. "Baby Angelina Carol Finn, born to Kathleen Ann Finn on February 18, 1950. Place of birth: Las Cruces, New Mexico."

Harrie's eyes widened. "Oh my word, look at the name of the father."

Ginger nodded. "Jacob Nathaniel Snow."

A barely audible sound caused Harrie to stiffen. "I thought I heard a door closing somewhere." She switched off the reading lamp and stood motionless.

"I didn't hear anything," she whispered.

Harrie moved quickly to the door of the safe room and turned off the humming fluorescent lights. Beyond the door, the library was bathed in a soft glow from the overhead fixture. The lamp on Philip's huge walnut desk made a tiny pool of light on the work surface.

Suddenly the library went dark except for the glow from the desk lamp. It didn't illuminate far enough beyond the desk to clearly see the figure of the man standing in the doorway. They heard a wispy male voice say, "Thank you ladies. You've saved me a lot of trouble. I knew I could count on you. Now please hand over the envelope and its contents. I'm in a bit of a hurry."

55

Harrie's adrenalin level shot up. Her brain bypassed the flight instinct in the first milliseconds and slammed directly into full combat mode. The arrogant order from the colorless voice sent her into a reckless fury. *Who is this insipid little bastard to think he can order us around?*

Harrie made a move toward the voice, but Ginger grabbed her arm and whispered. "Cool it. Don't go Rambo on me now."

Then Ginger spoke to the voice, her tone calm and steady. "Why don't you show yourself? I don't respond to faceless characters."

"You're not really in a position to give orders, Mrs. Vaughn. Now, be a good girl and hand over the envelope."

Harrie's anger flared again. "Why don't you come get it, tough guy?"

The man stepped closer, and Harrie saw an individual no more than five inches taller than her. He had on black from head to foot, including a hooded jacket and ski mask. A sudden, sickening recall of her nightmare flooded her memory. Why did she ever think that image was Nick?

"Ah, the volatile Mrs. McKenzie, or should I call you 'Harrie'? It would be fun to stay here and spar with you. I hear you're a real little spitfire. But alas, business before pleasure."

He shifted his arm. "You'll notice I didn't come without persuasion." The barrel of a revolver gleamed dully in the tiny pool of light.

The opening at the end of the barrel was big enough to drive a truck through. Harrie decided it had to be a 'Dirty Harry' gun. As she recalled, Clint Eastwood could shoot big holes with his. Her mouth felt incredibly dry, and her eyes seemed unable to look away from the gun.

Ginger put the two documents back in the brown envelope and held it out to the intruder.

"Okay, you win. Take it and go."

As he approached for the envelope, Harrie tightened her grip on the big flashlight she'd picked up in the safe room.

As he reached out his hand, Harrie swung the flashlight as hard as she could in the direction of his head. She heard a satisfying 'thwack' as it hit his skull. He stumbled backwards, flailing to keep his balance, and the gun fired. The desk light shattered, engulfing the room in darkness.

Harrie shoved Ginger back into the safe room and hit the button on the wall, causing the steel door to slide shut.

Harrie heard nothing but the roaring in her ears. *This must be what firing a cannon sounds like when you stand next to it.* She still had the flashlight, but she didn't dare use it. She dropped to the floor and crawled. If she could get behind the desk, maybe she could think of a plan. She bumped into something and reached out to feel her way. *Damn! I'm going the wrong way!* Her hand made out the form of Philip's leather lounge chair. She eased herself along the side. If she remembered the layout correctly, all she had to do was maintain a straight line and she would be at the door of the library.

Her eyes began to adjust in the darkness, but she still couldn't hear anything. She had no idea whether the intruder was moving around or if she'd managed to lay him out flat with the blow to his head. The doorway to the library loomed before her. She cautiously stood up and felt for the doorframe. She eased herself through and moved slowly down the hallway. Did she dare turn on the flashlight? If she could find her way to the living room, maybe she could hide until she figured out her next move. She remembered her cell phone was still in the secret room. *Wonderful! Good place for it in an emergency!* Her next thought gave her new hope. *I can use the phone in the kitchen!*

Harrie bypassed the living room and made her way carefully through the dining area. The ringing in her ears had diminished enough to hear the sound of her own movements. The kitchen door moved silently and she felt cheered when she saw that the streetlight faintly lit the kitchen. She caught her breath when the refrigerator motor started up. At least her hearing had mostly returned. The lovely sight of the wall phone almost caused her to cheer. She picked up the receiver and listened for the dial tone, but heard nothing. Harrie thought her ears were failing her again, and she frantically hit the switch hook.

"Forget it, Mrs. McKenzie." She stifled a scream. The voice was so close she could feel his breath on her neck. "I cut the phone line this afternoon when I came here in preparation for tonight. We don't want anybody crashing our little party do we?"

She felt something cold and hard pressed against her back. She toyed with the idea of swinging the big flashlight at his head again, but it was as though he read her mind.

"Give me the nasty flashlight. You don't want to risk using it again, believe me."

His left arm reached around her to take it. She tried to twist away and his arm closed around her neck in a strangle hold. She dropped the flashlight and clawed at his arm. He encircled her waist with his right arm, gun still in his right hand. She found herself effectively pinned against him, and she felt the blood draining from her head. His left arm squeezed against her neck, tighter and tighter, until the blackness overcame her completely, and she collapsed on the floor.

Harrie had shoved her into the safe room so quickly that it took Ginger several seconds to recover her wits. One moment the man was pointing a gun at them. The next, Harrie was swinging the flashlight, the gun went off and they were plunged into darkness. Another moment found her in the safe room, the steel door firmly in place, and the envelope still in her hand.

Her first reaction was to rescue Harrie. But how? She had no idea what was happening in the room beyond. She turned on the lights and looked at the security system. If she could just remember how to activate it, maybe she could see what was going on. *Damn! Why didn't I pay closer attention to how Harrie did this?*

She fiddled with first one switch then another. She finally tripped the master switch and was rewarded by a hum and flashing lights. The monitor showed a view of the library. She was stunned to see the overhead light was on, and the man in black was systematically pulling books from the shelves. How long would it be before he found the hidden switch that would reveal the steel door of her hiding place? Could he possibly enter the correct code into the keypad by trial and error?

She had to assume Harrie managed to escape, because the alternative was unacceptable. She reasoned the man wouldn't be back in the library if Harrie were still in the house and able to move. Ginger looked around the room, her heart pounding and her nerves pushed to the edge. Her gaze stopped at the telephone mounted on the wall beside the door, and relief flooded her. She grabbed the receiver.

Harrie opened her eyes, struggling to remember if she had been having one of her dreams. A faint light came in through a high window. Her neck hurt, and she was curled up on a cold, hard floor. She slowly pulled herself upright. She was in a small bathroom. This was definitely not a dream. She reached for the door. The knob turned but the door wouldn't budge. Something must have been wedged against it.

In the dim light, she surveyed her cell. The room consisted of a toilet and a pedestal sink. Under a small frosted window, she saw a waist-high cabinet. She took off her high heels—amazed they had somehow remained on her feet—and climbed up on the cabinet. She opened the window and looked down on the side yard. This must be the powder room off the kitchen. She'd been in this room just yesterday morning. She remembered Ginger telling her that Mrs. Sanchez kept a few personal grooming items in here for her convenience.

Harrie jumped down from the cabinet and opened the drawer. Did she dare turn on a light? Not knowing where 'ski mask' might be, she decided not to risk it. She reached in the drawer and rummaged around, identifying items by touch. She felt a comb, toothbrush and tube of toothpaste. Then she found the one item she prayed she'd find — a metal nail file.

She hopped back up on the cabinet and went to work on the window screen. She loosened its screws and let it drop to the ground. It made a small clanking sound and she froze, listening for someone to approach her prison. After a few agonizing seconds of silence, she stuck her head out the small opening and looked down. It was a long drop.

Just to the left of the window, Harrie could see the outlines of one of the large rubber garbage cans the City of Albuquerque so thoughtfully provides to homeowners. If she could squeeze out the opening, maybe she could hang on to the window frame and ease the garbage can over with her foot. *Great plan, Harrie! If you don't break your leg or knock the damn garbage can over!* She knew it was crazy, but her choices were limited. She had to escape and get help.

She hitched up her skirt and put one leg over the windowsill. She pulled her other leg out and clung to the window ledge. She reached for the garbage can with her foot and almost cried when it started moving toward her. When she judged it was close enough, she swung her body in that direction and let go. She landed on the lid, teetered, and half slid, half fell to the ground.

She picked herself up, took a step and collapsed on the ground again, rubbing her painfully twisted ankle.

In the next moment a blaze of light cracked, open the darkness. Brilliant spotlights bathed the house, and someone spoke through a bullhorn.

The loud noise made Harrie's ears ring again. Her heart slammed against her ribs. What was happening? People in dark clothing rushed toward her, rifles raised. The light was so bright and the noise so loud she couldn't tell who they were or what they were saying.

In the confusion, a face moved into her line of vision. It seemed familiar, especially that lock of black hair that caressed the forehead.

DJ's voice sounded strained but tinged with relief. The ringing had subsided enough she could now hear what he said.

"Am I destined to always be picking you up off the ground?"

58

Harrie leaned against DJ's black SUV, her neck showing signs of the bruises to come, her throat sore and her ankle throbbing.

Philip Lawrence's home in Canyon Estates was lit up like a movie set. APD and unmarked FBI cars were in the driveway and street. Deputies from the Bernalillo County Sheriff's Department added more muscle to the scene. Harrie saw Ginger and hobbled to meet her.

"Are you all right?" They spoke in unison and both laughed. Harrie felt some of the evening's tension leave her.

"I was so worried about you," Harrie said, hugging Ginger hard enough to make her squeal.

"You were the one in trouble. I was safely ensconced in the panic room. I didn't know if you got out or if that maniac found you. Tell me what happened."

Harrie told her as much as she could. Then she said, "I made my big escape from the bathroom and dropped into the set of the remake of *Die Hard*. I'm still not sure what happened and what's going on."

A very relieved Steve walked up and pulled his wife into his arms. "You scared me to death. Please, don't ever do anything like this again."

Ginger broke free from the bear hug. "Don't worry. No more detective work for this girl. From now on, we leave it to the experts, right Harrie?"

"No problem. I think I've had enough excitement for a lifetime."

DJ joined them and Harrie asked, "Who was that man? And how did you happen to show up just as I thought I was done for?"

"I showed up because Ginger called me."

Harrie looked at her friend. "How did you manage that? The phone lines were cut."

Ginger shook her head. "I don't know about the rest of them, but the one in the safe room worked just fine. I called 911, and then I called DJ and told him how to get me out." She grinned at Harrie.

"Great," Harrie blew out a big breath. "I'm trying to rescue you, and you were sitting cozy with help on the way. I, on the other hand, was being shot at and strangled. Not to mention twisting my ankle and ruining a perfectly good pair of pantyhose!" Harrie joined in the laughter of the others.

DJ said, "Safe rooms usually have a dedicated phone line independent of the main line. That's essential for the room to withstand a home invasion. As for your other question, the man who locked you up is none other than *El Jefe* himself. He wanted something from the senator's house, and he came by to get it before meeting up with his employees later tonight."

"Rotten timing for us. But why tonight?" Harrie asked.

"Remember Swannie told you about undercover guys imbedded in *El Jefe's* operation? They tipped us that a major shipment of drugs would arrive tonight from a Mexican cartel. All of *El Jefe's* lieutenants fanned out around the city to take possession of the shipment from various drop sites. *El Jefe* had arranged to meet them all later tonight."

Harrie wrinkled her nose. "Why not just one big drop site?"

"Because by spreading out, there's less chance of calling attention to any one transaction. This way, it's just a couple of guys meeting and talking. One guy buys a TV or some other piece of equipment and inside is a portion of the drugs. They didn't realize the task force knew all the drop points. As soon as the drugs changed hands, we rounded up *El Jefe's* gang."

"Okay," Harrie said. "What I really want to know is what does this thing with Philip have to do with *El Jefe*?"

"Philip hired Nick to find the identity of Chipper Finn's baby. Nick tracked that down and turned it over to Philip, but not before *El Jefe* found out he had it."

Ginger pulled out the brown envelope, now a bit bedraggled, and handed it to DJ. "We found this tonight in Philip's library. This guy, *El Jefe*, wanted it. He knew who we were, and he called us by name."

"Did you get a chance to look at this?" DJ asked.

"We saw a birth certificate for baby Angelina. *El Jefe* interrupted us before we got a chance to examine the second document."

"It was the other document he really wanted. He needed it to find out the current identity of baby Angelina."

Harrie didn't know if her shiver was from the night air or her sudden apprehension. "Why did *El Jefe* want to know that? Did you catch him?"

"They caught him, but stick with me. I'll get to that. *El Jefe* suspected the identity of Angelina's father, but he wanted to make certain. Philip told Nick about Becky Martinez and the baby being left at St. Anne's. Starting with that info, Nick found out the current identity of the baby. *El Jefe* wanted to eliminate anybody who knew and then eliminate the woman herself as well as Nick and Philip."

Harrie interrupted. "Only Daniel or Jonathan would want to know about the baby. Are you saying that *El Jefe* is connected to them?"

DJ said, "Oh, it's more than a connection. *El Jefe* and Jonathan Templeton are one in the same."

They were stunned into temporary silence. Ginger recovered first and posed a question. "Do you also know the identity of Angelina's father?"

"Yes," he said.

"How long have you known?" Harrie asked.

"Elizabeth Snow told me yesterday when I went to see her."

"Elizabeth knew Jacob fathered Chipper's child?" asked Ginger. "Why didn't she say something earlier?"

"Because," DJ said, "she's been trying to protect the woman that child grew into. She found out about Jacob being the father shortly after his death. It was in the journal taken from his office."

Harrie said, "So she must have read the journal before she turned it over to Philip. And Philip has known for the past year and a half who the child's father was." She had another idea. "If Elizabeth knew that Jacob was the father of Chipper's daughter, did she also realize that same child was turned over to the orphanage where she volunteered?"

"She did after she gave the journal to Philip. He told Elizabeth all about Becky Martinez and the things she'd done to protect the baby."

Ginger asked, "Did she try to find out who had adopted the baby?"

DJ sighed. "Yes, but not until recently. She said at first she wondered if the little girl had grown up to be a healthy adult. Then she wondered if perhaps she owed something to the person that child had become. She made inquiries through her contacts and pieced together enough information to discover the current identity of Angelina."

Harrie said, "So why didn't Elizabeth tell Philip who Angelina is today? Why did he have to hire Nick to find out?"

DJ hesitated a moment. "Well, frankly it was a bit awkward for her." He handed the envelope back to Ginger. "If you look in here, you'll notice the other document contains the adoption record of Baby Angelina. I think you'll see what I mean."

Ginger looked at the second document, the one they hadn't yet seen.

"What does it say, for goodness sake?" said Harrie.

Ginger wordlessly handed the document to her. "It says 'Caroline Ann Hanover'. Do we know who that is?"

DJ said, "Hanover is my mother's maiden name. Caroline Ann Hanover Scott Johnson was originally Angelina Carol Finn."

DJ went to confer with the task force commander and make sure it was okay for Harrie and Ginger to leave

Harrie turned to Ginger. "I forgot to ask DJ if Caroline knows."

Ginger shook her head. "I'll bet she doesn't."

Ginger's phone rang, and she checked the caller ID. "Oh, Lord. It's my parents. Steve, you didn't say anything to them about all this, did you?"

Steve shook his head. "I didn't have a chance. DJ called right after the boys and I got home. I dropped everything and raced over here."

Ginger flipped open the phone. "Hi, Dad." She brightened, a big smile spreading across her face. "Really? When? Is he talking?" She put her hand over the microphone. "It's Philip. He's awake and demanding to see us."

"Let's go!" Harrie said.

"Hold it just a minute," Steve said. "We have to wait until they release you officially. I'll go find DJ."

Ginger ended the call with her father by assuring him they would be at the hospital as soon as they could get there. He said he would tell Philip.

Steve returned with DJ. "We're cleared to leave."

Steve followed Ginger home so they could go in one car to the hospital, and DJ did the same with Harrie. When she joined DJ in his car, she broached the subject that had occupied her mind for the past half hour.

"Does your mother know who she really is?"

DJ shook his head. "Not yet. She's always known about being adopted, and it was only recently she started actively searching for her birth parents. She asked me to help her find them, and I've been working on that for a few months on my own time. I thought about telling her yesterday after I spoke to Elizabeth, but I decided it would be better if we waited until Jonathan was no longer a threat. I'll tell her first thing tomorrow."

Light traffic enabled a quick trip to the hospital. They met Ginger and Steve at the door of the private room Philip had been moved to.

Philip sat almost straight up in the elevated hospital bed. He looked a little pale and sported a bandage on his head but looked good for someone who had been through such an ordeal. When he saw Harrie and Ginger, he gave them a big smile.

"Thank you for coming. I hope it's not too late. Hello, Steve. Who's your friend?" He looked at DJ.

Steve introduced DJ. "Glad to meet you, my boy. So you're with the FBI? These ladies been giving you trouble?"

"Yes sir, quite a bit. But I think we have things under control now."

DJ explained what had happened since the senator's attack. When he got to the part about Nick Constantine being shot, Philip frowned.

"I'm very sorry to hear that." He reached for Harrie's hand. "What I said to you at Ginger's wedding was based on the way Nick as at that point in his life. But he turned his life around. He's been trying to make amends for his past mistakes. He impressed me as a sincere young man."

Philip turned to DJ, "How did it happen?"

DJ explained that Jonathan found out about Nick's investigation and panicked. Then he described the situation with Pablito and about Harrie and Ginger being overtaken by Jonathan at Philip's home just a few hours ago. Philip raised his eyebrows and looked at Ginger.

"It didn't occur to me you would go off sleuthing on your own. I expected you would bring the police in. I hope your parents don't know what you've been doing."

"No," Ginger assured him. "We were able to keep them from knowing anything about this."

Harrie said, "Sir, do you know why Jonathan Templeton was so desperate to know the identity of Chipper Finn's baby?"

Philip took a deep breath. "I believe he found out the terms of his uncle's will. You see, Daniel told me he made provisions that in case a direct heir of one of the Snows turned up, his entire estate would go to that heir. Everybody was quick to assume that Eric was the father of Chipper's baby, but Daniel began to doubt that after the murder. When Jacob went to him and threatened to expose him and Peter, Daniel suspected Jacob might have had a more personal interest in Chipper. I think Daniel felt guilty about the child, and did something that would ease his conscience. At least that's what Jacob said in his journal.

"In 1972, when Jacob asked me to run for the senate, he told me there were secrets in his family that, if they came out, would ruin them. I assumed it had something to do with Daniel's son, Eric. I knew from the days Daniel and I were friends that the boy had caused a great deal of trouble. He was wild, headstrong and spoiled. Jacob told me he and Daniel would throw their full support behind me, but that I was free to be my own person. With those assurances, I decided to run."

Philip stopped speaking as the nurse walked into the room. She made a big show of checking his IV, taking his pulse, and generally showing her disapproval of all the people crowded around the bed. "Ten more minutes, and then I want you all out of here."

With that, she stomped out of the room and shut the door.

The chastised visitors looked at each other and turned back to Philip. He chuckled. "Don't mind her. She's just very protective. Now where was I? Oh, yes. In 1972, after I won the election, Jacob told me all about Daniel's past with illegal gambling. He explained about the deal he made with Daniel that if he agreed not to run for the senate, Jacob wouldn't expose him for his past activities. After hearing all that I understood why they were so eager to have me run. At first I was angry they hadn't told me all this before I agreed to run, but in a way, it's just as much my fault. The fact is that the idea of becoming a senator had begun to appeal to me. I didn't press too hard about any deeper reasons Jacob might have had for asking me. After that, Daniel and I drifted apart."

Harrie asked, "How did you reconnect with the Snows?"

"Just before Jacob had his stroke, he asked me to come see him. He was agitated, and I sensed there was something he wanted to tell me, but he seemed reluctant. Before I left, he told me that someday he would provide me with all the information needed to see that Daniel could never hurt anyone again. By this time, Peter was already dead, and I could only speculate what Jacob meant.

"I was out of town when Jacob died. Elizabeth contacted me a few weeks later and told me about the sealed envelope Jacob left for me. When I went to meet her, she explained about the burglary in Jacob's office and how she managed to get the envelope before that happened."

"Did she tell you she'd hired Nick Constantine to retrieve it?"

Philip looked at Harrie. "No, my dear, not then. It was only recently she told me who she'd hired."

Ginger interrupted. "What was in the envelope?"

"It was bad—worse than I'd imagined. I knew Peter Templeton had a drinking problem. Everyone knew that was why Daniel sent him home from Washington. Peter worked as Daniel's personal aide, and he resented being sent home. He got drunk one night and admitted to Jacob that he and

Sheriff Hernandez had murdered Chipper Finn. He described how they staged a couple of episodes where they got Eric drunk and took him to the club where Chipper worked. They made sure Eric was seen fighting with her several times. The night of her death, he shoved her against a wall before Manny Salinas threw him out of the club.

"Later, Manny walked Chipper to her car. As soon as he left, Peter and the sheriff approached her. The sheriff knocked on her window and made her get out. Peter came up behind her and hit her over the head. They threw her in the trunk of the sheriff's squad car and drove out to the desert. When they took her out of the trunk, she moaned and they realized she was still alive. So Peter strangled her with her own scarf. They laid her body out on the desert floor and drove back to town."

Philip stopped talking and reached for his water glass. He took a few sips, shifted his position in the bed and continued.

"Peter went back and got Eric, who had passed out behind the club, and drove him back to Albuquerque. They told Eric he killed the girl, and he believed them. That's why he went to Europe and stayed away so long."

Harrie spoke up. "So you've known for at least a year who killed Chipper Finn? Were you going to reveal that in your book?"

"I hadn't made up my mind. I knew if I went too far, Daniel might find a way to take revenge on Elizabeth and on Chipper's daughter."

Philip looked at DJ. "What will happen to Jonathan?"

"There's a slam-dunk case against him for drug trafficking. We also executed a search warrant tonight on an apartment he maintained. APD found the weapon they believe was used in Nick's murder. Jonathan will go away for a very long time."

Philip had a faraway look. "So now Daniel is alone. What will happen to him?"

DJ shrugged. "We don't have anything on him. Even if we could prove the allegations of corruption and bribes in the 40s and 50s, too much time has passed. If we can connect him to Jonathan's activities, then that's another story. I'll have to get back to you."

Philip waved his hand. "I doubt it will come to that, but keep me posted anyway."

Ginger had one more question. "We found the birth certificate and adoption papers behind the photo of you and President Reagan. Did you figure out who Caroline Hanover is?"

He smiled. "Yes, my dear, and I almost choked the day you told me about your new office manager. I had verified her identity earlier that day, and I took it as a sign that something would happen soon. That's why I made the elaborate plan to have you find the documents. I hoped you wouldn't have too much trouble figuring it out."

Harrie grinned at Ginger before she responded. "Oh, no sir. We didn't have a bit of trouble. Did we, Ginger?"

60

Wednesday Morning, April 19, 2000

Harrie overslept after the long, tension-filled evening. When she pulled into her parking space the next morning, she noticed DJ's car and Caroline's. She debated about driving around for a bit before going in. DJ said he would tell his mother this morning about her newly discovered parentage, and Harrie didn't want to disturb them. She finally decided to chance it and went in.

She dumped her briefcase in her office and went for coffee. DJ and Caroline were sitting at the table in the kitchen, sipping coffee and talking.

Harrie said, "Oh, excuse me." She turned to leave, but DJ called out, "Wait. Don't go. Come in and join us."

Caroline came around the table, and hugged her. "Thank you so much for all you've done for me."

Harrie felt speechless. "I can't think of anything I've done for you. You're the one we should thank for helping solve the mystery."

Caroline said, "You have my gratitude for bringing closure about my childhood. Now I know where I came from and why I was given up for adoption. That's something I've wondered about for years."

Harrie said to DJ, "You must explain that Philip, Nick, and Elizabeth did all the investigating. Ginger and I just found what Philip hid for us." She looked at Caroline. "I'm glad you're okay with all this. It must have been quite a shock to find out your boss all those years was really your father."

Caroline said, "I always thought there was something about Jacob that seemed so loving and protective. He treated me with the kindness and concern I'd always longed for in a father. My adoptive parents were older people. They were strict and not comfortable with showing affection. I knew they loved me in their own way, but it was never enough. I had such a longing to be cherished. I'm sure that's why I ran away and got married at such an early age. Jimmy . . . that was David's father . . . was sweet and gentle. We loved each other so much, and he wanted us to make a home where we could raise our children with the love and tenderness I never had. When he was killed, I'm sure I would have died too if I hadn't been expecting this wonderful boy." She beamed at her son, and DJ put his arm around her and hugged her to him.

Harrie felt tears welling up in her eyes. Seeing the love that flowed between mother and son made her ache for the love she'd been missing so long. She tried to wipe away the tears before anyone noticed. DJ stood close enough to reach out and pull her into the embrace of his other arm. That scene greeted Ginger when she came sailing in moments later.

"Uh oh," she said. "What am I interrupting here?"

Ginger and Harrie declared it a day of celebration and closed the office. They decided to take everyone to lunch at La Esquina at the Galleria. Ginger called Steve and asked him to join them and invite Swannie to come along. Ginger wanted her parents to meet them there, too. After the previous evening's operation, DJ was back on vacation and free for lunch. Only Philip would be missing. Ginger said she'd save him a sopapilla and smuggle it to him at the hospital later in the afternoon.

Harrie went to her office to collect her briefcase. In her haste, she didn't realize it was unlatched. When she grabbed the handle, it spilled its contents on the floor. As she bent down to pick up the mess, she saw the bundle of mail she'd stuck in there on Friday. She noticed a fat envelope with no return address, postmarked in Santa Fe. She opened it and discovered a three-page letter. The handwriting looked vaguely familiar and her breath caught in her throat when she looked at signature: Nick.

61

Wednesday Afternoon, April 19, 2000

"My Dearest Harrie,   &

You're probably thinking, 'Where does this jerk get off addressing me that way?' Of course you're right, but I still feel a connection to you and sadness for the way I left. I also regret the financial disaster I dumped on you. I hope you'll read this letter all the way through and try to hear my words, not to excuse me, but to understand the transition that occurred because you were in my life.

Harrie, I was literally running for my life, and in a way, yours too. I knew that if I left, some very nasty people I worked for would leave you alone. The bastards were closing in, and the only way to keep us both safe was to disappear. Unfortunately, that meant not giving you any notice and leaving behind an enormous trail of debt you would have to handle. So I left like a coward in the night and tried never to look back. After a while, it began to penetrate my thick skull that I had to make significant changes. It didn't happen all at once, of course. It took me another five years to clean up my act to the point I could find a good job and begin to climb out of the mess I created. During that time, I went home to see my grandfather. He was skeptical at first, but even he could see that I wasn't the same conceited jerk I had been when I left his house. I told him I only wanted to redeem myself in his eyes, not to be put back in the will . . . I didn't care about that anymore. I just wanted to win his respect. He was the only family I had, and I wanted to make him proud of me before he died."

Ginger rushed into Harrie's office. "Hey, what's the holdup?" She stopped in her tracks when she saw Harrie's face, cheeks wet with tears, and pale as a winter shut-in. "My God, what's wrong?"

Harrie wordlessly handed the letter to Ginger, who started reading it then looked back at Harrie. "What the . . . where did this come from?"

Harrie explained about the mail she'd picked up from her house and just now rediscovered. "Why don't you read it to me? I'm having a little trouble focusing right now."

Ginger found the place Harrie had left off.

"Eventually, I began practicing law again in a small town in Nebraska. The only attorney in that town needed an associate, and I begged him to let me work with him. Then my grandfather became very ill, and I went home to upstate New York to be with him. He only lasted for six months, but I was there with him that entire time. And don't laugh, Harrie, but I took care of him. I sat by his bed at night, cleaned him when he needed it, gave him his medicine and held his hand when he was delirious. Just before he died, he had two good days when he seemed to rally. We talked for hours, and he told me things about my mother and father that I never knew. He told me how kind and gentle my mother was and how much she loved me. He also told me about my father's coldness and his willingness to abandon my mother and me for money. I was ashamed when I realized how much like my father I had become without ever knowing the man. I decided to return to Albuquerque and see if I could make amends.

"If you wonder why I didn't try to contact you or Steve, it was because I didn't want you to know I'd returned until I was in a position to really make amends to all of you. There were people here in town who expected me to go back to my old habits, and I had to handle that situation carefully. I heard about your remarriage and the death of your husband. Harrie, I'm sorry for your loss. After what I put you through, it doesn't seem right. Maybe someday I can apologize in person, but for now, I just wanted to say I regret all the heartache and trouble I've caused.

"In the meantime, please accept the enclosed check. A small part of it covers the financial debt I owe you. The rest is for the emotional debt, although there is not enough money in the world to settle that.

"Harrie, you were a gift to me that I threw away. Please know that I'm very much aware of what I lost."

Ginger dropped the letter on Harrie's desk. "Where's this check he mentions?"

Harrie blew her nose and picked up the envelope. She handed a check to Ginger who looked at it and let out a shriek. "It's a million dollars!"

DJ and Caroline rushed in, concern on their faces. DJ said, "What the hell is going on? It sounded like someone being murdered."

Harrie took the check back from Ginger and said, "No, actually, it's a kind of rebirth. I think the past is finally behind me, and suddenly, I feel wonderful. Could we get out of here now? I'm starving!"

"Yeah," said Ginger. "And she's definitely picking up today's tab."

They gathered at the restaurant, a small treasure tucked away in the basement of the Galleria. They sipped Margaritas from fat, salt-rimmed glasses. The waiter kept them supplied with baskets of tortilla chips and fiery salsa that was a specialty of the chef. Harrie told them about the unexpected letter and check from Nick.

They were still chewing on that news when Caroline spoke up. "I forgot to tell you I heard from my friend at the publishing house in New York. She found out who Francis Black is."

Harrie said, "So who is he really?"

"Well, believe it or not," Caroline said, "it's Peter Templeton."

There was a stunned silence. Ginger said, "But why would he write a book pointing to Eric as the killer? That doesn't make any sense at all."

DJ said, "No, actually that's pretty clever. In view of what Philip told us last night, blaming it on Eric was one way to deflect suspicion away from Daniel, Peter, or even Sheriff Smiley Hernandez. Peter maintained all along that Manny Salinas and some unknown acquaintance did the deed. Nobody would suspect him of writing a book with a completely different theory, especially one that accused his own nephew. It was brilliant."

They were still talking about the book when Swannie joined them.

"Sorry I'm late but an interesting call came in just before I left. It's a bit of a shocker. Our old friend Daniel Snow died this morning. He left a note saying he had been diagnosed with an aggressive form of cancer and didn't wish to stay around for the end that awaited him. He secured a hefty quantity of barbiturates and took them during the night."

"My God," Caroline broke the silence. "I guess he was my last living relative except for sleazy Jonathan and the institutionalized Eric. I suppose I should feel something, but I don't. I only remember how much Jacob disliked the man and how much he distrusted him."

DJ spoke up. "Well, there's one more surprise, Mom. I neglected to mention to you earlier what Philip Lawrence told us last night. Daniel made a will in which he left his entire fortune to any surviving children of the Snows. Jonathan was excluded from any inheritance unless absolutely no one else survived. Elizabeth says Daniel set up a trust fund years ago for

Eric's care. That means you are the sole inheritor of Daniel Snow's considerable fortune."

Caroline's face showed surprise and disbelief. Harrie started to giggle.

"I'm sorry," she said when the others turned to look at her, "but think about it. Just a few days ago, none of us would have guessed we'd be sitting here today, sipping Margaritas together with new friends like Caroline and DJ and that Caroline would be the long lost child of the woman in Senator Lawrence's book. Then there's the additional strange communication from Nick, ending years of speculation about why he left and what happened to him."

Ginger added, "And we also had no idea that Harrie and Carline would be wealthy women. I said in the office that Harrie would be picking up the tab today, but—"

Caroline held up her hand. "I know what you're going to say. I'm going to share the expense with Harrie."

Ginger nodded then stared at DJ. "Somehow I get the idea that isn't all you two will be sharing in the future."

"Ginger!" Harrie yelled, her face as red as the salsa.

When the laughter subsided, DJ said to the whole party, "Now that Harrie has riches to go with her beauty, I better make my move before all the other men come running"

Harrie sat back and folded her arms. She studied the handsome man beside her and thought of all the reasons she had avoided entanglements. She thought of the loneliness she'd felt and the opportunities she'd rejected. All those years of trying to protect herself could not suppress the warm feeling emanating from her heart. Something had melted inside her, and she didn't even try to suppress the grin that creased her face.

"I have a question for you." She brought her face up close to his. "How do you feel about women who love cats and have strange dreams?"

You may also enjoy these books from Aakenbaaken & Kent

The Pot Thief Who Studied Billy the Kid
by J. Michael Orenduff
The 6th book in this wildly-popular and award winning series

While illegally digging for Anasazi pots in a cliff dwelling, Hubert Schuze grasps a human hand. He was hoping for an artifact, not a handshake and is puzzled by his discovery. The Anasazi did not bury their dead in their living quarters. A more pressing problem confronts him when he hears his truck drive away from the plain above the cliff. The rope he was planning to use to return to the surface was attached to the truck's winch. After a bizarre escape from the cliff dwelling, he is convinced to return by his sidekick Susannah who suspects the body was not a mummy but a contemporary person. But when Hubie descends a second time with her help, what he discovers defies all logic. It takes Hubie, Susannah, a coyote and Billy the Kid to finally figure out who was dead and why.

Bought Off
By Roger Paulding

Suave, buttoned-down Alex Upchurch seems an odd match with his position as Assistant District Attorney of Galveston, a city some say is like the antique store on the north end that advertises "Mostly Junque, a Few Jewels." But when a dead John Doe is discovered naked in the bedroom of Alex's baronial mansion, District Attorney John Henry Davenport has to cover up the crime to save not only his able assistant but also to placate Alex's Mother, Honey Upchurch, whose money bought John Henry's position. Figuring out who is dead and why proves almost as challenging as keeping that information from becoming known, especially when Alex is appointed to prosecute a former lover who knows all but tells nothing. Fortunately, Leon McAdoo, known as Miss Starlight because of a gossip column he (or she?) writes, is on hand to guide us through the maze of power, money, sex and corruption.

Touching the Moon
by Lisa M. Airey

A gifted healer with a genetic secret and a haunted past, Julie Hastings takes her new veterinary degree to South Dakota hoping to bury memories of a physically abusive stepfather and un-protective mother. Although intending to lead a quiet life, she finds herself relentlessly pursued by two unwelcome suitors: the Chief of Police and a powerful member of the Sioux Indian Nation. The man she chooses shatters her world-view. Her stepfather taught her that not all monsters run on four legs. Now Julie must face another truth—some beasts are good.

Making Story
edited by Timothy Hallinan

It's often said that everyone has a book inside him or her — but how do you plot it? In *Making Story*, twenty-one novelists – who have written more than 100 books among them and sold more than a million copies – talk about how they go about turning an idea into a plot, and a plot into a book. This is an indispensable book for aspiring authors and the first in a series, each focusing on a different writing challenge.

Ghosts
Strange Tales of the Unnatural, The Uncanny and The Unaccountable
edited by Lynne Gregg and Julian Kindred

Is there a ghost in your life? Do you see people who aren't there? We warn you, don't read these tales when you are home alone. Stories by writers who understand where and when ghosts may bring good or evil to your daily routine. Or sometimes, just a laugh.

The Pot Thief Who Studied D. H. Lawrence
by J. Michael Orenduff
The 5th book in this wildly-popular and award winning series

D. H. Lawrence wrote of the winter on Taos Mountain, "In a cold like this, the stars snap like distant coyotes." Hubie's official reason for visiting the Lawrence Ranch high on that Mountain is to entertain donors with a presentation about ancient pottery. But his real goal is to find the pot Fidelio Duran presented to D. H. Lawrence as a welcoming gift. Then a snowstorm strands Hubie at the Lawrence Ranch Conference Center, and his new goal becomes survival. Are the guests dying of accidents or is there a murderer among them?

The Pot Thief Who Studied Escoffier
by J. Michael Orenduff
The 4th book in this wildly-popular and award winning series

Old Town Albuquerque potter Hubie Schuze agrees to create unique chargers for the table settings in a soon-to-open Austrian restaurant in Santa Fe. Once onsite, Hubie is immersed in the politics of the restaurant business. In an effort to negotiate the egos and agendas, Hubie invites the *grillardin* for cocktails. The inebriated grill cook insists on snoozing in Hubie's truck, but the next morning, Hubie finds the *garde manger* there instead… not breathing and as cold as his menu items. Before Hubie can recover from the shock, things spiral out of control at *Schnitzel*, forcing the eatery to close its doors. Unwilling to cede defeat, the kitchen staff convince Hubie to help them convert to a Mexican-Austrian fusion menu. The reviews are rave and the money rolls in, but Hubie is soon faced with that old prophecy …no good deed goes unpunished.

The Pot Thief Who Studied Einstein
by J. Michael Orenduff
The 3rd book in this wildly-popular and award winning series

Maybe it was the chance for an easy $2500. Or maybe it was the chance to examine a treasure trove of Anasazi pots. Or maybe it was just a slow day at his Old Town Albuquerque shop that enticed Hubie Schuze to be blindfolded and chauffeured to meet a reclusive collector looking for a confidential appraisal. Sure, it was an odd setup, but what could possibly go wrong? Hubie s devil-may-care attitude fades fast when he finds three of his own Anasazi copies among the genuine antiquities. Worse, when the driver drops him back home, what he doesn't find are the twenty-five crisp hundred dollar bills the collector paid him. Hubie is determined to recoup his cash, but Detective Whit Fletcher interrupts, dragging Hubie to the morgue to identify a John Doe. When the sheet is pulled back, Hubie is stunned to see the collector. Hubie is not a suspect yet. But the longer he pursues his missing appraisal fee, the more tangled he becomes in the collector's shadowy life.

The Pot Thief Who Studied Ptolemy
by J. Michael Orenduff
The 2nd book in this wildly-popular and award winning series

The pot thief is back, but this time Hubert Schuze' larceny is for a good cause. He wants to recover sacred pots stolen from San Roque, the mysterious New Mexico pueblo closed to outsiders. An easy task for Hubert Schuze, pot digger. Except these pots are not under the ground—they're 150 feet above it. In the top-floor apartment of Rio Grande Lofts, a high-security building which just happens to be one story above Susannah's latest love interest. Hubie's legendary deductive skills lead to a perfect plan which is thwarted when he encounters the beautiful Stella. And when he is arrested for murder. Well, he was in the room where the body was found, everyone heard the shot, and he came out with blood on his hands. Follow Hubie as he stays one step ahead of building security, one step behind Stella, and one step away from a long fall down a garbage chute.

The Pot Thief Who Studied Ptolemy
by J. Michael Orenduff
The books that started it all

Pot hunter and trader Hubert Schuze knows he should decline the offer of $25,000 from a shady character to steal a pot from a local museum. He may be a pot thief, but he isn't a burglar. But he visits the museum just to see how difficult the job might be. After deciding the museum is impregnable, he returns to his shop where a federal agent is waiting to accuse him of stealing the 1000-year-old pot. When the agent is found dead in a hotel room, theft charges escalate to murder. Hubie must use his strong deductive skills and overcome his weak nerves to solve the murder.